Thea and Denise

CAROLINE BOND was born in Scarborough and studied English at Oxford University before working as a market researcher for twenty-five years. She has an MA in Creative Writing from Leeds Trinity University, and lives in Leeds with her husband and three children.

Also by Caroline Bond

The Forgotten Sister
The Second Child
One Split Second
The Legacy

Thea and Denise

caroline bond

CORVUS

Published in hardback in Great Britain in 2022 by Corvus, an imprint of
Atlantic Books Ltd.

This paperback edition published in 2023.

10 9 8 7 6 5 4 3 2 1

A CIP catalogue record for this book is available from the British Library.

Paperback ISBN: 978 1 83895 407 9
E-book ISBN: 978 1 83895 406 2

Design benstudios.co.uk
Printed in Great Britain

Corvus
An imprint of Atlantic Books Ltd
Ormond House
26–27 Boswell Street
London
WC1N 3JZ

www.atlantic-books.co.uk

To my friends.

Prologue

THE SKY was filled with purple-tinted clouds.

The sun was coming up.

The roof was down.

The roads were clear.

Thea drove fast, following the smooth contours of the coast road with ease. Denise tilted her head back and felt the warmth of the new day hit her face.

They were mistresses of their universe.

As the sun rose higher, the road started to narrow and climb. After a few miles, Thea turned off. A plume of dust rose in their wake as they rolled and bumped along the unmarked track. Denise had no idea where they were. They drove on, away from or towards something – she no longer cared.

After another ten minutes or so Thea swung the car around a bend and brought it to a stop.

They'd reached the end of the road.

In front of them was a stretch of scrubby grass, the sky and the cliff edge. Away to the left, on the headland, sat a lighthouse, a curiously squat affair topped with a black-capped dome. Beyond it the coast unfurled in a seemingly never-ending series of rocky inlets. Denise heard the sea heaving and crashing somewhere far below. Above them the gulls wheeled and screamed.

'Where the hell are we?'

'St Abb's Head.' The wind whipped Thea's hair across her face. 'Isn't it beautiful?'

'It is.'

They sat, side-by-side, taking in the view. The grandeur of it silenced them both. They'd been travelling together for barely a week, but in that moment Denise felt closer to Thea than she had to anyone else in her entire life. She wanted Thea to know that. 'You're a good friend.'

Thea smiled. 'You too.'

Denise breathed in the fresh, sharp air. She caught sight of her reflection in Thea's sunglasses: her hair a mess, not a scrap of make-up on her face, her nose and cheeks tinged red with sunburn. She looked good. Even more importantly, she felt good – the best she'd felt in a very long time. So much had changed since they'd left home, not least Denise herself. She was a different person, happier, freer, braver, and that was due, in large part, to the woman sitting next to her.

They fell silent again, reflecting on what they'd learnt about themselves, and each other, over the past few hectic, revelatory days.

Indifferent to the presence of such wise women in their midst, the gulls rose and fell at the cliff edge. Their screaming and flapping reminded Denise of the problems mounting and massing at their backs. Real life was going to catch up with them eventually. They couldn't keep running for ever.

Although up on that wild, isolated promontory, with the sun shining down on them and the wind blowing in off the sea, it felt like perhaps they could.

'So,' Denise finally asked, 'what do you want to do now?'

Thea looked at the limitless sky stretching out beyond the cliff edge and said, 'Keep going.'

PART ONE

Chapter 1

SHE WOKE up on fire.

Desperate to get some air onto her molten skin, she began kicking at the bedcovers. Her nightie clung to her like a sick child. It fought back as she attempted to drag it off, entangling itself with her arms and sticking to her face. She panicked. Her heart thudded and her breath caught in her throat. For a split second she wondered if this was what waterboarding felt like, but immediately discounted the thought as hysterical. Free at last, she threw her nightie on the floor. She reached for the glass of water on her bedside table and glugged down as much as she could manage, trying to put out the flames. The sensation of the cold water trickling down the insides of her stomach was unpleasant. Stripped and doused, she leant back, closed her eyes and waited for the inferno to die down.

It did so quickly, the heat radiating off her in waves. The slick of sweat that had coated her body only minutes earlier evaporated, leaving behind a deep chill and a tightness that felt like black pepper under her skin. She reached for the duvet and pulled it up around her. As the shaking subsided and her body slowly unclenched, something close to normal bodily function finally returned.

Released from the grip of her night sweat, Denise regrouped and began her second battle of the night – hand-to-hand combat with her brain.

Tonight the battalion of worries was fronted by a number of seemingly intractable work issues, but soon other concerns joined the assault, chief amongst them her sons. There was Aaron's stormy relationship with his girlfriend, Millie – they seemed to do nothing but fight, make up, then start all over again, often over the course of a single day. There was Lewis's future – if his A-level results were as bad as she was expecting, God knew what he was going to do. He couldn't play golf for the rest of his life. Next her mind pivoted to her youngest, Joe, and his persistent acne, and the impact it was having on his confidence. The weight of worry never seemed to get any lighter. Indeed, as her sons headed into adulthood, she found herself increasingly at a loss as to how to help, what to do or say to make it better. A hug and a kiss no longer cut it. Then there was Eric, her ageing father-in-law, who consumed so much of her time and offered so little in return, other than bad temper and military statistics. And down there, right at the bottom of a list that she should surely be near the top of, was her eighty-three-year-old mother, Lilian, hundreds of miles away in the North-East, alone in her little cottage by the sea. How long was it since Denise had spoken to her mum properly, without having her eye on her emails or her attention directed elsewhere? How long since she'd been to see her? Months!

Having exhausted her stock of family anxieties, Denise's brain fought wearily on, skirmishing with a myriad of smaller guilts and concerns. Before she knew it, she was worrying about the cracked drawer in the freezer, and whether she'd texted the joiner with the right measurements for the shelves they were having fitted in the dining room.

Enough! She knew worry was wasted energy.

She scrunched up her toes and released them ten times. She focused on each vertebra in her spine, imagining them aligned in a smooth curve. She tried to breathe from her diaphragm, resting her hand on her belly to check she was doing it correctly. She visualised being by the sea, imagined the soothing sound of the waves, the fresh air, the sense of peace she always felt when she was close to water. She rolled over onto her front and tried to channel her inner child. She rolled onto her side and counted her blessings.

Nothing worked.

She threw in the towel at 1.16 a.m. She simply couldn't face lying there any longer, staring into the darkness, listening to her husband, Simon, sleep, peacefully unaware of her nocturnal battles.

Trying to get to sleep was such a contradiction. Sleep was not responsive to effort. Once you started trying, you were doomed, as she knew from bitter experience. She slid out of bed, mindful of not disturbing Simon. He had a meeting down in Southampton in the morning. The alarm was set for 5.45 a.m. Four and a half hours. Not long if you had an early start; an eternity if you were awake and fretting. She shrugged on her old towelling dressing gown, crossed the landing quietly and crept downstairs.

A darkened house, with everyone else dead to the world, was one of the loneliest places on the planet. Denise chided herself for the thought. Of course that wasn't true. A teenager sleeping rough on the streets, a prisoner in a locked cell, a security guard patrolling an empty office block, an arthritic old lady sitting up in her chair, alone with her fading memories – the list of lonelier places and circumstances was endless, and deeply depressing. She really needed to limit her news intake before bed.

She switched on the under-cupboard lights in the kitchen, feeling reassured by their warm glow. As she waited for the kettle to boil, she moved the plate and knife from someone's evening snack to the sink, swept the crumbs off the worktop into her hand, threw them away and returned the loaf to the bread bin, twisting the bag shut as she did so. Then, despite having made a pact with herself that she wouldn't, she looked at her phone. There was, as always, a tranche of new emails. The downside of dealing internationally was that someone, somewhere, was always awake, working and awaiting a response. She skim-read through her messages, mentally prioritising them. That done, she composed a polite, but firm email to the supplier in San Francisco, reiterating her take on the latest supply issues and stressing the importance of it all being sorted before the next shipment.

Having corralled some of her 'work monkeys' into order ready for the morning, she felt a little better. She slipped her phone back into the pocket of her dressing gown and made herself a mug of tea. Proper tea, not camomile for Denise – it was bad enough being awake in the middle of the night, without drinking hot bath water. These small acts of distraction helped. The relentless, flickering spool of things to be done or sorted that played almost constantly inside her head slowed, their projection dimmed.

Denise knew she was lucky.

She had a close family: a faithful husband, three strapping sons and a mother who, although old, was fit and independent. She lived in a nice home and had a good job that, although busy and demanding, fitted around her family responsibilities. She had safety, security and more than enough money to keep the wolf from the door. Indeed, she – or, rather, they as a family – had the financial resources to track any wolf that might be found lurking in the manicured gardens of St Albans, humanely capture it and ship it off to Alaska, to be released back into the wild with its brethren. She was essentially a well-off, moderately healthy middle-aged woman. She had absolutely nothing to complain about. Nothing substantial going on in her life to explain her current sense of frustration, dissatisfaction and all-round off-kilterness.

Cradling her drink, Denise wandered through to the lounge. It was cast in silvery-grey moonlight, which made it look like an old black-and-white film set, although she was hardly rocking a Joan Crawford housecoat and chignon. She was wide awake now. She walked over to the window. Glanced out. The garden looked tempting. She imagined the cool grass under the soles of her feet, her dressing-gown hem soaking up the damp, the breeze on her skin. Perhaps she'd have a chance encounter with some nocturnal creature: a cat, a fox perhaps, maybe even one of those pesky wolves of her overactive imagination. Isn't that what always happened when characters in films went on solitary strolls in the moonlight? An image of a beautiful tousled-haired, footsore Reese Witherspoon and her equally beautiful red fox encountering each other in the snowy expanses in *Wild* popped into Denise's head.

No! She couldn't start wandering around the lawn in her dressing gown. That really would be tantamount to accepting that she was going slightly insane.

Denise raised her gaze from the empty lawn. The houses over the road were in total darkness. There was no face at an upper window, no crime of passion taking place for her to observe and become embroiled in. She was a witness to nothing. It was still and quiet and exactly what you'd expect of a good area, with nice neighbours, who – beyond the occasional polite 'hello' – kept themselves, and their business, very much to themselves.

Denise pulled herself away from the lack of drama, accepting that she was destined to while away the next couple of hours awake and unaccompanied by man or beast, or at least not by any real ones.

Chapter 2

Thea was late back. Very late. She clattered up the stairwell to her front door and let herself into the apartment. Once inside, she unstrapped her pretty, but excruciatingly uncomfortable sandals and kicked them off. They made a satisfying noise as they bounced along the floor, before coming to rest against the base of the huge brushed-steel plant pot that was artfully positioned in front of the middle window. Bullseye! Able to walk once again without wincing, Thea roved around the apartment switching on lamps, flooding her high-ceilinged, tastefully furnished home in light. There was no one else around to disturb, despite the late hour. Ella was with her father, again. It was, apparently, *more convenient for hockey practice.* She seemed to be staying with him more and more often these days. Thea crushed that vein of thought before it could start pulsing and pushing the old familiar jealousy around her well-dressed body. Tonight was not about her being a mother and the co-parent of a teenage daughter.

Music! That's what was needed. Some tunes to prolong the mood.

She chose Beyoncé, 'Best Thing I Never Had'. Not a bad anthem, at any time of day or night. Thea whacked up the volume, letting her spiritual sister sing out loud and proud. There were upsides to living in the middle of town. The primary one being that she had no real neighbours to speak of or consider. Her apartment sat on top of a row of offices that were empty outside of working hours. Admittedly there was no outdoor space, but there was what felt like acres of space inside.

Thea had found the apartment by pure chance a few years back. She'd been walking past the estate agent on Catherine Street when she saw one of the sales staff in the window adding a new property to the display boards. An architect-designed, newly converted 'unique living space' on the High Street, at a price she could in no way afford. Thea's attention had been snagged. After months of arguing that it was imperative she and Ella stay in the family home, she found herself going inside and asking to view the property. She'd fallen in love with it the minute she stepped over the threshold, negotiated as best she could – given that it was blindingly obvious she wanted the place – and had her offer accepted that same evening, all without saying a word to daughter, or her estranged husband, Marc.

Some things were just meant to be.

Despite the ongoing stress of paying the mortgage, not once in the intervening five years had Thea ever regretted her decision. The apartment was as different from their old house as it could possibly be, but that had been the whole point. A fresh start, of her own choosing, in surroundings with no memories and no associations, 2B The High Street, Harpenden had lived up to its promise. It had gifted Thea light and space, and the perfect mix of privacy with a simultaneous sense of being in the middle of things. Living in the apartment, she found the constant thrum of other people's lives going on outside reassuring, soothing even. Its position above the action, but not removed from it, gave her connection without direct contact. Most people were unaware that there was residential accommodation above the office fronts. Very few ever looked up and wondered who lived behind the tinted windows on the upper floors of the stylish old buildings that lined the High Street.

So what, if living on a different level from everyone else led to complications.

The day she and Ella had moved in, the removal van had caused a tailback all the way to the Common. Deliveries were a nightmare – parcels ended up left in dustbins or with one of the shop owners. And the parking at the back of the building was a very tight squeeze – hence trading in her much-loved Audi for the Mini. But none of the hassle of town-centre living really bothered Thea, because she loved her new home. It made her feel invincible.

Free of her vertiginous heels, Thea danced around her expensive, but very lovely home, feeling the buzz of alcohol and excitement zipping around her bloodstream.

She had been on a real date.

The first in a very long time.

A nice restaurant.

A nice man.

A nice evening.

Small things, perhaps. No, that wasn't true – they were big things.

Men paid Thea quite a lot of attention. She had the looks and the attitude that attracted them. In theory she had plenty of options and opportunities, but in reality the type of men who showed an interest in her wanted sex more than they wanted anything else. True, she sometimes wanted sex too, but rarely did she want it badly enough to lower the reassuring barriers that she'd built around herself since her divorce. The couple of drink-oiled encounters that she had gone through with – in hotel rooms far away from her home, her daughter and her professional life – had been okay, but who wanted a life based on okay and the cover of darkness?

Thea shimmied another circuit around the sofas, swaying her hips and shaking her ass – once more for luck. Not that she believed in random good fortune, but she didn't want to jinx this tentative feeling of excitement and hope.

Tonight she had spent time with a nice man.

A man who seemed to like her.

A man she liked in return.

A man who wasn't Marc.

For a start, the nice man was taller than Marc – that was a bonus. His height had made her feel dainty. He had the kind of physique that seemed eminently capable of encircling you and keeping you safe. It was so Mills & Boon she should be ashamed of herself, but she wasn't. He had made her feel feminine, and Thea had liked that. True, the nice man did have hair that was worryingly similar to Marc's – close-cropped, lightly greying – but that similarity was offset by his totally different face. The nice man had a more prominent nose, slightly thinner lips and less noticeably blue eyes. That wasn't to say he wasn't good-looking. He was, just in a different way. Because, somehow, despite his physique, the nice man had seemed slightly less masculine – though not in a bad way. Perhaps that was down to his voice, which, though warm, educated and courteous, was not as deep as Marc's.

Yes, all in all, it had been a very pleasant surprise that the nice man had been as nice in person as he had seemed on his profile and in his messages, and that was something worth celebrating. Thea threw herself down on one of the sofas and stretched out.

And he had asked to see her again.

He'd come straight out with it, in the middle of the meal, laying his cards face up on the table, no bluffing or faking or playing games. She'd liked that about him as well: the directness. She'd declined to give him an immediate answer, of course. Instead she'd excused herself and gone to the Ladies to... *freshen up*. A phrase she never used. *Coy* was not in her repertoire – *hard to get*, that was a different matter. In the harsh glare of the mirror she'd studied herself, trying to see what he was seeing, to work out what it was about her that was calling to him. In it she saw a woman who looked good for her age, which was forty-nine. Or perhaps good for any age. Almond-shaped, blue eyes. Good brows. It was a strong face with well-proportioned and positioned features. Features she had inherited from her mother. Thea had seen a programme once about the science of attraction and had been proud to be able to tick many of the 'required' boxes to qualify as a conventional beauty, totally aware – even as she was congratulating herself – that her face was purely the product of genes.

What were this woman's faults? Or at least what were her visible flaws? Her internal flaws could wait – wasn't that the joy of a new relationship, the ability to keep things hidden, at least for a little while? Thea rotated her head through 180 degrees to get a better view of herself. There was her mouth. It was a touch too wide and filled with gappy teeth that 1980s orthodontics had never quite fixed. And there was her nose: it had a bump on the bridge – the legacy of an old hockey injury – that no amount of concealer could conceal. On balance, Thea thought these imperfections added character to her appearance.

But the key ingredient that the mirror captured was confidence. The woman in the mirror met Thea's scrutiny full on and returned it, with interest. Hopefully it was that strength of character, as much as her conventional good looks, that was intriguing the nice man, who was – as she preened – sitting at their table in the crowded restaurant fiddling with the stem of his wine glass, waiting for her. Thea touched her lips with a dab of colour and adjusted her neckline – in his favour.

She'd returned to the table, slid into her seat and they'd talked on long into the night, convincing themselves of each other's potential. And as they chatted and sipped their wine, and were sublimely oblivious to the other customers finishing their meals and melting away, Thea had given the nice man, who was not Marc, a hundred small gestures of encouragement, but no actual promises.

At the end of the evening, when the last waiter left standing finally ushered them out of the restaurant and locked the door behind them, she'd declined to allow him to escort her home; indeed, she'd insisted that he didn't, thereby asserting her independence and protecting, for now, the sanctity of her address.

Beyoncé started in on 'Sorry'. Thea clicked her off. The apartment fell quiet, or as quiet as it ever got with the almost constant sound of traffic and the sporadic bursts of drunken shouting from the street below. It was time for bed. She had work in the morning. She retraced her steps, turning off the lights as she went. She didn't extinguish all of them. Thea always left the floor lamp near the front door on. A nightlight for a daughter, who no longer needed it, especially when she wasn't there.

Despite the late hour, Thea stuck to her routine. She undressed, slipped on her dressing gown, hung up her dress, threw her underwear in the laundry basket and laid her clothes out ready for the morning. She removed her make-up thoroughly, slapped some moisturiser on her face, then brushed her hair twenty times, silently saying goodnight to her mother as she did so. Night-time ritual complete, she climbed into bed and turned off the light.

Thea was reliant on her own body heat to take the edge of the coolness of her king-sized cotton sheets, just as she was reliant on herself for so many things. It took a little while. In the darkness she brought her hand to her face. She followed the bony contours of her cheeks and her nose with her fingertips, explored the smoothness of her cheeks and the fullness of her lips. She ran her fingers along her jaw

19

and down her neck. She lightly stroked the fragile thinness of the skin of her breastbone, before moving on to the soft weight of her breasts.

Gently, slowly, lovingly she traced herself into existence.

She stopped, broke contact with her body, arousal crowded out by more complicated emotions.

She laid her hand on her stomach, let it rest there for a few seconds, feeling her tummy rise and fall. Instinctively her fingertips found the top of the scar. She ran her fingers along the full length of it. Each dent, bump and pucker was as familiar to her as her face. The skin along the ridge was smooth and shiny now, the passage of time reducing the violence done to her to something almost, but not quite, benign.

The scar was her proof of life, but it was also a marker of how close to death she'd been.

She had fought and won.

She had been hurt, but healed.

Whether she'd fully recovered was another matter entirely.

Chapter 3

DENISE WAS on her way out to visit Eric, her father-in-law, when she heard Joe and Lewis in the lounge. She paused, although she really didn't have the time, hoping to catch what her sons were talking about. Her boys rarely actually spoke to each other, at least not in her presence. They seemed to prefer to communicate physically. Shoves, head slaps, punches, kicks, finger flicks. It was often hard for Denise to tell what was mock fighting and what was real. They'd be casually, amicably sprawling next to each other one minute and battering each other with real intent the next.

It was her and Simon's fault. Her sons were too close in age. Sixteen months between Aaron and Lewis, fourteen between Lewis and Joe. When Aaron was home from university the brawling ticked up another notch – all of them trying to assert their alpha-male credentials. The amount of testosterone in the house was so high that Denise sometimes thought she could actually taste it.

When they were young, Denise used to watch the mothers with only one child enviously, especially those with daughters. The calm, the sense of peace, the gentleness, was sometimes too much for her to bear as she presided over her pack of sons. It was a jealousy she would have vehemently denied, had anyone commented on it. She'd hoped they would grow out of the physical stuff as they got older, but it hadn't happened. Indeed, the fierce competition had only grown worse, the contact between them more boisterous. At nineteen, seventeen and fifteen, they behaved like unpredictable children in men's bodies. She loved them as fiercely as ever, of course, but she felt she understood them less and less as they grew up and away from her.

'Told ya.' Lewis's languid tones.

There was a pause. 'Yeah. I see what ya mean.'

She disliked their lazy drawl. To her, it seemed put on – a fake to indicate confidence.

'How old do you reckon?' Lewis again.

'Not sure. It's hard to tell. Have you seen her without her make-up on?'

'Nah.'

There followed a contemplative silence.

It was Joe who spoke next. 'Old enough.'

It was the tone as well as the sentiment that shocked Denise. She clumped into the room, deliberately creating a disturbance. The pair of them were kneeling up on the sofa, looking out through the bay window. At the sound of her approach they moved fast – which was a sure sign they were up to no good.

'What are you doing?'

They both collapsed into liquid-limbed indifference on the sofa. 'Nothing,' they said in unison.

She moved towards the window. The new family who'd just moved into number nineteen were unloading a supermarket shop from the car. As the teenage girl lifted out the last bag, there was a flash of taut, tanned midriff. The girl slammed the boot and followed her mum down the side of the house. Denise stared at each of her sons in turn. 'Well, I'd *like* you to stop doing "nothing" quite so blatantly and do something more constructive.' They didn't move. 'Now!'

The sharpness of the last word finally provoked a response – albeit a languid one. They unfurled slowly into something resembling an upright position and loped across the room, out of her sight.

In the hall she heard them laughing. She grabbed her jacket from the hook and headed out, one more worry added to her list.

Chapter 4

WHEN THEA arrived, Nancy was dancing to Dean Martin, dressed to impress in a pink satin ensemble, with a jade silk scarf trailing behind her like fag smoke. Only the four necklaces today. She looked perfectly serene as she swayed around her room, bumping into the furniture occasionally. As requested, the staff had pushed everything they could to the edge of the room, to give her mother more room to dance. They were good that way; they tried their best to recognise and accommodate the people the residents used to be, not the ones they'd become. When Nancy caught sight of Thea, she beamed, not with recognition, but with the pleasure of having a guest. Thea was used to it. It didn't hurt any more. Well, not so much. Thea had brought flowers with her, as she often did. It was an easy shortcut to bring joy into her mother's randomly spotlit life. Music, flowers, chocolates, perfume – Nancy still like to be courted.

'Come. Join me,' Nancy beckoned.

Thea put down the anemones, bought because they used to be her mother's favourite. They sashayed together around the carpet to Dean's crooning – Nancy lost in the raptures of her past, Thea doing her best to join her there, through the veil cast by her mother's dementia. Nancy felt insubstantial in her arms, a paper-cut-out version of her mother. When she laid her head on Thea's shoulder, there was waft of hairspray, perfume and old age. When she raised her head and smiled, there was the scent of Gordon's. They danced for five tracks, including the incessantly sunny 'Volare', before Thea managed to convince her mother it was time to take a breather, pleading weariness – her own. As she gently guided Nancy to her chair, Thea also contrived to turn down the volume a notch. Frank usurped Dean. One lush followed by another.

'How was last night?' Thea asked.

Having smoothed her skirt and patted her hair, her mother drew a fluttery breath, leant forward and began, as she always did, 'Well...' – a conspirator's glance left, then right – 'there was, I'm afraid to say, something of a furore. Giovanna was not happy. Not at all. And I can't say I blame her, not after all the effort she'd gone to.'

Thea sat back and listened as her mother told a fluid, but incomprehensible tale of fantasy and glamour with a liberal scattering of random, incorrect nouns and the insertion of the occasional fact. The *cold custard* and *that horrid man with no manners* being two such realities. Thea let it wash over her, smiling and nodding at what felt like the appropriate junctures. When the story petered out, Nancy sighed dramatically and raised her hand to her throat. A touch of Dame Margot today.

Thea recognised the signal. 'Are you thirsty, Mum?'

'Do you know, I think I may be.'

'Shall I go and fetch you a tea or a glass of juice?'

Nancy pretended to give it some thought. 'No. Not tea.'

Thea relented and went over to the mahogany drinks cabinet in the corner of the room. Nancy had insisted that it be transported with her when she'd moved into Cherry Trees, despite its evident inappropriateness and ugliness. Thea opened the drop-leaf front and fixed her mother a weak gin and tonic. The vellum was littered with old ring marks, a ghost map of social gatherings in happier times. Perhaps that was what her mother had been trying to hang on to – not the cabinet itself, but the memories it contained. From her handbag Thea extracted a small Tupperware box. Inside were fresh slices of lemon. Another small treat.

When she passed the G&T to her mother, Nancy glanced at it with both gratitude and a touch of disappointment. 'No ice?' She still had her standards.

'Sorry, Mum. It's an expensive handbag, but it has its limits.'

Nancy sipped, adding a smear of baby-pink lipstick to the rim of the glass, graciously resigned to a life where her pleasures were curtailed. It was up to Thea to introduce the next, non-taxing topic of conversation. She went with Nancy's grooming. 'I see they haven't been to cut your hair yet?'

'Am I booked in with Harry?'

Harry hadn't styled Nancy's hair in more than thirty years, owing to the fact that his salon had been situated in central London, which had become too much of an inconvenience once Nancy stopped going up to town so often; and because he'd been dead for a quarter of a century. Nancy had cried elegantly into a lace hankie at his funeral whilst wearing a hat that would have been more suited to Ascot than a crematorium in Tottenham. But there was nothing to be gained from reminding her mother of this fact. It would only make her sad all over again.

'No, he's away on holiday. Barbados, I believe.' Why not let Harry have some sun, after all this time? 'But the girl you like is booked to do it.' Thea had no idea which mobile hairdresser would be visiting the home that week and whether Nancy liked any of them or not, but it was all about positive reinforcement. It would, no doubt, be fine, given that her mother thrived on any and all attention, so long as the hairdresser was true to their profession and a good listener.

'Ah, yes.' Nancy joined in the fiction willingly enough. 'It'll be Clare. Such a lovely girl. Though she has rather fat ankles. All that standing, I suspect. Does it look a fright?' She patted her hair like it was a dog that might bite. It did have a touch of Bichon Frise about it.

'No, Mum. It looks lovely, as always, it's just getting a little long at the back.' Change of tack. 'And have you been going through to the dining room for your evening meal, like we discussed?'

Nancy hid behind her drink, which, given that it was gin and tonic, provided little cover for her fib. 'Oh yes. Most evenings. Though your father prefers the food at The Metropole.' Thea smiled. If her father was still squiring her mother out to dinner in her dusty, but seemingly happy memories, so much the better. Her parents had eaten out, or gone dancing, or attended concerts most weekends throughout their marriage. They had had that sort of relationship: dedicated, loving, romantic to the end. Thea felt a rush of affection for her mother's loyalty to her father. Appropriately enough, a round of applause filled the room. On the DVD player Frank handed over to Sammy Davis Jnr. Nancy set down her glass absent-mindedly. It toppled over and fell onto the carpet. Thea left it there. One of gin's many benefits was that it didn't stain. Nancy stood up and reached out her hands. Her nails were newly varnished, a pretty, iridescent pearl colour. Regular manicures were another habit that Thea maintained for her mother. 'I love this one.' Nancy's eyes sparkled cloudily in the sunshine.

And despite the aching boredom that came from having listened to the same DVD a hundred thousand times before, Thea stood up and stepped back out onto the dance floor of her mother's flickering imagination.

Chapter 5

'HOW'S HE been?' Denise asked the same question every time she visited the home, although the answer was never the one she wanted, which was 'dead'. The horrifying cruelty of wishing her father-in-law gone was merely one of Denise's dark secrets. She harboured a few such unkind desires, though no one ever seemed to detect the malevolent vein that ran through her – obscured, as it was, by her polite, self-effacing demeanour. This particular ardent death wish reared its head every time she stepped into the overheated lobby of Cherry Trees and braced herself for yet another round with Simon's seventy-nine-year-old father, Eric.

This was her second visit in as many days. She'd been summoned by an urgent request from the manager of the home, more of a demand really, to supply Eric with supplementary Blu Tack. Karen, the manager, had added *at your earliest possible convenience*. Politeness and insistence: they were an irrefutable combination. Eric's preferred method of fixing things to his walls – good, old-fashioned drawing pins – had recently been banned after he'd pressed a tack into the bent head of Cheryl, one of the cleaners. She'd unwisely attempted to pick up some of the 'paperwork' that encircled Eric's armchair like a porch-drop of indoor snow and had been pinned in the head for her trouble. The Blu Tack was a testily negotiated compromise that had created a seemingly unquenchable appetite for the stuff. On the call, Karen had explained that Eric had run out, again, and as a result had been getting 'very agitated' about his inability to make headway on his 'project'. This, to the ill-informed observer – namely, anyone brave enough to enter his room – appeared to be a commitment to cutting out every single article on military spending in Europe, the Balkans, Russia, Japan (his interest was old-school but global) and annotating these articles with a spider's web of comments and calculations. His aim being to demonstrate that the UK was woefully unprepared for the next big conflict, which he repeatedly predicted was only a matter of time. These scribbled-on articles were then stuck around the walls of his room in classic crime-drama fashion. Unfortunately, with the recent move to a bigger room, Eric had upscaled his efforts.

It was costing Denise a fortune in newsprint, Blu Tack and, most importantly, time.

Julie, the care assistant, shrugged, 'Same as usual.' Julie was one of the most tolerant, more experienced members of staff. She must have seen and put up with it all before. 'Though he did comment on the size of my arse this morning. And it wasn't a compliment.' Denise instinctively apologised, but Julie flapped the 'sorry' away with her small, blue-gloved hands. 'Shall I bring you both a cuppa?'

Her kindness caused a rush of tears to fizz up Denise's nose. She turned away, embarrassed. These bouts of sudden emotion – sadness and rage, about the smallest of things – were increasing in number and unpredictability. 'No, you're busy. I'm not staying long.' She vehemently hoped this was true as she tapped on Eric's door.

'What?' he shouted.

She took this as her invitation to enter.

The room was worse by 10 per cent than it had been when she'd last visited on Tuesday. It wasn't just the mess, she was used to that; it was the frenzy reflected in the mess. The chaos Eric created around him spoke of frustration and anger, of things not dropped absent-mindedly, but hurled with intent. As always, this physical display of his distress enabled Denise's sympathy to scramble over the top of her irritation. Eric hated being old – detested it – and, as a result, his furious response guaranteed that everyone who came into contact with him also had a hateful time. Which impacted on people's willingness to visit, which increased his isolation, which made him more miserable, et cetera, et cetera. It was the true definition of a vicious circle.

'Afternoon, Eric.' Denise stepped into the room warily, nervous of disturbing some pattern of paperwork that only he could discern in the layers of stuff on the carpet. She left the door open, preferring to be able to see out, and be seen by the passing staff.

'Have you brought it?' He held out his hand, blue veins bulging beneath his crêpy skin. She dug the Blu Tack out of her handbag. He snatched at it and proceeded to count the packets. 'Is this all they had? Five packs!' She had thought it a lot. 'It'll have to do for now. But I'll be needing more, with the Spending Review coming out next week. Can't you bulk-buy the stuff? It'd save time, and money.'

'I'll look into it.' Placatory – that was the way to go, with her father-in-law.

Minimally satisfied by her offering, Eric put aside his new supply on top of a pile of papers and fumbled open a pack. He pulled a lump of Blu Tack off the sheet and began rolling it between his fingers. Denise noticed that his nails needed cutting, but quailed at the thought.

'How's it going?' She had to ask. This was his 'work' now, and not asking was tantamount to disrespect.

'I'm making progress, but the review will stir up a shitstorm, so I want to be ready for it. The head of the MOD is already doing the rounds, setting his stall out. They're obviously not happy.'

Denise nodded as if she had some clue what he was talking about – but not enough, obviously, to offer a valid opinion. Eric was used to women who were seen, not heard. Simon's mother, Maggie, had fulfilled that brief perfectly. Even her death had been a quiet affair: a soft crumpling onto the kitchen floor in the middle of crimping the edge of an apple-and-blackberry pie. A massive heart attack at the age of sixty-five. No one heard her fall. Eric, who eventually found her when he went in search of his lunch, had been devastated. But his genuine and heartfelt sorrow had not softened him. Instead, his grief had hardened around him like a carapace. And with every year that passed of his miserable, lonely, angry old age, it seemed to grow thicker and sharper.

It was all very sad.

It was also a major pain to have to deal with on a regular basis.

Denise wondered if leaving within five minutes of arriving was acceptable and knew it was not. You had to sign in and out of the home – a public register of familial duty observed. Added to which Eric's new room was, unfortunately, just across the corridor from the communal lounge, and so the brevity of her stay would be noted by the ever-vigilant staff. When your family member was on the 'challenging' end of the spectrum, you were expected to share the load.

Karen had positioned the room switch as a way of giving Eric more space for his project, but Denise suspected it had more to do with the staff wanting to keep a closer eye on his interactions with the other Cherry Trees occupants. Her father-in law's drive to proselytise was rarely met with much enthusiasm. Quite naturally, most of the residents preferred conversations about gardening and the royals to diatribes on the dangers of reduced defence spending. Eric's loudly voiced categorisation of his neighbours as *brain-dead* also did little to endear him to them. And when, as it inevitably did, Eric's rudeness caused serious offence, it always fell to Denise to deal with the problem – Simon's relationship with his father being too combative for him to bring up the old man's intolerance. These increasingly necessary, painfully awkward 'little chats' about Eric's behaviour never went down well. At least today she wasn't having to tackle his rudeness head on, merely live with it for half an hour or so.

Denise accepted her fate and moved a stack of books off one of the chairs. 'May I?'

'Give them here.'

She passed him the pile and sat down. 'How have you been keeping, Eric?'

'You asked me that on Tuesday. Nothing's changed in the space of two days.' Small talk was not one of Eric's fortes.

'Yes. You're quite right, I did – sorry.' But what the hell else was there to say? So she lied. 'Simon and the boys send their love.' For a second the old man paused in his restless wandering. His faded blue eyes settled on her and she felt a draught of discomfort and sympathy. Eric might be old, but he wasn't stupid. She rushed on. 'The gardens are looking nice. Do you fancy a walk? Outside,' she clarified pointlessly.

'The grass will be wet. I don't want my turn-ups ruined.'

'Okay.' She cast around for another topic and found herself struggling. Her attention wandered. Through the open door she heard music. Sinatra whooping it up in New York. 'Sorry, Eric.' She had missed a question.

He came and stood over her – making the most of his still impressive six-foot-plus height. Simon had inherited his father's stature. Denise wondered, with an involuntary shiver, whether he would develop the same short fuse.

'I asked about the business,' he said testily. 'Did Simon get that problem with the US supplier sorted?'

Mather's had been set up by Eric. It represented his life's work. He still held a non-exec director title, out of respect. Denise had told him about the issues they'd been having with a supplier in San Francisco, as a distraction when she'd last visited. There was nothing wrong with his memory, just his grasp of her role in the business. 'It's being sorted.'

Eric did not look convinced by her reassurance. 'Simon needs to be careful they're not shafting him. They're renowned for it, the Yanks. They think we're all wet behind the ears.'

'I'll mention it to him,' Denise said. She obviously had no intention of doing so. Simon had endured more than his fair share of his father's advice and guidance over the long years they'd worked together. His relief when his father had finally retired, after considerable pressure to do so, had been immense. That fraught period went some way to explaining Simon's reluctance to spend anything other than the bare minimum of time with his father now – explained, but did not excuse it. She glanced at her watch. Had she really only been in his room fifteen minutes? She felt her phone burr in her bag: another missed work call. But she didn't get it out to check. Eric had a passionate hatred of mobile phones, as he'd forcefully demonstrated a couple of months back when she'd got sucked into a long conversation about an issue with a shipment. She'd been so intent on resolving the problem that she'd forgotten to keep an eye on the old boy. Her shock when he'd ripped the phone out of her hand and hurled it across the room, smashing the screen in the process, had been intense. In an immediate reflex attempt to calm things down, she'd been the one to apologise for taking the call in the first place.

Eric had resumed his patrolling around the room. He stopped every now and again to peer at one of the cuttings plastered on the walls. The image an old lion pacing up and down the bars of his cage came to Denise. It was the same restless toing and froing, with no real purpose. She saw her 'get out' and took it. 'Well, I can see you have a lot to get on with. I'll not disturb you any longer. I'll look into a bulk-buy of the Blu Tack, as you asked.' It was just like the old days when he'd been her boss. Family businesses! If only she'd known about their very persistent and peculiar challenges when she'd first offered to help out in the office. She stood up. 'I'll call in again next week, Eric.'

He switched his attention back to her, briefly. Nodded, curtly. 'Very well.' Then he resumed his circuit.

Dismissed, she made a hasty exit, relieved to have fulfilled her duty – until next time.

Out in the corridor she heard clapping, followed by someone whistling. The whistling gave way to the swell of violins, then Sammy Davis Jnr began crooning 'Mr Bojangles'. The music wasn't coming from the residents' lounge, as she'd first assumed; it was coming from one of the rooms further along the corridor.

Denise didn't mean to intrude, but, with the door open and the strains of a full orchestra drifting out, it was only natural to glance inside as she made her way past. What she saw made her smile. An elegant old lady, wearing a pink dress, dancing with someone who had to be her daughter. The two women were spotlit by the sunshine streaming in through the big bay window. The daughter held her mother in her arms with real tenderness as they swayed together to the music, eyes closed, full of grace, in a world of their own making.

It was such a picture of contentment that Denise stopped and watched them for a few seconds, before turning away.

Chapter 6

THEY WERE going to have breakfast together, for a change, which should be nice. Or at least Thea hoped it would. Pain au chocolat and croissants, bought fresh from the deli on her morning run, proper coffee, a proper conversation. As she laid out the plates and cups, the sun streamed in through the open windows and the sounds of the already-busy High Street rose up from below. She paused, made herself appreciate the moment. She supposed it was a good sign that she had to remind herself to stop and smell the roses these days.

She was going into work late because she had a long day ahead of her. There was a do at The Grosvenor that evening, 250-plus carefully selected guests. Canapés and wine to oil the wheels. Chamber music to ease the hard sell. Government money to pump-prime the private investment. Her department was the event sponsor. It was one of their formal events of the year. The Department for International Trade still did a surprising amount of business the old way. If you were female, a dress and heels were de rigueur. She had an oyster silk Whistles shirt dress hanging ready in her office. Ella was going over to Marc's to sleep, again. She refused to stay in the apartment on her own when Thea was going to be late back, which was, Thea supposed, understandable, but surely she could have slept at a friend's or had a friend over to the apartment instead of fleeing back to her father's? That they were still fighting over their daughter's time and affection, after all this time, made Thea sad. If she thought about it too much, it would make her bitter.

Not this morning.

This morning was about spending time together. 'Ella! It's ready.' The smell of buttery pastry and coffee filled the apartment. She heard her daughter's footsteps clattering along the hallway, away from and not towards the kitchen. Thea poured a cup of coffee for herself and an orange juice for Ella, then tore the end off a croissant, enjoyed the layers of flaky pastry filling her mouth. Ella clumped into the room, the post in her hand. She climbed onto one of the stools, dumped the mail on the work surface, then turned her attention to her breakfast. The mail looked like the usual pile of nonsense – takeaway fliers, a cellophane-wrapped copy of a marketing magazine that Thea still subscribed to, but never read and, ominously, an official-looking envelope with her name printed on the front. She knew what it was. She reached for the pile, turned it over, pushed it to one side and concentrated on her daughter.

Their conversation was sporadic at first, driven by her, but that was normal. Ella was in some ways a typical fifteen-year-old and making small talk ten minutes after waking up was not on her list of favourite activities, but after she'd consumed her first croissant with butter and jam she rallied and started chatting. Thea learnt about a school trip she'd been unaware of – *Macbeth* in Watford, it was one of their set texts – and about a gross injustice involving a girl called Sabine on the hockey team, who had been picked to play on Saturday despite rarely coming to training. *And* – Ella went for a pain au chocolat next – *when she did deign to turn up, she didn't put in nearly enough effort, but stood around criticising other players.* Thea nodded sympathetically and watched, with pleasure, as Ella ate and drank and shimmered – full of life and righteous indignation.

Half an hour later, gripes aired and stomach full, she set off for school. Thea was left with the dirty crockery and the post. But instead of addressing either, she got up and walked over to the windows. She was just in time to see Ella emerge onto the High Street and set off in the direction of the bus stop – weaving in and out of the other pedestrians – her ponytail swinging, her oversized backpack making her look smaller than she really was. She soon disappeared from sight, but Thea continued to stare out after her, safe in her eyrie, watching the slow traffic and the fast eddies of people coming and going. A lethargy descended on her. The warmth of the sun was seductive. She felt disinclined to move. She rested her forehead against the glass, glad of the support. A thought occurred to her. She could call in sick, go back to bed, pull the duvet over her head, give the reception a swerve. She could message Ella, tell her to come home instead of going to her father's. She could take a brief sabbatical from her professional life – focus on the personal, for a change. The temptation was there, whispering softly but insistently in her inner ear.

But, of course, she had no intention of listening to that siren voice. That way lay depression. It would be a sign of weakness, and Thea's defining characteristic was that she was not weak. She was strong, resilient, motivated, professional. Taking sick leave – never again. She had a case to prove, if not to anyone else, then to herself. She was formidable and she intended to stay that way.

She straightened up and turned back to the room. Time to move.

She cleared up the plates and cups, put the butter and jam back in the fridge, stacked the dishwasher and ran a cloth over the countertops. As she tidied, her gaze was inexorably drawn to the small stack of post near the fruit bowl. That needed dealing with as well. Kitchen clear, she slid the pile along to the end of the counter near the bin and depressed the pedal to lift the lid. She picked up the business mag first, dropped it in, vowing as she did so to cancel her subscription. The Indian takeaway menu went in next. The *Harpenden Hub* newsletter didn't even touch the sides. That left the letter, the only proper piece of actual correspondence. She picked it up, recognised the postmark, knew – with a churn of her stomach – what it denoted and, without giving herself time to waver, proceeded to rip it into a hundred tiny pieces. The confetti of words floated the same way as the rest of the junk.

Knowledge was power, but so was wilful ignorance.

Chapter 7

IT WAS the last thing Denise wanted to do. It already felt like a long week and it was only Wednesday. She glanced longingly through the steam at her faithful old dressing gown hanging on the back of the bathroom door. If only wishing made it so.

She couldn't put it off any longer, it was time.

She twisted the dial and gasped as the cold hit her. Despite the months of practice, she was still unable to control the initial, violent recoil. Physical shock was obviously not tameable. Her body contracted and her heart rate rocketed. A self-induced panic attack, all for the benefit – allegedly – of her increasingly wonky internal thermostat and the lump of cardiac muscle buried deep inside her chest. The things she did to keep age at bay. She rested her palms flat against the tiles and made herself lean into the needles of icy water. Her snatched breathing echoed around the shower cubicle, channelling Janet Leigh. Despite the pain, Denise forced herself to keep her body under the torrent. As she endured the freezing water she tried to distract herself by summoning up some little-known facts about *Psycho*.

From the messy, overflowing film-trivia archive that was squashed into the boxroom of her brain, she dredged up the fact that it hadn't been Janet Leigh who'd filmed the infamous shower scene, but a body double. Denise's breathing was less panicked now, though she was still holding herself rigid under the water. It had been another nubile blonde, a Playboy bunny, if her memory was correct. Name unknown, by Denise at any rate. The blood was now pooling in her feet and her heart seemed to have rattled to a complete stop, but the shock had at least receded and what remained was a deep, bone-penetrating chill. There was a story that Hitchcock's naked stand-in had, some years after the film had been released, been raped and murdered by a man obsessed with the infamous scene, but in true Hollywood style there had been a twist. The girl who had actually met such an awful end had been the lighting stand-in, not the body double.

Pleased with herself for being able to retrieve this complicated piece of grisly movie folklore, Denise snapped off the water and lunged for a towel. Heart exercised and body thermostat hopefully reset, it was time to get dressed to impress.

The function was being held at The Grosvenor on Park Lane. Of course it was. Economies waxed and waned, governments came and went, the sea rose and rose some more, but the Department for International Trade glided on as if Britain still had an empire, and the respect and influence that went with such global power. Of all the aspects of Simon's food import/export business, this was the part that Denise disliked the most. Glad-handing and networking, while trussed up in an uncomfortable outfit bought especially for the occasion, were not Denise's idea of fun. Although, loath as she was to admit it, she no longer had any notion of what was fun any more.

Occasionwear. In the early years of her marriage, the description had made no sense to Denise. She came from a family where clothes were either *everyday* or *best*. The nonsense of buying exceptionally expensive suits and dresses that you only ever wore 'occasionally' still struck Denise as odd, despite the fact that she now had a section of her wardrobe dedicated to such outfits. Tonight's choice, prompted by the upscale venue and the gold-embossed invitation, was a fitted, floor-length black crêpe-de-Chine evening dress and a pair of matching heels, finished off with a splashy patterned pashmina, which would no doubt spend the whole evening slipping off her shoulders. The description of the outfit sounded far more glamorous than the end result looking back at Denise from the full-length mirror, but she was used to such disappointments. Her eyes were drawn to the stretch of fabric across her stomach and the way the dress clung to her rear – and not in the flattering modern way. She was also worried about how much of her upper arms were on display. But it would have to do; she had her game face to apply. She set to work with skill, rejuvenating her skin and making the most of her indifferent features.

Never did Denise feel more like a wife, and less like a person, than at upmarket business junkets.

In contrast, Simon loved the whole performance. The slipping on of an immaculately pressed shirt, the selection of the right cufflinks, the deliberation about which cologne to wear, the 'driving up to town' – though not the driving back, that was her department – the valet parking, the rooms loud with the buzz of other entrepreneurs (as business owners were now called), he genuinely enjoyed it all.

Hence his good mood as they left the house, and her subdued one.

An hour and a half later, standing on the threshold of The Grosvenor's huge gilded ballroom, which was full of people who might be of use to them, Denise couldn't shake the familiar trepidation that always assailed her before such gatherings. But she knew that it was the price of doing business and, more importantly, of doing it profitably. To stay afloat you had to keep swimming, so she smiled, slipped her arm through Simon's and they plunged in.

After three rounds of paddling around the room she retreated to the sidelines, found herself a little niche to hide in and drew breath. Standing alone, grasping the slender stem of a wine glass full of warm, no-longer-sparkling water, she watched the endlessly shifting eddies of Paul Smith suits and Reiss dresses. Simon was somewhere in the melee, but she had given up trying to maintain contact with him. He'd be onto his third or fourth glass of champagne by now, working the crowd with his insightful, witty anecdotes and his charm. It was what he did best. He no longer needed her by his side, cheering him on. After twenty-four years of marriage they knew what each other's strengths and weaknesses were and played to them. They were a good team. Besides, it was a relief not to have to laugh at the punchline to stories she'd heard a hundred times before.

Denise glanced at her watch and wondered how much longer he'd be. The drive back to St Albans would take them more than an hour. She had an early call in the morning. The thought of it drove her to check her phone again. Eight new emails since she'd last checked. She glanced at the contacts, mentally sifting them by priority. The logistics were her department, which meant that most of the problems were hers to sort out. She decided she would get up at 6 a.m. to clear at least of a couple of the straightforward process issues, before her call.

It was as she slipped her phone back into her bag that it happened. No warning. Just the sensation of a trapdoor opening, and a gush. Simultaneously she heard her name being called.

'Denise! It's been an age. How the hell are you?'

The man looked familiar. Peter Something. In baking ingredients, if she remembered correctly. It was too late to pretend she hadn't heard or seen him. She smiled and took a step towards him. Felt another gush. 'Well. And you?' Desperately she squeezed her thighs together.

'Mustn't grumble.' He looked past her. 'Simon not with you?'

Thank God for the old boys' network. 'Yes, he's here somewhere. He might be at the bar.' Which was, helpfully, in the other room. 'I'm sure he'll want to say hello and have a catch-up?' Denise was confident that he wouldn't, but needs must.

Peter Something hesitated, perhaps waiting for her to lead the way, but there was no chance she was going to walk in front of him anywhere. 'I'll be through in a minute. I need to make a couple of calls.' She drew her mobile out of her bag and waggled it. Permission to re-join the pack granted, the man who made money from powdered eggs turned away. 'See you in there.'

The second his back was turned, Denise began her slow, but urgent progress around the edge of the ballroom. She kept her legs clamped together so tightly that she had to hobble as if her feet had been bound at birth. With each limited step she prayed that no one else would recognise her.

After what felt like an age, she made it to the ladies' powder room. Just. Once on the other side of the door she stopped for a moment, glad to have made it to safety without her predicament becoming obvious. Her relief was almost immediately replaced by an acute rising panic as she realised that her stylish evening bag contained nothing of any use for the torrent of menstrual blood that was now flowing out of her – again. Fifteen days since her last period. She should have been okay, but equally, given how unpredictable her cycle now was, she should have come prepared. As she took a tentative step towards one of the cubicles, the door opened and in strode a woman who seemed horribly familiar. The effortless, shiny chestnut-coloured hair, the willowy height, a certain unmistakeable poise, which was accentuated by her figure-hugging oyster-grey dress. It was the woman Denise had glimpsed dancing with her mother at Eric's care home. Denise was stranded.

The woman nodded a greeting. 'Hi.' She seemed about to head over towards the sinks, but hesitated. Obviously bemused by Denise's static pose. 'Are you all right?'

'Yes, fine,' Denise lied. 'Just, you know, a touch of stomach cramp.' She straightened up in an attempt to prove it was nothing, which released another pulse of blood.

The woman's beautiful face smoothed into a hesitant, if somewhat bemused smile.

'You're here at the do?'

'Yes. We're distributors. Retail and trade customers. Nuts, dried pulses, spices. That sort of thing.' Denise didn't know why she was waffling on about Mather's, given her predicament, nor why she decided to ask, 'And you?' Politeness was a curse sometimes.

'I work at the DIT.'

Denise heard herself say 'Ah' at the same time as the flow of blood that had been making its way down her leg finally reached her ankle. It was imperative that she move. 'Well, it was nice talking to you.' She desperately wanted to make it into the cubicle and shut the door.

'Yes. Enjoy your evening.' At last the elegant DTI woman turned away and Denise was free.

She'd never been so grateful to slide a lock on a door. Sanctuary at last – although she didn't properly breathe out until she heard the woman's heel high heels signalling her exit.

Five minutes later, as Denise sat on the loo looping toilet roll around her hand, she heard the door to the Ladies open and the click of heels again, a pause, then a tap on the door to her stall. 'Are you still in there?' She was back.

Denise hated the hesitancy in her voice as she answered, 'Yes.'

The footsteps pattered into the next cubicle, then a hand appeared under the divide, bearing a small John Lewis carrier bag. 'One of the benefits of working in an all-female team. We keep supplies in.'

Denise took the proffered 'gift'. She barely had time to say 'thank you' before the heels were on the move again, out of the cubicle and out of the Ladies. The door shut with a muffled thud. She looked inside. Pads and tampons. And, to her discomfort but deep gratitude, a pack of tights. Sheer black. One-size. Ten denier. And underneath the tights, a pair of knickers. Plain, cotton, new. A rescue package.

She could have cried.

Ten minutes later she emerged from the powder room restored and able to walk upright.

She went on a husband hunt.

She found Simon, pink-cheeked and relaxed, leaning against the bar, the epicentre of a circle of faces she didn't recognise. Networking or, more accurately, just plain working. He was adept at disguising trading as socialising. He kissed her cheek and introduced her to Edward, Seb, Katherine and Nisham. They all beamed at her as if she was exactly what they'd been waiting for. Denise endured another twenty minutes of shop talk, before an opportunity to leave finally presented itself when they realised their glasses were empty. As Simon turned and began to raise his hand to summon the barman, Denise made her move by announcing that 'Lovely as it has been, we really need to be going as we both have early starts in the morning.'

Simon immediately lowered his hand. Message received and understood. He smiled. 'The boss has spoken.' He straightened to his full six-foot-three height and shook each of their hands. 'I'll drop you a note tomorrow, Seb, with the contact details for that guy in New York. Honestly, he's so much cheaper than Gardeners.' With goodbyes and handshakes dispensed, he followed Denise out of the ballroom at her pace, which was swift to the point of being Cinderella-ish.

To her immense relief, Denise did not see her glamorous saviour again.

It was only when they were back in the car, and she'd swapped her heels for her flats and pulled the seat closer to the steering wheel, that she felt better. She could sense Simon watching her as she got herself settled. He waited until they'd pulled into the surprisingly heavy traffic, given that it was gone 11 p.m., before he made a comment, as she knew he would. 'They weren't that bad. Not by Peter Stansfield standards. Thank you for sending him over, by the way.'

'They were perfectly fine, but I was tired and I'd had enough.'

He let it go. His gaze drifted to the night-time economy, which was still very much in full swing outside the confines of the car, the first properly warm evening of the summer having brought everyone out onto the streets. Simon was quite drunk, but you'd have to have been his wife for quarter of a century to tell. There was no slurring or slumping, no loosened tie or untucked shirt. Indeed there was nothing dishevelled about Simon at all – there rarely was. He was like a TV anchorman: calm, in control and fond of the occasional catchphrase. After a few minutes of people-watching, his attention returned to her. She shifted in her seat, concentrated on her driving and on the random hazard of pedestrians who threw themselves off pavements at this time of night in central London. He reached over and stroked her neck affectionately. 'Are you all right? You look a little pale.'

She said, 'Yes, fine' and made an effort, despite her discomfort, to sound brighter and sit up straighter.

He accepted her reassurance. Why would he not put two and two together and come up with four? She could hardly blame him for not noticing something she was hiding from him. 'Nearly the weekend.'

She nodded and carried on driving, avoiding eye contact.

Denise didn't fully relax until she finally pulled off the North Circular onto the M1. As she did so, she felt another torrent of blood, but this time her secret was safe, due to the kindness of another woman.

Chapter 8

THE FOLLOWING Sunday found Thea parked up outside Marc's house like an Uber driver. She was, as she so frequently seemed to be these days, waiting for Ella, but the only meter ticking was the one that enumerated her frustration. She'd texted Ella and got no response. There was no sign of either Marc or Jenny's car. The house seemed as quiet as a grave. She tried calling again. It went to voicemail. She threw her phone down on the passenger seat. Denied the true object of her anger, she chose to take out her bitterness on the neighbourhood and the prosperous, conventional family homes of Prospect Crescent, St Albans. The neat hedges, the soulless over-mown lawns, the child-friendly lack of traffic or life – or action of any sort.

Domesticity raised up on a pedestal.

The perfect place to raise a family.

The location of Marc and Jenny's new for-ever home.

It was the top rung of a ladder that Marc had been climbing ever since their separation five years ago. She remembered each and every step he'd taken away from her – the bed in

51

the den of their old house, the room at the Premier Inn, the tiny serviced apartment behind the station, the flat on Glebe Street, the rented house in London Colney and now here. How many of these abodes Jenny had shared with him, Thea still wasn't sure. In the official version of their relationship, Jenny did not put in an appearance until Glebe Street.

Yeah, right.

It was impressive really, the speed with which he'd built a totally new life with the new love of his life. Although Jenny was not, as yet, his wife. That fact still gave Thea a pathetic sense of satisfaction. Though it was probably simply because they hadn't had time – being far too busy conceiving children (plural) and moving. Perhaps the wedding would be the next big event, or maybe they'd squeeze in another child first. The house looked plenty big enough.

Surrounded by sunshine and birdsong and suburban pleasantness, Thea sat and stewed in the fresh juice of old resentments.

She'd been shoved to the kerb by a woman with a soft, fertile body and a gift for home economics. Even her name, Jenny, spoke of homeliness and goodness. Charming, spontaneous, thrill-seeking, career-driven Marc had chosen comfort over passion, a good cassoulet over a feisty conversation. Marc, who she'd loved passionately and wholeheartedly, had opted for an easy life as opposed to an interesting one – in direct contravention of everything he'd claimed mattered to him. Five years on, and she still didn't truly understand or accept it.

And now, to make matters worse, Ella was following his lead.

Where the hell were they?

Thea picked up her phone. Put it down again. No message. No apology. No respect.

Suddenly there was a face filling the passenger window. Some middle-aged woman, busybodying for the local Neighbourhood Watch no doubt. She looked the type. Reluctantly Thea pressed the button and the window slid down.

'Hello.' The woman smiled, nervously. Thea studied her. She had a pale complexion and a fine mesh of worry lines surrounding her light-blue eyes. Her hair was blow-dried into an exact bob that was so neat it made Thea want to ruffle it. Her voice was sprigged with anxiety. 'I thought it was you, but I wasn't sure.'

That's what jogged Thea's memory. It was the woman she'd helped out at the DIT bash.

The woman went on, a little breathlessly, 'What a coincidence! I live across the road. Number twenty-four.' She gestured at a large, double-fronted detached house. Thea nodded. The woman's skin mottled red. 'I just wanted to say thank you. For the other night – the do. At The Grosvenor. It was very kind of you.'

'No worries.' Thea meant it. It's what she hoped anyone would do.

'I'm Denise.' The woman looked expectant.

Thea felt obligated to volunteer her own name and offer her hand. 'Thea.' It was an awkward handshake through the gap in the window.

Still the woman lingered. Thea was disinclined to explain why she was sitting, parked in her car, outside an obviously empty house, no matter how stalker-ish her behaviour might appear. The situation smacked of desperation.

'Well, thank you again.' Denise's face started to retreat from view. Thea's hand moved towards the button. 'If you need anything. Like I say. Number twenty-four.'

The window purred shut.

Half an hour later, Thea was regretting her lack of sociability. There was still no sign of Ella and Marc, but there was every indication that if they didn't arrive within the next five – or possibly, at an upper limit, ten – minutes, then she was going to wet herself. Drinking a couple of cups of coffee before she set off had been a bad idea. Her options were to drive off and try and find a garage or to shlep all the way to the big Sainsbury's at London Colney (that thought really didn't appeal), or she could take up the offer of help 'if you need anything' from a relative stranger.

A stranger who had a ringside view of Marc and Jenny's lovely new home.

Another five minutes sitting with her pelvic floor muscles clenched decided the matter.

It was a relief when her knock at the door was answered by Denise herself. Thea really hadn't wanted to explain her situation to anyone else. As expected, Denise was welcoming and, joy of joys, the toilet was downstairs. Trying not to actually run, Thea dashed inside, locked the door, fumbled with the belt of her jeans and sank with gratitude onto the loo.

As she relaxed, she took in her surroundings. This was no ordinary downstairs loo. The basics were, of course, the same – a toilet, a washbasin, a mirror and a towel rail – but the decoration was unique. At first glance, Thea thought the walls were covered in a bold, some might say brave, choice of wallpaper. She'd seen similar in bars and hotels, faux shelves of leather-bound books. But on second glance, this room was actually lined with real built-in shelves that were filled, not with novels, but with hundreds (no, thousands) of DVDs. On closer inspection, Thea discovered that the DVDs were all films, neatly categorised by genre: comedy, drama, thriller (US and UK), horror, romance, foreign-language. There was also a large section of black-and-white classics. It was like being inside the tiniest, tidiest, cleanest Blockbusters ever. As Thea washed her hands, her attention was snagged by a shelf of family movies. There were a number of titles that she, Ella and Marc had watched, camped under their fluffy blankets on the sofa, when she'd been recovering. *Wreck-It Ralph*, *Brave*, *Hotel for Dogs*. Christ, how many times had they happily watched that pile of cheesy nonsense, snuggled up together, Thea book-ended by the small solidity of Ella and the larger block of Marc's reassuring presence?

She heard a cough and realised she was taking far too long. She dried her hands and stepped out into the vanilla-scented and painted hall. Denise was loitering in the doorway to the kitchen, obviously waiting for her to reappear.

'Thank you.'

'No problem,' Denise replied. There was a pause.

Thea had to say something. 'It's quite a collection.'

Denise smiled. 'Yes. They're my one vice. I always tell Simon it could be worse – it could be shoes or expensive handbags.' Involuntarily Thea glanced down at her own bag, a slate-grey Mulberry tote, bought to celebrate her promotion to Head of the East Asia Division. A red speckle of heat rash appeared in the V of Denise's shirt and she hurried on, obviously worried she'd committed a social faux pas. 'My sons think I'm mad. They're the digital generation. But I refuse to get rid of them. It was either in there or the garage.' The rash was now racing, rather than creeping, up her neck.

Thea smiled and quipped, 'So you're a closet film buff.' Not the funniest joke in the world, but surely not so bad as to cause Denise to redden even further. Thea tried to make amends. 'They look great. Men have their caves, so why shouldn't you have your loo full of movies?'

Despite having reached peak blush, Denise seemed keen to prolong their conversation. 'I love films. Have done since I was a kid. There's no better feeling than being able to escape into another life entirely different from your own, even if it's only for a couple of hours.'

Thea nodded, but felt she had nothing to add. She didn't think a review of *Hotel for Dogs* was going to cut it. 'Well, thanks again.' She made a move to leave. Denise opened the front door for her. 'It was nice bumping into you again.'

They stood awkwardly on the threshold. Thea glanced out across the street. There were still no cars. No sign of life. Compelled by a strange mixture of motivations, foremost being her perverse desire to have some sort of foothold in Marc's new world, she added, 'It doesn't look like they're back yet?'

Denise blinked and looked puzzled, as well she might, as she still hadn't a clue why Thea was hanging around the neighbourhood.

Thea explained, 'My ex-husband has recently moved into number nineteen.' She gestured at Marc's new home. 'That's why I'm here. I was supposed to be picking up my daughter, Ella, at three p.m.'

'Oh.' Denise glanced at her watch. It was 3.40 p.m. Kindly she added, 'I was about to make myself a coffee. You'd be very welcome to stay and have one – if you'd like to. It would save you waiting in your car.'

Thea didn't need to be asked twice.

Chapter 9

They were totally unrelated issues. Jenny and Marc's new St Albans idyll had nothing, whatsoever, to do with Thea agreeing to see the nice man again for dinner the following Saturday evening. It had nothing to do with Ella choosing to spend her weekend with her father rather than at home, yet again. Nothing to do with her increasing sense of being cut off from life and people.

The nice man had booked the new French restaurant. Soft lighting, great service, fine food and interesting conversation: all the hallmarks of assiduous seduction. The nice man was not letting up, or letting her down – not yet. Anyone looking at them would have thought they were a loved-up couple. Which was why, at the end of their date, she'd let things go a step further. She'd shared a taxi with him back to her apartment, where she'd kissed him, long and slow, then said goodnight, quickly. The look of pure frustration on his face as she'd exited the car had been satisfying to see. She hadn't looked back as she'd walked away, although she'd been sorely tempted to. He was nice. And because he was nice he would wait, at least for a while; and while she kept him waiting, she had control – and Thea liked being in control, needed it to feel safe. Besides, she was enjoying the romance, the attention, the tension.

But that restraint was why she was now alone on Sunday morning. It was the reason why there'd been no lazy waking to the sunlight coming through the curtains. No tentative rekindling of the previous night's passion. No drifting half asleep in his arms. No reluctant getting up, taking a shower. No breakfast together. No walk on the Common, holding hands. No us. Just her, and an empty apartment. She thought through her list of friends and discounted them, one by one. They'd be busy with their families; and besides, none of them seemed likely to offer the distraction she was seeking.

Her thoughts zeroed back to what would currently be happening over on Prospect Crescent, St Albans, AL1 2UB – Marc and Jenny's house-warming party. Ella had told her some of the details. They were having a barbecue. A fancy new outdoor grill had been purchased specially for the occasion, and for all the other family parties they were obviously envisaging celebrating in their new home. A bouncy castle had been hired for the kids. They were going to fill the old Belfast sink that the previous owners had left in the garden with ice to keep the beers cold. It was going to be a lovely, sunny early-June day, with temperatures in the high teens and a light breeze from the south-east. There was not a drop of rain in the forecast. Thea had checked, hoping to see a line of little grey clouds.

Ella was helping with all the preparations. She was, according to her latest text, currently on bunting duty. Jenny had been hand-making her own by cutting up old duvets and curtains for the past fortnight. Was there anything – domestic – that the woman couldn't, or wouldn't, do? Ella's bubbling enthusiasm about the party over the past week had been touching, and hurtful.

There were, apparently, a lot of family and friends invited.

Not Thea, obviously.

She wasn't family any more.

Though as she stood in her empty, extremely tidy breakfast-and-lover-free kitchen, drinking her coffee, Thea started coming round to the idea that she had as much right as anyone to see her daughter's new second home. The maggot of an idea began to wriggle and twist. She wandered over to the fridge and opened it. The bottle of champagne, a recent purchase, bought on a whim, was sitting there, inside the door, waiting idly for the right moment or event.

What better occasion was there than a house-warming?

The noise from the back garden signalled that the barbecue was in full swing when Thea arrived. A roaring success, by the sound of it. There was music and bursts of laughter and the intermittent screams of kids running wild, no doubt hopped up on an excess of unsupervised crisps and sugar. Thea had to ring the doorbell three times before anyone came. She was about to walk around the side of the house when Jenny opened the door. She had Maisie, her youngest, stuck, limpet-like, to her hip. If she didn't start putting that child down occasionally, she was never going to learn to walk. Jenny's reaction on seeing her partner's ex-wife standing on her doorstep was a facial stutter and an admirably quick recovery. 'Thea! How nice to see you. Come in.' By the end of the sentence she'd managed to force some warmth into her words. It was quite impressive really – she very nearly sounded pleased to have an unexpected, uninvited guest.

Thea waggled the champagne, her passive-aggressive offering. 'I won't stay long. I just thought it'd be nice to see the new place, properly.'

'Of course.' Jenny turned round. Thea followed her through the house.

Jenny moved remarkably quickly for a woman carrying a fourteen-month-old, and quite a lot of baby weight. There was no 'of course' about Jenny's welcome. They hadn't invited Thea to the barbecue. They hadn't, until now, even so much as let her set foot inside the bloody house, despite the numerous times she'd dropped Ella off and picked her up.

There were, however, lots of people who had been welcomed into Marc and Jenny's lovely new home. The kitchen and the back garden were thronged. Faces turned towards Thea that she didn't recognise. Judging by their reaction, they had no idea who she was, either. Perhaps this had been a bad idea. But she was here now, which meant she had to brazen it out. She added the champagne to the cluster of bottles on the side, pleased to see that her contribution stood out amidst the sea of prosecco.

'Help yourself to a drink. I'll go and find Ella for you.' Jenny seemed keen to get away.

Thea poured herself a glass of red. The kitchen was a mess, dirty plates and cutlery on every surface, bowls of smeary coleslaw and crushed crisps, empty cans and bottles. There was also a large sticky patch on the floor from something spilled and only half-heartedly mopped up. Thea tiptoed around the unidentified spillage on her way outside.

She scanned the garden, looking for Marc. She found him easily enough. He was working the posh new grill, tongs in one hand, beer in the other, surrounded by a coterie of barbecue acolytes, all of them blokes – the classic man-of-the-house image. She watched him chatting and flipping burgers, looking relaxed and happy, feeling the oh-so-familiar rush of conflicting emotions. This was the man who'd shared the best and the worst of times with her, who had been her joy and her support, her lover and her best friend, and yet now he was a worse than a stranger. It was hard to process, even harder to accept.

It took the best part of five minutes for him to notice her, and he only did so then because Jenny – finally without Maisie in tow – appeared at his side and whispered something in his ear. That something obviously being 'Thea's here'. Their eyes met across the crowd. Thea raised her glass to Marc, and after a second he responded in kind by saluting her with his beer bottle. One glance, that was it. His attention returned to his burgers. His indifference hurt, more than it should. Time was supposed to heal, wasn't it?

Thea lifted her chin, flicked her hair out of her eyes and set off to mingle. The slight problem was that she knew hardly anyone. A couple of the men's faces looked vaguely familiar, possibly work colleagues of Marc's, but there hadn't been much socialising towards the end of their marriage, so she couldn't be sure of their names. The guest list for the party seemed primarily made up of couples. They all looked so young. No real surprise there. There was a twelve-year age gap between Marc and Jenny. These people laughing and chatting and celebrating the new home with the happy couple were primarily Jenny's family and friends. Marc's reboot of his life had been ruthlessly efficient, very little from his old incarnation had survived the cull, except of course Ella.

'What are you doing here?' So it was possible to conjure up your daughter simply by thinking about her. If only it worked like that more of the time.

'I thought I should show my face. Say congrats on the new house. I brought champagne.'

Ella's expression tightened as if her discomfort at her mother's unscheduled appearance was literally contracting her skin. 'Mum! You can't just turn up.'

'Oh, but I can.' Thea waved and smiled at a man she thought she recognised. 'And I have.'

Ella leant into her, her lovely face close to Thea's. 'Well, now you're here, please – whatever you do – don't cause a scene.' Thea hoped that anyone watching would imagine it was a nice moment between mother and daughter.

Thea took a sip of her wine. 'I'm not going to. Would you show me around? I want to see where you're spending so much of your time.' Even to her own ears, the last comment sounded snarky.

Ella hesitated, obviously trapped between wanting to get Thea out of sight and her desire to avoid doing anything that might jeopardise the upbeat atmosphere. Her loyalty to her father, as always, won. 'Wait here,' she whispered. She hurried over and spoke to Marc, her lips so tight it was a wonder she could get the words out. She was back at Thea's side in a matter of seconds, taking her arm and guiding – some might say pulling – her back inside the house.

In the hall, away from the audience of the other guests, Ella paused. 'Dad says I can show you round, but after that you have to leave.' It was unclear whether the injunction to get lost came from Marc or from her own daughter.

'Okay.' There was no point arguing. Thea was hardly having fun and whatever her feelings about Marc, or Jenny for that matter, she didn't want to upset her daughter. Their relationship was fragile enough as it was. Having regained control of the situation, Ella also regained her composure. 'Where first?' Thea asked. Ella glanced at the half-drunk glass of red in her hand. Sometimes it felt as if their roles were reversed. Thea drained her glass and plonked it down on the radiator cover, hoping it might leave a ring. Red wine was a bugger to get off matt paint. Still Ella wasn't satisfied. She glanced at Thea's sandals. 'Really?' Thea queried.

'Yes.' Ella had kicked off her own flip-flops in the kitchen. 'House rule. No outdoor shoes upstairs.'

Begrudgingly Thea obliged.

Ella gave her the full tour. It was like a perverted version of a house viewing, with Ella cast in the role of the enthusiastic estate agent. Thea was spared nothing; not the house bathroom with the stack of fluffy towels and the five toothbrushes nestled in the pot. Not the master bedroom – that had been a swift glance, long enough to detect more of Jenny than of Marc. Not Teddy's room, with its boxes of plastic toys and monster-truck bedding. Not Maisie's nursery, with its sea of pastel teddies and tulle, and Maisie herself, fast asleep in her cot, her thumb wedged in her mouth. Thea was shown the cosy lounge, plenty of squishy sofas for them all to nestle up on, and the practical and obviously much-needed utility room. Five shirts a week for Marc, Jenny's Boden-Mum wardrobe, Ella's various sports kits and an endless slew of sicked-on and soiled toddler and baby clothes – their Whirlpool must be swishing away all day. Then there was the study where Marc allowed Ella to do her homework, so that she could get some peace and quiet; and the dining room that – surprise, no surprise – contained an eight-seater table, which must be perfect for family get-togethers, and a piano, great for family singalongs. They thankfully gave the large kitchen/diner at the back of the house a miss: too many people about for Ella and, besides, Thea had already seen its light and lovely aspect.

Fifteen minutes later the tour was complete, the pitch for the perfect family home made, the customer not buying, and Thea was in the hallway again, her sandals back on her feet. She had no option but to accept her fate. 'Well, have a good time. Just text me when you want me to come and pick you up?'

Ella avoided looking at her. 'There's no need. Stella said she'd run me back.'

'Whose Stella?'

'One of Jenny's friends. They live in Bower Heath, so it's not a hassle for them.'

'But won't she have been drinking?'

Thea couldn't be 100 per cent sure, but she thought she saw Ella glance at her abandoned wine glass on the top of the radiator cover. Teenage judgement had sharp teeth. 'No. She's pregnant, so she's not drinking.'

'Okay. I'll see you later then.' Thea kissed Ella's cheek and felt a ripple of longing to hold her daughter tight and keep her all to herself.

But the moment passed.

Ella escorted her to the front door. On the windowsill sat Thea's bottle of champagne. Jenny's work? It didn't have a sign hung around its neck, but if it had, it would have read, *Don't forget to shut the door behind you on your way out!* Thea obviously wasn't the only one who could rock a bit of passive-aggression. Thea grabbed the bottle, shouted a cheery, 'Bye. See you later' and left. Her dignity, if not her emotions, intact.

She walked down the drive, trailed by the smell of charring meat and the shouts of other people having a good time, and stood beside her car. She was about to get in and drive away, as instructed, when a thought occurred to her.

The sun was shining.

She had nowhere she had to be.

No one waiting for her return.

But she did have a perfectly good bottle of champagne and a standing invitation *to call round any time*, from one of Marc's neighbours.

Chapter 10

'THEA.' DENISE put an exaggerated emphasis on the 'Th' and did a flourish with her hand, à la someone French. They'd been sitting – correction, lounging around – outside long enough to have made it on to a second bottle.

'What?'

'I was just saying your name.'

'Tell me about it.' Thea shrugged. 'But the one thing you can't blame someone for is their name.'

Denise wriggled upright. 'It's unusual, though, isn't it? I've never met a Thea before.'

'We're not a separate breed!' A good portion of Thea's face was covered by her sunglasses, but Denise could tell she was smiling

'It's such a confident thing to do: give a child such a distinct name. Imagine what your life would have been like if you'd turned out to be chubby and short-sighted. What does it mean?'

'I can't remember.'

That was so obviously a lie. 'I'll google it.' Denise reached for her phone.

'Please don't.'

'Here we go. *Thea means a gift from god. Thea is the Greek goddess of light. The mother of the sun and the moon.* Wow! Not much to live up to then.'

'Like I said, you can't choose your parents, or be responsible for their pretensions.'

Denise dropped her phone in her lap and took another sip of her champagne. 'My folks can't have had too many aspirations when it came to me. I don't know what on earth possessed them. I don't even have any uncles called Dennis.' She'd always hated her name. She'd sounded like a middle-aged woman all her life. Now that she was one, she hated it even more.

'It's not so bad.' Thea was being kind.

Thea versus Denise. Denise knew which name most women would opt for, given a choice. 'Isn't it? Go on, name me one gorgeous, feminine, strong woman called Denise.' Before Thea could offer up the *Big Breakfast* blonde bombshell, Denise cut in, 'Apart from Denise van Outen.'

'Denise Welch.'

'Um.'

'That's harsh!' Thea laughed, seemingly determined to do better. 'Wait. I've got a good one. Denise Lewis. A gold medal in the Sydney Olympics. Commonwealth Games champion, twice. Beautiful. Talented. And a better commentator than Steve Cram,' she added.

'Wow there – back off the Geordie golden boy, will you?' Denise took another drink and happily returned to her half-mock moaning. It was fun to talk crap and drink champagne with the smell of a neighbour's barbecue drifting on the warm air. 'It's just such an ugly word. A woman with a bloke's name.'

'I don't imagine it holds Misses van Outen, Lewis or Welch back.'

They laughed. Denise looked up at the clear blue sky and the treetops rippling in the breeze. She was happy. The afternoon felt like a small, surprise, perfectly judged gift – something to be treasured.

After another half hour or so of chatting and mentally drifting in a haze of champagne and warmth, the sound of Simon shouting reached them in the garden. Denise pushed herself upright, twisted round and looked back at the house. He emerged through the patio doors. Thea pushed her sunglasses down her nose and peered over them. She smiled, but didn't shift her position, which was stretched out on one of the sun loungers, her long legs tanning in the afternoon sunshine, as befitted the goddess of light.

Simon strode across the lawn towards them. As he got closer, Denise noticed a ridge across his forehead where his cap had dug in and left a mark. His hair was sweaty. For a second she felt self-conscious on his behalf. Simon looked good in a suit and a crisp white work shirt. He looked less attractive in a mint-green polyester polo and baggy cream golf trousers.

Denise shielded her eyes from the glare. 'You're back early.'

'No I'm not.'

She squinted up at him. 'What time is it? She hadn't looked at her phone since Thea arrived.

'Gone five.'

'Oh.' Three hours had slid by without her noticing.

The shift in atmosphere probably wasn't his fault, it was more to do with the awkwardness of him standing over them. Denise saw Simon glance at Thea. 'Sorry. This is Thea.' Simon nodded, though he obviously had no idea who this leggy, reclining woman with the Jackie O sunglasses was. 'Marc's ex-wife.' This additional information didn't help. 'You know Marc. The family who recently moved into number nineteen.'

'Ah.'

Denise wished that Simon was better at disguising his thoughts, because it was clear from his expression that he couldn't see how Marc moving in opposite would lead to Thea being in their garden, drinking champagne, topping up her tan. Denise stepped up her game. 'Thea and I bumped into each, quite by chance, at the DIT do last month and got talking.' There was absolutely no need for her to get into about what.

Simon seemed to have regained his equilibrium, and his usual politeness. 'Hello. Very nice to meet you, Thea. I won't shake hands.' He held out his hands, palms up, to demonstrate that they were covered in grass stains. Then he hesitated, as if uncertain of his next move. Denise was slightly ashamed to realise that she had no desire for him to join them. Thankfully Simon seemed to have no such intention. 'I'll go and grab a shower. Get cleaned up. Enjoy the sunshine.' And with that, he turned and walked back inside the house.

After he'd gone, the atmosphere in the garden felt different. Denise no longer felt as carefree. Simon reappearing had triggered thoughts of meal preparation and email checking, and a sudden awareness that when he stripped off his sweaty golf kit he would find the laundry basket full. She swung her legs over the side of the sunbed and sat up. Thea didn't move. Denise detected defiance and relaxation in her new acquaintance, which both impressed and slightly bothered her. Thea reached for the bottle and held it up to the light. There was about one-third left.

'It'd be a shame to waste it,' Thea said and smiled.

Denise looked back at the house, which was now in full shadow, then up at the sun softening the outline of the trees at the bottom of the garden, and made her choice. She picked up her glass and held it out for Thea to top up. The washing and Simon could wait.

When she walked into the kitchen an hour or so later, she found Simon peeling potatoes. By the set of his shoulders, she could tell he was in a mood. She chose to ignore it. 'How did you get on?'

He spoke without pausing in his vigorous peeling. 'Not great. Eighty-nine.'

'What par was it?'

'Seventy-two.'

'Well, at least you broke ninety.' Look at her, talking golf.

He threw another skinned potato into the pot. 'Has she gone?'

'Thea? Yes.' *She* did have a name. Perhaps he'd already forgotten it. 'She ordered an Uber. She'll pick up her car in the morning.'

'Um.' Another spud went under the knife. 'I hadn't realised you'd arranged to see anyone today.'

Denise leant against the cutlery drawer. She wondered what he was planning on making, other than a vat of mashed potato. 'I hadn't. She called round on the off-chance that I might be in and free.'

'Right.' The last potato having been dispatched, Simon clattered the lid down on the pan.

'What are we having?' Denise asked.

At that, he did turn around. 'I don't know. I just thought I'd better get *something* started. The boys are back.' The thump of music attested to that.

His tone made Denise feel defensive. One afternoon off – that's all she'd had. One single afternoon, but those few self-indulgent hours had somehow put her behind, and in the wrong.

Instinctively, but unhappily, she walked over to the freezer. She opened it and began rooting around for the components of an actual meal. Sausages. They were frozen solid, but if she got them on now, they'd do. They'd have to. She turned on the grill, ripped open two packs – one was never enough – and threw the sausages into the pan. Having underestimated their rigidity, and her anger, the clatter they made ricocheted around the kitchen like gunfire. She was aware of Simon watching her. 'I'll do some veg as well.'

The switch from sun-dappled silliness to household drudgery made Denise unreasonably sad. Hormones were a bugger. Add in daytime alcohol and, well, she only had herself to blame. These days wine often seemed to trigger a downward swing in her mood, and her sense of perspective.

Gone were the days when drinking was a thoughtless leapfrog into a good time. She was half cut. Simon was hungry. That was all. As the grill heated up, the sausages began to crackle and spit.

'Do you think it's wise?' For a second she thought Simon was talking about cooking the sausages from frozen, until he elaborated. 'Making friends with the new neighbour's ex-wife?'

'I can't see the harm in it.' She rattled the sausages around.

'It just seems a little odd to me, her popping round so soon after they've moved in.'

'That's not the connection. Like I said, we met at the DIT do. Then I bumped into her again outside on the street, when she came to pick up her daughter last weekend. She was having to wait. They were late back. We got talking.' Again there was no need to elaborate.

'But why was she back again today?'

'Well... it was such a nice day.' Thea hadn't actually provided a reason for her impromptu visit, she'd simply appeared on the doorstep waving a bottle of champagne. Simon still looked bemused, which – to be fair – was understandable. It was unusual for Denise to be so spontaneously sociable. 'We'd mentioned meeting up again for a coffee or lunch, but given that she was in the neighbourhood, she called round. She's an interesting person to talk to. And she knows lots of people in the business.' Denise threw that in deliberately. Simon might be less cool about Thea if he realised she might be a useful contact to cultivate. Not that Denise wanted that to be the focus of their burgeoning relationship. 'We get on,' she added. It sounded so lame, but it was true.

'Okay.' He straightened the salt-and-pepper grinders. 'I didn't really need chapter and verse.' It was a good job she hadn't mentioned seeing Thea at Cherry Trees as well. Simon wouldn't want there to be any overlap between his private life and the business. Piece said, he walked away, but not without one last parting shot. 'I'd be a little wary of getting too involved. You've no idea what sort of post-divorce relationship she and her husband have.'

Thank you for your sage advice, Simon, Denise said – in her head, while watching the sausages begin to leak fat.

The lightness of the afternoon now well and truly extinguished, Denise switched on the hob under his meticulously dismembered potatoes and got on with the evening meal.

Chapter 11

'WHERE WERE you earlier?'

On the commute home Thea had promised herself she would leave it, she had enough on her plate; and yet here she was, only minutes after stepping through the door, challenging her daughter.

As she could have predicted, her abrupt enquiry did not go down well. 'We went to Starbucks, to do our homework.'

'You could've messaged me.'

'What... to say I was going to be home seventy-three minutes later than usual.'

'Yes.'

'Why? You weren't even here.'

'That's not the point.' Frost descended on the apartment, despite the warmth outside. Her grip on her daughter was loosening day by day. As normal as that might be, it bothered her. The sense that Ella was deliberating freezing her out of her life hurt. Trying for a more chatty tone, Thea asked, 'Did you get much done?'

'Yes.'

'Good. Who was there?'

'Only me and Lucy.'

'Are you planning on making it a regular thing?'

'Maybe.'

Thea suddenly felt tired. She leant against the countertop. 'Well, next time maybe you could text me. Just so I know where you are.'

Ella sighed. 'Why do you need to know where I am, twenty-four-seven?'

'Because I like to know that you're safe when I'm at work.'

'Only when you're at work? Aren't you bothered the rest of the time?'

Thea tried hard not to rise to Ella's sarcasm. One of them had to be the adult in their relationship and, as she was the mother, that responsibility fell to her. 'You know what I mean.'

Ella began gathering up her stuff, preparing to flee. 'I'm fifteen!'

'And you think that makes you safe?' Thea couldn't think of anything less safe than a fifteen-year-old girl in her school uniform on a summer's day. The thought was so depressing that it made her angry for Ella, and at her. 'I only say these things because I care.'

Ella started walking away. 'Do you?' Thea heard her mutter.

'Pardon?' Her daughter knew which buttons to push.

Ella stopped and turned round. 'I said, "Do you?"'

That stung. 'Of course I do.'

'Well, you've got a funny way of showing it.'

This, again! Ella resented her full-time, full-on job and as a result she rarely let an opportunity pass to comment on the contrast between Thea's career-focused absence and the other mothers' homely presence. It pained Thea that she'd raised a daughter with such old-fashioned views on the role of women. Without her salary, Ella's lifestyle would be very different – Marc's maintenance payments only went so far, and then there was the apartment. And the bills, which all had Thea's name on. The stresses of being single-handedly responsible for covering the many and mounting costs of their lives were very real.

But it was a pressure she kept to herself, because that's what good parents did: they kept the world at bay, at least for a while. 'Please, Ella. I don't want to fight. Come and sit with me. Let's have a proper talk.'

'About?'

'Anything. Your day? School? Whatever you want to talk about.'

Ella dropped her bag on the floor and climbed onto one of the kitchen stools. She composed herself – her expression, in profile, suddenly serious. 'There is actually something I want to talk about, but I'm worried that you might not like what I have to say.'

'Try me,' Thea countered. She'd been reading her Caitlin Moran and was determined to practise what had been preached. Listening, not trying to fix. Empathy instead of energy. Calm, not panic. She walked round the kitchen island and came to stand opposite her daughter, keeping her shoulders down and her posture relaxed, giving Ella space. A clear *I'm here to listen* pose. But having taken up their positions, the next step proved far harder.

'Go on,' Thea prompted gently.

'Okay.' Ella took a breath, then said quietly, 'I've been thinking about this a lot. I really don't want to upset you, but I think it would be better, for everyone, if I went to live with Dad.' She raised her hand to her throat, a sure sign that she was feeling anxious.

Thea was shocked into silence, her brain processing what in her gut she'd always feared was inevitable. In truth, she was surprised it had taken this long for Ella to voice her desires out loud. The suspicion that she wanted to move in with Marc and Jenny had been there for months, festering between them, causing jealousy and tension. The new house made it all the more doable.

But it was Thea's fault as well – she knew that. She hadn't been around enough, been 'emotionally available' for Ella, and as a consequence her daughter had bonded with her father more than with her. The two of them had always been close, and the divorce had done nothing to weaken that connection. Indeed, it seemed to have strengthened it. The awful, but simple truth was that Ella loved Marc more than her.

Ella sat tensely on her stool, obviously waiting for the explosion. Thea dredged up a facsimile of composure from somewhere deep inside herself and managed to speak in a tone that was carefully neutral. 'What about school?'

Ella flicked her hair off her face, feigning a confidence she was obviously not feeling. Thea recognised the gesture. She had, after all, taught her it. Her daughter's voice was impressively controlled. 'There's a bus. Lots of other people travel in. And Jenny says she should be able to drop me off some mornings.'

Thea's studied calmness shimmered at the mention of Jenny. 'So you've already spoken to them about this?'

Ella hung her head, but the desire to make the move happen was obviously far stronger than her fear of Thea's reaction, because after a second or two she looked up and tried to sweeten the bitter pill of her request. 'Can't we just try it? For a month or so? Maybe we'd get on better if we flipped it round, with me staying there in the week and us doing nice stuff together at weekends, when you've got more time and you're less stressed out. It doesn't make much sense, the way we're doing it at the moment. Does it?'

Thea said nothing. She didn't trust herself to.

Ella honed her argument. 'You're never here during the week. You're always at work. So I'm stuck on my own. I'm lonely.' She had never wanted to move to the apartment. 'Please, Mum. It's worth a try, isn't it? It would take some of the pressure off you.'

Everything she said was true, but Thea wasn't giving in that easily. She couldn't. If she allowed it, she would have lost – she would *be* lost. She relied on Ella. She loved Ella. She rallied. 'I'm not late that often. Not any more.' She'd been trying hard to be home most evenings so that they could eat together. Only the week before, she'd laid on that nice breakfast for them both. 'We get on fine, most of the time. I really don't see why we need to change things.'

Ella did a double-take. 'Mum! Get real. You're late back all the time or you're away. I go over to Dad's a lot, as it is. And when we do spend any time together, all we do is argue.'

'But that's normal. Mothers and daughters bicker. It's the female equivalent of Oedipus.'

Ella shook her head. 'No it isn't. Not the way we argue. You don't like anything I say. Or do. Or wear. You don't even seem to like the way I think. Everything is a war with you.'

'Oh, come on. Now you're exaggerating. I thought you liked our debates.'

'That's an example of exactly what I mean. You *never* listen to me – to my opinion – you just want to turn me into a mini version of yourself. Dad doesn't do that. He listens when we talk, lets me be *me*.'

'Well, bully for your dad.' It was easy to be laissez-faire about your kids when you only did the fun stuff.

Ella sighed. 'I knew you'd be like this.'

'Like what?'

'Jealous.'

She was spot on, but Thea was never going to admit it. 'It's not that bad living here, is it?' She could hear the pleading in her voice.

Ella swallowed. 'I'm sorry, Mum, but yes, it is. I'm not happy here. I am when I'm with them. And they're happy to have me.' The tears came. 'Don't you want me to be happy?'

Thea wanted to shout, *Why can't you be happy with me? It's not all my fault. I would have loved to give you a sibling. Would have loved to have stayed married to your dad. It's not my fault that it's just you and me. Why can't I be enough?* But she didn't because she didn't want to hear Ella's answer. 'It was your dad who suggested this, wasn't it?'

Ella lost it. She flung her hands up in a gesture of frustration. 'No it wasn't. Don't start in on Dad. It's what I want.'

Thea believed it, but she refused to accept it. It was less painful to blame Marc. His campaign had worked; he'd turned Ella against her, with his subtle blend of charm and gentle persuasion. It was a paternal seduction that had been going on for years, even before they split. Ella and her daddy against the world. Ella and her dad thick as thieves. Ella and Marc closer than she and Ella had ever been. It was a campaign that Thea had been unable to counteract. She had a very clear image of Ella being sucked into the powerful vortex of Marc's shiny new family, with Jenny fulfilling the role of understanding, patient stepmum, and with Teddy and Maisie as her adoring younger siblings. Christ, Jenny probably had a matching pair of sweet, grey-haired, compos mentis grandparents to complete the set.

If Thea let this happen she knew, with absolute certainty, that her daughter would never re-emerge from their soft, suffocating embrace. Okay, so she might not be naturally maternal, and she did encourage Ella to try her hardest at whatever she did, but that was because she wanted her to get every ounce out of life, for her to build her confidence and her resilience. It was important. And no one could say that she hadn't tried – that she hadn't been there for the hard-slog aspects of raising a child. She'd done all the mundane crap: the childhood ailments, the practical chores, the homework, the form-filling and appointment booking, the constant worrying. All she ever thought about was Ella and how best to protect her from the shit in life.

It was not fair. She would not – could not – let it happen. She straightened up and looked directly into her daughter's eyes. 'No.'

'What?'

'No, you can't go and live with your father. I forbid it.'

Ella frowned. She paused. Sniffed back her tears. The sound of traffic on the High Street inserted itself into the gap. Then she said, very firmly, 'You can't stop me.'

'I have a court order that says I can.'

'You wouldn't.' Ella climbed down from the stool, using her now-matching height to face up to Thea.

'Try me!' If her daughter thought that all she did was fight, well, Thea might as well live up to her reputation.

Ella flushed. 'Dad will go the court and get them to redraft the terms of the custody order.' As the child of a divorce, Ella had picked up plenty of insight and understanding along the way. 'Besides, I'm old enough now. They'll ask me where I want to live.' The tears had stopped. 'Do you really want me saying I don't want to live with you any more? That you're impossible to live with.'

Of course Thea didn't. In her heart she knew the battle was already lost because here she was, standing in her rather nice kitchen, issuing empty threats to her much-loved daughter. She knew she was behaving like the worst kind of overbearing mother, but she was only doing it because she was desperate.

And when Thea was desperate, she got reckless. Very reckless.

'There's something you should know.' Thea stepped up to the edge of the precipice, fully aware of quite how dangerous it was, for them both.

'What?' Ella stood, trapped in a shaft of sunlight, wanting to flee, but standing her ground.

Knowing what she was about to say next, Thea didn't blame her daughter for wanting to run away. Indeed, the rational, non-panicking, non-raging-with-impotency part of Thea's brain hoped Ella would make it out of the room before she spoke.

It was not to be.

'I've never wanted to tell you this, but I think, given the circumstances, you have the right to know.'

'What?' Ella looked shaky.

She was frightening her own child, but it was the only weapon she had left. Thea took a shallow breath and stepped over the edge. 'Your dad isn't the man you think he is – who he pretends to be. He cheated on me, and on you.'

Ella's face drained of colour.

Thea paused, thought about the damage she was doing, then said it anyway. Why should she keep protecting him? 'He had an affair, with Jenny. That's why we broke up. It wasn't a mutual decision. He started seeing her when you were nine. Or at least that's when I think it started. He's never come clean about it. It doesn't fit with the image he likes to project. I'm sorry, Ella, but the painful truth is… your dad left us for her. He's the one who broke up our family.'

Chapter 12

THEY WERE sitting at the dining table eating together, which was a rare occurrence for a midweek evening. Aaron was back from uni for a few days to see Millie. The mood was relaxed, the boys talking – sure, it was about football, but Denise could live with that. It felt good. Like the old days. Simon smiled at her and she smiled back. Pride in their pride. A basic, shared instinct.

In a lull in the conversation Aaron asked, 'Have you spoken to her yet?'

'Yeah, a bit,' Joe mumbled.

Lewis dug him in the ribs. 'That means he's said hi to her under his breath, when she was on the other side of the street.'

Aaron grinned. 'So you're having to make do with perving over her out of the lounge window then.'

'Fuck off.' Joe rarely swore, at least not in front of them.

Simon and Denise both cautioned, 'Language!' at precisely the same time.

Lewis grabbed another slice of garlic bread. 'You know she's actually moved in now, don't you?'

Aaron grinned. 'You lucky boy. Might give you the time to work up the nerve to actually speak to her properly, like a fully functioning real boy.'

Simon intervened, 'Leave him alone.'

He was alert to them picking on Joe. He ignored their roughhousing, didn't even seem to hear it most of the time, but he wouldn't tolerate anything that smacked of bullying. Denise suspected it brought back memories from his own childhood – not of his siblings, because there weren't any, but of his father. She put down her knife and fork. 'Are you talking about Ella?'

'Ella?' all three of them queried in unison.

'The girl who stays over at number nineteen some weekends,' Denise prompted.

They stared at her, surprised by her knowledge. Aaron finally said, 'Yes. If that's the name of the fit girl across the road that Joe is in lurve with.'

'What do you mean... *she's actually moved in now*?' Denise asked, circling back to Lewis's earlier comment.

'I saw her dad unloading a heap of her stuff out of his car on Saturday evening. Looked like she was coming to stay – for good.' Lewis dipped his bread in his pasta sauce.

Thea hadn't said a word about any of this to Denise and they had been in touch by text a number of times over the past week. Surely she would have mentioned something so momentous as her daughter moving out. Denise didn't want to think it was true or, if it was, that Thea hadn't felt able to talk to her about it. Hence her rebuttal. 'She often stays over on the weekends.'

'No, she's been there all week. I've seen her setting off for school.' Lewis had the decency to flush after volunteering this piece of information, which had obviously been gleaned from spying on Marc and Jenny's house, just as much as his younger brother did. They were as bad as each other. The unnerving image of her sons as a pack of young lions, heavy-pawed and strong-jawed, lazing around, eyeing up their prey, crept unwanted into her brain. She blinked it away.

Simon must have had the same thought – though perhaps with less fanciful illustrations – because he chipped in with, 'Don't be making a nuisance of yourselves. Any of you!'

Subject closed, they moved on to asking what was for dessert.

Ten minutes later Denise found herself alone at the table – two family-sized sticky toffee puddings having put up little in the way of resistance to their voracious appetites. She reached for her phone. The problem was... what to text? She didn't want to seem, or *be*, interfering, but at the same time if Ella had really moved in with her father, that would surely imply something had gone badly awry. This was, of course, precisely the sort of thing Simon had cautioned her against, getting involved in other's people's private lives, but Denise felt she had established a connection with Thea – a mutual one, she hoped – and if she was having a difficult time, then surely she should reach out to offer some support, as a friend.

But did she know Thea well enough to do that?

Caught in a dilemma, she defaulted to the most innocuous of messages. Hi. Just checking in. Are you ok?

The response, three seconds later – a thumbs-up emoji

– hardly spoke of family trauma. The boys must have gone the wrong end of the stick.

But whatever the facts surrounding Thea's daughter's living arrangements, Denise made a mental note to keep her eyes open for any signs of interaction between Ella and her sons. She simply couldn't see how such contact would be a good thing.

Chapter 13

THEY WERE gathered in one of the big conference rooms on the south side of the building. The panorama across Whitehall towards Big Ben was as impressive as ever, but Thea was immune to the grandeur. She was too distracted. The room was stuffy. The huge windows might be good for breathtaking views of London, but they didn't open and there was no air con. She poured herself a glass of water and took a sip. It was lukewarm, having sat in the sun for far too long. Her head hurt. One of the division heads, Ross Allinside, was walking them through the revised strategy for South Korea. He'd been speaking for more than an hour. It was technical stuff, but this was her area of expertise; hence her presence at the meeting. This was the third iteration of the strategy so far, but they still had a long way to go before they would have anything ready to take to the Minister. Things never moved quickly within the DIT. Thea tuned out Ross's voice. In her current mood she hadn't the mental energy to focus on the intricacies of the changing market conditions in the Far East, although she made sure to nod her head every now and again, indicating interest. Her mind was focused far closer to home. As the presentation ground on, she sipped her tepid water and kept an eye on her phone.

She was still on tenterhooks waiting to hear from Ella. It had been five days since they'd spoken, or more accurately fought, and the lack of contact was killing her – as it was intended to.

Thea stared at the sunlight reflecting off the Thames and let the presentation wash over her.

For years she'd kept her counsel. Through all of the pain and anger of her marriage collapsing, she had colluded in, even helped to embellish, the myth that Marc and Jenny had got together after she and Marc had separated. *A mutual decision* was the lie they agreed to tell Ella when they sat her down and told her they were breaking up. It was a kind fairy story, but one without a happy ending. In calm, controlled, reassuring voices they'd reassured her that they would always be her parents and they had solemnly promised that neither of them would ever stop loving her.

And they hadn't.

But they had, from that point forward, never stopped fighting over her.

During the intervening years – despite plenty of provocation – Thea had been unwavering in her silence, not out of any residual loyalty to Marc, but to protect Ella. She hadn't wanted her daughter to have to deal with the irrefutable evidence of the shittiness of adults, not on top of everything else she'd been through. But Marc had forced her hand, by wanting all of Ella. Thea blurting out the truth had been a last, desperate throw of the dice.

Of course it hadn't worked. It had backfired, massively. Because Ella was wise enough to see Thea's allegation of infidelity for what it was – an attack. The veracity of what she'd said was irrelevant; it was her intent that had damned her. And Thea's intent, in that moment, had been to knock Marc off his pedestal and, in doing so, weaken his relationship with Ella. She had been motivated by jealousy, not love.

Thea had known instantly that she'd gone too far – those seemingly never-ending seconds of Ella's silent disdain as they'd faced each other in the kitchen were proof of it. Her beautiful, mature, bright daughter had blinked and swallowed, but there had been no outburst, no tears and, most worrying of all, no questions.

Thea had reached out to touch her, wanting to snatch the words back, but Ella had moved away.

That's when Thea had panicked. 'I'm sorry. Please, sweetheart, say something.'

'Like what?' Ella's voice had betrayed her, but her expression had held firm.

'I don't know. Anything.'

Ella took another breath. 'It makes no difference. I still want to live with Dad and Jenny. That's where I'm happiest. And I'm going to. With or without your permission.'

And she had.

That evening.

Without a word of goodbye.

She'd sneaked out of the apartment while Thea was in the bathroom trying to put on a brave face, taking only a rucksack and her old teddy with her. As soon as Thea had opened the bathroom door she'd known she was alone. The air had felt different, the atmosphere dead.

It still was.

Gabbie Merchant stood up and took over from Ross Allinside. A different voice spewing more data and valuable insight. Thea's attention turned back inwards.

In the days following Ella's departure the only communication Thea had was with Marc. Their exchange when he came to pick up Ella's stuff was frosty to the point of Arctic. He informed Thea that what she'd done was selfish and deeply damaging and, as a consequence, she must stay away. He coldly explained that Thea had no option other than to allow time for the shitstorm she'd so recklessly and cruelly stirred up to die down. Above all, Marc stressed that it was up to Ella to decide how she wanted things to be, going forward. He was of course right, but it didn't make taking her punishment any easier.

And so began the waiting and wondering, and the long, lonely hours in the apartment.

Ella had finally relented and phoned on the Tuesday evening, which was a relief, but a painful one. On the call Ella gave vent to her shock and disbelief, eloquently and very coherently. Trust was the word she used again and again, without irony. There was little Thea could say in response to her daughter's hurt and anger other than 'Sorry' – which she did, repeatedly and at length.

She said she was sorry for the pain she'd caused.

Ella sniffed.

She acknowledged that there had been times when she'd been less than understanding of Ella's needs and emotions.

Ella did not disagree.

She swore she was profoundly sorry for everything that had gone wrong in their relationship and acknowledged that Marc was not to blame for their difficulties.

Ella did not waver.

Eventually Thea ran out of apologies.

With nothing left to offer up to her unrelenting daughter, a stony silence descended. It was a void that told Thea she was not forgiven, more clearly than any barrage of words could have done. When Thea said, 'Goodbye. Speak soon. I love you', Ella had simply disconnected.

Since then she'd heard very little from her daughter, other than a couple of curt responses to her text messages. There had, however, been the call from Marc. It was not a conversation. He had spoken to her briefly and very firmly. He informed Thea that they needed to formalise the new living arrangements. He said Ella wanted her school to know about the change in her circumstances. He didn't bother to specify the change – they both knew he meant Ella's permanent move in with them. He said the new arrangement needed to be agreed ASAP, and he was very explicit on this point. He stressed it was incumbent on each of them to demonstrate to Ella that – although things had been said in the heat of the moment and, as a result, feelings had been hurt and would take time to heal – they both wanted what was best for her.

'Ultimately, our responsibility is to show her that we are her parents and we love her... whatever might have been said or done.' He left a pause. Was that an acknowledgement of his part in the mess they had both created? If so, it was a brief and tangential one. 'Don't you agree?'

She had acceded to his demands. It was the only way Thea was ever going to be allowed to set foot inside the fortress of happiness ever again.

In their ongoing tug of war over Ella, Marc had finally won.

Thea's caller ID lit up – the burr of the vibration yanked her back into the boardroom. She scrambled for her phone.

It was not Ella.

But it was a number she recognised, purely from having ignored it for the past fortnight. She stood up, overwhelmed by the need to be anywhere other than trapped in this oppressive room, pretending to concentrate on the complexities of international trade as her life fell apart. Her colleagues all looked at her, startled by the sudden scrape of her chair. Her life was closing in on her, each problem bleeding into the next. Her instinctive reaction was flight. She was committed now. 'I'm very sorry, but I'm afraid I need to take this.' You could bury a bomb, but that didn't mean you couldn't still hear it ticking away beneath your feet.

She gathered up her stuff. Let them think what they liked... that she was playing the ego card of the really important person who receives calls that simply have to be taken, or that she was just another frazzled working mother. She didn't care, either way. They all watched as she made her way around the huge board table and out of the room – grandeur came with a lot of carpeted acreage.

By the time she reached the corridor the call had gone to voicemail.

Going back to her desk wasn't an option; it was an open-plan office and she didn't want an audience for the next incendiary that was about to blow up in her face. Instead she made for the stairwell. A good choice – it was cool and quiet and, most important of all, empty. But despite the privacy it afforded she kept moving, as far away from other people as possible. Up one flight, then another, then another. At the very top, out of breath from the climb, she sat down on the step. She took care not to lean against the door that led out onto the roof – she didn't want to be setting off any alarms. Her stomach muscles were clenched, waiting for the incoming blow.

She dialled her message service. She reasoned that she might as well get it over with, unleash all the mayhem in one fell swoop.

She recognised the voice immediately. Mr Tennant. The head man himself. A sure sign of how serious things were. 'Thea, it's Damien Tennant. You're a very hard woman to track down. We've been trying to get hold for you for a while now, with no success.' Three letters and five texts, a number of calls – she'd ignored them all. 'We really need you to contact us and arrange to come in. ASAP.' Even on voicemail he was authoritative, a man not used to being ignored. He sounded irritated that he was having to chase her himself. 'We look forward to hearing from you – very soon.' He cleared his throat and she thought he was finished. But no. He had one last warning for her. 'Thea, ignoring this isn't going to make it go away.'

A click, then silence.

Her phone informed her that she had no new messages.

They weren't going to leave her alone, she knew that. The hounding would go on. More letters, more calls, more emails. It wasn't going to stop. Would they resort to turning up in person? She doubted it, but she wouldn't put it past them. She didn't want to think about how that would play out. Having to have the conversation in her own home, the place where – up until now – she had always felt safe. What if they started trying to contact her at work? She couldn't stand the thought of that. Her privacy, her control over her own future was being eroded, relentlessly. And this was merely the beginning.

But she was only trapped if she let them catch her.

Fight or flight? She still had options.

She stood up.

She rammed down the bar on the fire exit and pushed it open. The alarm triggered, an ear-splitting wail that reverberated around the stairwell. She didn't so much as flinch.

She went out onto the roof, into the sunlight, leaving the door wide open behind her. The security guys would find her soon enough. Then she'd have some explaining to do – security was not something that was taken lightly in a government building. But in the meantime, she was free. Free to walk over to the edge of the roof, lean against the parapet, feel the sun on her face, breathe and start planning her escape. With Ella gone, there was nothing and no one left to stop her.

Chapter 14

THE SCREECH of baboons filled the office. Simon glanced sharply at Denise across the top of his computer screen. She scrambled to kill the volume on her phone. Thea often sent Denise random things to make her laugh: YouTube clips, Twitter links. She was currently having a run on *primates doing the funniest things*. Simon went back to his Excel spreadsheet without comment. Denise returned to her invoices. She was glad it was the type of routine work that freed her mind.

The speed with which Thea had become part of her life was surprising. Denise didn't normally make friends easily, and she certainly did not make them quickly. Her social circle was dominated by women she'd met through the boys – friendships developed through shared expediency rather than personal choice. Added to which, Thea was really not her type. That sounded wrong, as if friends had to fulfil a specific criterion to make the grade, like potential partners on a dating app, but for Denise that had probably been true, in the past. She had a habit of sticking to the safely familiar in friendship, as she did in so many other areas of her life. Denise opened another file of invoices and began working methodically through them, her brain able to focus and drift at the same time. Thea possessed so many of the attributes that Denise normally found intimidating. Confidence in herself, and her opinions, volatility, unpredictability – all bound up in an attractiveness that drew attention. She was vocal, unapologetic and funny.

All the things Denise wasn't.

All the things Denise wished she was.

But – and it was a troubling 'but' – for all Denise was enjoying having Thea in her life, she was very aware that their relationship was flimsy. They liked each other, or at least she hoped they did, but there was still a lot that Denise didn't know about her new friend. Or, more accurately, a lot Thea seemed determined not to share. Time. That was what they needed. More time. And more trust.

Denise sped through the invoices. She needed to get a wriggle on. She was going over to Cherry Trees in her lunch break. She was looking forward to it: not the seeing Eric part, but the meeting Thea bit, in the café in the park along the road from the home afterwards. Two birds, one stone – how was that for multitasking? She hadn't mentioned her coffee date to Simon. What she did in her lunch break, other than pick up some bits of shopping and visit his father, was none of his business. Another half hour and she would be done.

Thea wasn't there when she arrived at the café. Denise was running late herself, thanks to Eric's insistence on reading aloud, in full, an article in *The Times* about falling fitness levels amongst army recruits, but by now Denise knew Thea well enough not to be surprised, or overly concerned, by her absence. Timekeeping. Another area of dissonance. Denise ordered an iced green tea for herself and a flat white for Thea and carried them over to one of the tables. She chose one that was half in the shade, half out, and opted to sit out of the sun. She had enough trouble keeping cool without courting trouble. And although a tan might make you look healthy, Denise knew that the UV light was as ageing as smoking and stress. Two out of three abstentions – it was all she could manage. She shook the sachet of collagen into her tea and stirred it. Was her hair thicker, her skin smoother, her mood better? It was hard to tell. But it was worth a try. Settled with her drink, and a view of the play area and the lake beyond, Denise was content to unhook her brain and wait.

A few minutes later the crunch of gravel signalled Thea's arrival. 'Sorry. I got stuck on a call.' She dropped into her seat, took a sip of her coffee, then fell silent. She seemed to be staring at the playground, though with her sunglasses on, it was difficult to be certain what she was looking at.

'Are you all right?' Denise asked.

'Yes. It's nice to have a day at home, for a change. I should do it more often. You?'

There it was again, Thea's tendency to deflect direct enquiries about herself. 'Fine.'

Thea nodded, flicked her hair off her face. 'How was the old bastard?'

Denise had shared with Thea some of her frustrations

about her father-in-law. It was nice to be able to talk honestly about how hard she found it all.

'As cheerful as ever. He's on another warning: an incident with one of the night shift.'

'Racist or misogynistic comments this time?'

'A bit of both, from what Karen said. I dropped off a card and some flowers to apologise on his behalf.'

'Does Simon ever visit his father?' Thea was also, Denise was beginning to realise, not afraid to stir a bubbling pot.

'When he can, but it's difficult with work.' It was equally awkward for her, of course, but she still went every week without fail, rather than once in a blue moon. Again, the sense surfaced of Thea pushing Denise to face realities that she normally preferred to ignore. Which prompted her to add something a little closer to the truth. 'They don't have the best of relationships. If anything, it tends to make things worse when Simon speaks to Eric – about most things. There's too much history between them.'

Thea didn't comment. She went back to staring off into the distance. Denise felt unsettled by the curious mood she seemed to be in. The lightness and humour that normally characterised their interactions was missing. She was definitely not her usual upbeat, ebullient self. Perhaps there *was* something going on with Ella? Should she ask Thea outright? But that might lead to questions about how Denise was suddenly so au fait with the comings and goings over at Marc's house. The anxiety about what to say lit a spark that, try as she might, Denise could not extinguish. To her dismay she felt the furnace inside her start to glow. Within a couple of seconds she was burning up. She dug around in her bag and found a leaflet that she must have picked up somewhere or other. Sweat beaded on her forehead. She began fanning herself.

Thea seemed to zone back in, summoned no doubt by the sight of Denise combusting. 'Shall I fetch you a glass of water?'

Denise fanned faster as the flames raced up her chest and neck and continued up to her ears and on over her scalp. 'No. I'll be okay in a minute.' A drink would make little difference, although the lake looked tempting. The cool hit of water. The plunge downwards out of sight. The release from the embarrassment. But she could hardly streak across the park and throw herself in – people would call the police. The blaze under her skin crackled and roared.

Denise dragged her overheated mind back to the present. Thea was looking at her, sunglasses off now, her gaze unwavering. Normally this would have caused Denise to get even more flustered, but given that she was in the grip of a full-on hot flush she couldn't get any more uncomfortable.

'Does anything help?' Thea asked.

Denise, who was heading up to the peak, mutely shook her head. The lake still looked very tempting, perhaps it would be worth it, but finally, blessedly, at the point where she was about to stand up and start running, the mercury topped out and began to drop. Thea continued to watch her. The heat lost some of its intensity, which allowed Denise to speak. 'I'm sorry.' She mopped the sweat off her forehead with a scraggy tissue that she'd found in the bottom of her handbag.

'What are you apologising for?'

Whether it was meant well or not, Denise felt chastised. 'It's just that when I have a flush, I can't concentrate.'

'I should imagine you can't.' To her discomfort, Thea asked the next, most obvious question. 'When did you start with them?'

Denise looked longingly at the lake. 'These last few months.' She could feel Thea studying her.

'How old are you?'

There was no dodging it. 'Forty-seven.' It might have been Denise's overheated imagination, but she could have sworn she saw a flicker of disbelief flit across Thea's face. It stung that Thea obviously didn't think that forty-seven was credible. It also worried her. She hurried on, 'They're not too bad, most of the time.' Minimising her symptoms was so much second nature to her that it was difficult to do anything else.

'Are you okay now?'

'Yes. Thank you.' Apart from feeling and looking like a sweaty mess, especially sitting next to the composed loveliness that was Thea.

'Are you taking anything?'

'You mean HRT?'

'Yes.'

'No.'

'Why ever not?' It was classic Thea, direct to the point of rudeness.

'I'm not sure that I want to go down the medical route. I'm not discounting it as an option, in the future, but I'm not at that stage yet.' Who was she kidding? Well, Thea and everyone else, obviously.

Thea didn't look convinced, which was understandable, given what she'd just witnessed. She pursed her lips, a sure sign of disagreement. 'A lot of the bad press surrounding HRT is total bollocks, you know.'

'I know.' Denise did.

Thea hoisted her handbag – another designer one, Denise assumed, although she didn't know which brand – onto her knee and began searching around in it. 'Here. You could give these a go.' She was holding out a box of tablets or patches, or something. She waggled them in the air as if they were sweets, entreating Denise to take them. For a second she reminded Denise of the kid-catcher in *Chitty Chitty Bang Bang* trying to lure the children out of hiding with his fistful of lollipops. 'They're the oestrogen-only ones. Perfectly safe. Well, maybe not "perfectly", but what is? They really make a difference.'

The conversation had suddenly taken an acute swerve into very personal territory, territory that Denise was very uneasy in. She knew she was sensitive about her age, but what woman wasn't – if they were being honest. Added to which, she was confused by Thea's offer. On the surface it was kind, but it was also odd. Rational people did not go around offering their prescription medicines to their friends. Did they? Although Denise wasn't surprised that Thea was on HRT. She was the type of woman who would decide she wasn't going to tolerate the many and varied indignities of the menopause and would head them off before they got started. Perhaps that's why she looked so good – it was all that oestrogen whizzing around in her bloodstream. 'Thank you.' Denise smiled to indicate her appreciation of Thea's gesture. 'But they're yours. I couldn't.'

Thea shrugged and dropped the box into her bag. 'Suit yourself. But suffering in silence is unnecessary in this day and age.'

Denise felt that she had let Thea, and the sisterhood, down by rejecting her offer and her advice. HRT might very well be the solution to her current, increasingly turbulent symptoms, but it would be an uncomfortable admission – one that Denise wasn't sure she was ready to make. By way of recompense, she offered, 'Maybe it is time to speak to my doctor. See what she recommends.'

Thea seemed indifferent to Denise's lukewarm response to her offer, which stung ever so slightly. Subject discussed and dismissed, she switched tack and began talking about the local MP, who was being investigated for harassing his junior staff. She seemed to know him personally and declared herself inclined to believe the allegations. Denise listened to her wax eloquently and angrily about how misogynistic and archaic the whole system was, impressed and unnerved by Thea's eclectic knowledge. Her capacity to switch gear so quickly and confidently, unfazed by any disagreement, was so different from her own cautious tiptoeing through conversations. She wished she were half as brave.

Conscious of the time, Denise glanced at her watch. She had been away from the office for more than an hour and a half. She was about to text Simon when Thea freaked her out by saying, 'I'm sure he'll cope without you for another few minutes.' It was like she could read Denise's mind sometimes. Read it and find it wanting.

Denise's smile in response was a little tight. Some residual bitterness must have been left behind by her burn-up. Not everyone was like Thea – cool, composed, in total command of her life, her views and her hormones. Denise might not be plugged into the latest gender politics, but she lived with the reality of them every day. She had stresses and strains that Thea had no concept of.

As if to underline the wide disparity in their lives, Thea finished her coffee and, in yet another gear shift, announced, 'I'm going away this weekend.'

'Oh. That's nice.' Denise injected more enthusiasm than she felt into her response.

'I need a change of scene.'

Something about the way she said it struck Denise as off. Perhaps there were problems between Thea and her daughter after all; that would explain what Lewis claimed to have seen. Her curiosity got the better of her and she risked asking, 'Is that why Ella is staying with her father at the moment?'

There was a nanosecond when Thea didn't say anything. Denise sensed that she'd strayed over some invisible, inviolate line, but as strong as the sensation was, it disappeared almost immediately because Thea simply crossed her legs and nodded. 'Yes. It made sense for her to go and stay with Marc this past week while I've had so much on.'

So it was simply a jaunt. 'Where are you heading?'

'Just away. I've booked a nice hotel for the Saturday night.'

'Sounds nice.' What else could she say? It was an appealing thought – buggering off for a while, leaving it all behind.

'You could come with me. If you wanted to. It might do you good.'

Denise was taken aback yet again, and confused. Here she was, being snippy about Thea, while Thea was being open-hearted. Regardless of her pleasure at being asked, Denise's first instinct was panicked refusal. 'I couldn't.'

But Thea seemed to be warming to her own idea. Her tone brightened and strengthened. 'Yes, you could. I'm not heading off until mid-morning. You wouldn't have to take any time off work. The hotel's not far away. It has really nice grounds, a spa, two good restaurants. I could check availability. Just come for a night. Treat yourself, for a change.'

Denise started to fluster. 'It's very kind of you, but...' Suddenly it occurred to her that she didn't know what to say, because she didn't have a valid reason why she couldn't have a night away.

Other than...

It was too-short notice. Denise couldn't simply up and go. It wasn't possible. She had the boys to think about, and Simon. Then there was Eric. And what if there weren't any free rooms? She couldn't possibly share. Surely Thea wouldn't want that, either. And what with her hot flushes and her sweats, any trip away would be fraught with potential embarrassment. Never mind the fact that although she and Thea were friendly, they weren't friends. Look how awkward this conversation had been at times.

Thea had said something.

Denise hadn't heard because her head had been too full of noise.

Thea stood up.

Denise stood up as well. 'Sorry.' Generic apologies, so useful in all circumstances. She felt foolish, and inexplicably sad. Thea's offer seemed to have been rescinded, as casually and as swiftly as it had been made. 'I'll see you when you get back then,' Denise heard herself assert weakly.

Thea didn't say anything in response. She appeared to be in a rush to get away now, gathering her things and staring at something beyond Denise's head. Their conversation was at an end. Thea set off walking, striding along the path towards the park gate, her hair shining and wafting in the sun. Denise had to break into an undignified trot to keep up with her.

In the car park Thea's Mini Convertible was parked alongside Denise's old VW van, a vehicle chosen, at the time, because it was useful for ferrying the boys around to the various after-school activities, and never replaced, because she was still ferrying the younger two and their friends around. 'I hope you have a lovely time.'

Key fob in her hand, Thea paused. She leant on the roof of her car, arms folded, eyes hidden by her shades. 'There's more to life than doing what Simon says, you know, Denise.'

There was a beep.

Thea opened the car door and slid inside, throwing her expensive handbag onto the passenger seat as she did so. Denise noticed – because that was the type of thing she was alert to – that it slid off the seat into the footwell with a thud. If she wasn't careful, it would mark. Thea backed out of the space, at speed, and was gone in under five seconds – leaving Denise standing alone, in her wake, aware that she had failed an important friendship test, and regretting it.

Chapter 15

THEA HAD been sticking to her plan, aside from her random, off-piste moment in the park when she'd inexplicably invited Denise along to the hotel. What the hell was that about? A craving for one last night of company? An instinctive belief that Denise's presence might make her feel better? A bit of both, perhaps. But that was weak and redundant thinking. When you were cutting ties the last thing you should be doing was attaching new threads. Predictably, Denise had helped Thea out by being totally thrown by the suggestion and declining her spontaneous and ill-judged invitation.

Which was, of course, for the best.

Aside from that uncharacteristic wobble, she'd achieved most of what she'd set out to get done.

Work was sorted. Her colleagues briefed. Projects handed on. Someone else could listen to Ross and Gabbie drone on about Korea. Questions about why she was taking leave at such short notice and how long she'd be away had been dealt with, deftly, or so she hoped. She had lied and said her brother had been taken ill and she was needed up in Scotland. It was, after all, none of their business why she was taking some time off.

She'd messaged her friends with a suitably vague I'm going away for a few days R&R text and received Have fun! responses from most of them.

The flat was clear and clean.

The fridge was virtually empty.

The post was dealt with, or shredded. Ella was unlikely to be back in the flat any time soon, but Thea wanted to be on the safe side.

And the flowers from the nice man had been thrown away – which was a shame, as the irises had only just begun to unfurl.

He was next on the list.

She was not looking forward to it.

It did not go well, but that was her fault. If she'd had more time to think it through, she wouldn't have suggested an early-evening stroll on Dunstable Downs. Innocuous as it sounded, it was the wrong setting for a break-up. She knew it wasn't going to be straightforward from the moment she pulled into the car park and saw him standing, waiting for her, looking tall and really quite handsome. His expression when she got out of the car, in her walking boots and jeans, with her hair pulled back in a simple ponytail, had been crushingly hopeful. She could almost hear the cogs in his brain calculating that a daylight date, without the props of wine and soft lighting, was a big step forward. Then she went and made it worse by greeting him with a kiss on the cheek and setting off as if everything was fine, thereby stretching the moment out and stringing him along. For half an hour she allowed them to walk and chat, and enjoy being away from the noise and normality. All they could hear were the birds and the breeze and their breath. All of which let him think that they were heading somewhere, rather than simply to the top of a ridge, then back down to their own cars and on their separate ways.

She told him it was over as they were standing side-by-side looking at the view. She kept it short, and as kind as she could make it. Namely that, lovely as it had been, she simply didn't feel the spark with him; and, sorry as she was, she didn't think it was fair to keep seeing him if she wasn't committed to investing in a relationship. She positioned her decision as not wanting to waste his time.

He listened and looked crestfallen.

They stared out across the Downs in silence for what felt like a long time. It was very scenic.

Then he surprised her, by fighting for her.

He said that he liked her more than any woman he'd met for a long time. That spending time with her made him happy. That if a relationship wasn't on the cards, then friendship would be enough for him. He said it would be a waste to have made a connection like they had and then sever it, just because he wasn't her type. He was eloquent and determined without being overbearing, and as they walked the long march back to their respective cars she felt herself weakening. As they said their goodbyes, without a kiss, he asked if he could keep in touch. She had every intention of saying 'no', but at the last minute she caved in and said 'yes', reasoning that at least it would put an end to their conversation.

And for that weakness she was ashamed.

Back in her own home, away from him and the soft seduction of the view and the summer breeze, she realised that what she'd offered him was false hope. She fully intended to put that right by texting him, to end it properly and finally. She would say that messaging her would make no difference; indeed, it would make her think less of him. It was over – before it had really begun.

That she hadn't delivered the final *coup de grâce* yet was purely a matter of time and timing. She would contact him on Saturday before she departed.

That left two more goodbyes.

Her mother and Ella.

She went to Cherry Trees on the Friday morning, armed with presents for the staff as well as for Nancy. Even Karen, the normally stony-faced manager, came out of her office to coo her thanks for the large fruit basket and the chocolates. While she had Karen's attention, Thea double-checked that her mother's meds and fluids chart were up to date and asked, politely but firmly, that they keep monitoring her weight. Nancy really couldn't do with losing any more. Having bribed the staff to keep up the good work, Thea walked down the corridor bearing the gifts for her mother: a small crystal vase filled with lily-of-the-valley, a litre bottle of gin, some tonic and a net of lemons. The lemons would last at least a couple of weeks – after that, Nancy would have to make do with her mid-morning tipple being light on vitamin C.

Nancy's room was quiet. No Rat Pack this morning. Her mother was up and dressed, if somewhat haphazardly, in a pair of moss-green slacks teamed with a teal-coloured blouse and a red cardigan – to match her red slippers. The slippers were bought as a joke, a poor-taste one perhaps, but one that Thea and her mother had been able to share in more coherent times. When Nancy had first moved into Cherry Trees she'd hated it. The rigid daily routine, the lack of action, the same people day in and day out – she'd found it all very depressing. Because, try as they had and did, there was no way of disguising the fact that a care home shared many of these characteristics with a prison. To mock and manage her lack of independence, Nancy had got into the habit of closing her eyes and clicking her heels together, like Dorothy, wishing herself elsewhere. Hence the slippers.

Today there was no wishful thinking going on. Nancy was sitting in her chair, her dancing feet up on a stool, her powdery cheek pressed against a cushion, her eyes closed. Whoever had got her settled had taken care to make sure she was comfortable. That heartened Thea. It showed they were caring well for her mother. She put the vase on the table by Nancy's bed so that the smell of lilies might fragrance her dreams, and stowed the G&T supplies in the drinks cabinet. Her mother didn't move while Thea pottered about. The room was very hot, a combination of radiator and summer heat. Thea opened a window, then pulled a chair across the room so that she could sit beside her mother. Still no movement.

Thea bided her time. There was no rush. The sounds of the home seeped into the room: the TV in the communal lounge, the cleaner banging a Hoover around in one of the other residents' rooms. There was a waft of cooking smells

– something meaty. It was only 10 a.m. Everything in the home happened ahead of time, although what they were rushing for, Thea didn't know.

She studied her mother. She saw a generic old lady. Frail, wrinkled, white-haired, with paw-like hands, rings loose on her fingers. It was the lack of movement that robbed Nancy of her essence. Only when she was dancing or telling a tall tale did her true character reappear. Inactive, she was a caricature. But as much as it upset Thea to see her mother so diminished, she was loath to poke and cajole her back into life. Requiring Nancy to live in the present, performing the same old routines, seemed selfish and pointless. She was happier when she was somewhere over the rainbow. Content to wait, Thea watched the fabric of her mother's blouse ripple. It was the only clue that she was still breathing.

But this was a goodbye. Much as Nancy wouldn't remember, Thea felt compelled to tell her mother her plans, or at least a simplified version of them. And what better way to tell her than when she was asleep – so much easier for both of them.

'I'm going away for a few days, Mum. I hope that's okay.' Nancy didn't stir. 'Not abroad this time. Just in the UK.' The hoovering next door stopped, thankfully, which allowed Thea to lower her voice. 'I thought I might take bit of a road trip, like you and Dad used to. See the sights here for a change. Do you remember that old Jaguar we used to have? You were always heading off somewhere in it. Dad used to insist on wearing those weird leather driving gloves with the mesh on the back. You hated them. You said he looked like something out of *Jeeves and Wooster*.' If Nancy was listening, she made no sign of it. Thea went on, 'They'll look after you while I'm away. Please try and eat, at least your puddings. You need some more meat on your bones. I've brought fresh lemons for your G&Ts. I'll ask one of the girls to slice them up for you. Please don't attempt it yourself.'

Through the open window a mechanical voice warned of a vehicle reversing. Thea hoped it was a delivery van rather than an ambulance. When the noise stopped, she found she had nothing else to say.

Before sadness had a chance to overtake her, Thea stood up. 'How about some music?' Still her mother didn't respond, but everything was better with music, even the gap where a relationship used to flourish. She searched through Nancy's CDs. She had to open each of the cases to find what she was looking for. The discs were never put back correctly. She eventually found Nat hiding inside a Buddy Holly cover. She put on the disc and went to sit beside her mother again. The swell of strings filled the room. Nat began singing 'Smile'. Thea had an overwhelming urge to kiss her mother, but she didn't want to disturb her dreams, so she made do with resting her head against the chair. Leaning thus, the crowns of their heads nearly touching, Thea listened to Nat sing about the importance of putting on a brave face.

At the end of the CD she made a move. She swapped Nat out for Benny Goodman. 'Sing, Sing, Sing' – one of her mother's favourites. Thea needed a contrast in tempo to give her the momentum to leave the room. Even the sound of an orchestra at full blast didn't rouse Nancy, but it gave Thea some comfort to think that when her mother did eventually choose to re-join the real world, it would be to the sound of swing.

'I'll see you soon, Mum. Keep dancing.' As Thea turned to leave, she could have sworn she saw her mother start tapping one of her red-slippered feet.

On her way out of Cherry Trees she encountered Denise's father-in-law. The corridor was narrow, so there was no avoiding a greeting. 'Hello.'

The old man stopped and peered at her. 'Who are you?'

'I'm Thea. Nancy's daughter.'

'Which one's Nancy?' he barked.

Thea didn't hesitate. 'She's the beautiful one.'

The old man stared at her, his watery eyes appraising and unfriendly. He made a guttural noise, as if clearing an obstruction from his throat. 'Too old to be any lookers in this place,' he announced. Then he limped past, presumably on his way to the lounge. Thea pitied whoever was sitting in there. He really was as obnoxious as Denise had described.

The thought of Denise pricked Thea's conscience. Her comment about Denise only doing what Simon said had been rude and presumptive, her lecture on HRT hectoring, but there was something about Denise that provoked Thea. Beneath all that hesitancy and endless apologising there was a pulse of energy, a hint of potential rebellion. What intrigued and infuriated Thea was that Denise so steadfastly refused to let it out. But timid as she was, there was no denying that she had a good heart. Knowing that she was just across the road from Ella made Thea feel better. Ella and Denise had never met, as far as Thea was aware, and even if they did bump into each other, they were unlikely to have much in common, but regardless, Denise's proximity to her daughter felt like a positive thing.

Thea signed out and headed back to her car.

It was a pity she and Denise hadn't met sooner.

They could, perhaps, have become friends.

Chapter 16

It was dark, or very nearly – the incessant glow from the street lights prevented proper darkness ever truly descending on Prospect Crescent, even at 2.30 a.m. As Denise paced around the garden, she found herself longing for the pitch black of the nights up at her mother's house on the Northumbrian coast. There you genuinely couldn't see your hand in front of your face, or the person walking alongside you.

Denise recalled leaving a pub on the outskirts of Bamburgh with Simon one night – it must have been on one of their rare trips up to visit Lilian before they had the boys. The sensation of stepping into a world transformed had been profound. The darkness had been so absolute that it had been disorientating. She remembered being both scared and excited by the sudden plunge into sightlessness. She and Simon had instinctively reached out for each other, his arm across her shoulder, hers around his waist. Thus anchored, they'd made their way back to Lilian's, concentrating on the road under their feet and listening to the unidentifiable nocturnal sounds. As they walked, Denise had been aware of the vast arc of blackness above them, reducing them to mere dots. At one point Simon had pulled her to a stop. Standing in the middle of an empty country road, bordered by tall hedges of hawthorn, far away from any electric light, they'd kissed. It had been a moment suspended in time and space. The memory made her yearn for the couple they used to be. But for now, the diluted darkness of her well-tended St Albans front garden was all that was available.

Tonight it wasn't a hot flush that drove Denise out of the house, it was the bulky parcel of anger that was wedged under her ribs. It had made sleep – always a struggle – an impossibility. As she wandered barefoot around the lawn, mocked by the calls of an unseen owl, she tried to unwrap and decant her anger.

It had all started with the freezer drawer.

She'd been preparing the evening meal when Simon called to say he was stuck in a traffic jam, some problem around Heathrow. He sounded tetchy, understandably. Denise put the meal on hold. Ever one to make use of any 'free' time, she dealt with some work emails, did their online shop and put on another load of washing. As she multitasked her way around the kitchen, the boys kept appearing and disappearing, reaching across and around her to get into the cupboards to scavenge for snacks. Her requests that they 'wait until dinner' went unheeded. Their greedy demands had irked her.

Her spiky irritation with them had, in hindsight, been a warning that she unwisely chose to ignore.

When Simon eventually walked through the door more than an hour later she began rushing around, in a bid to get the meal on the table as soon as humanly possible, while he stood, a beer in his hand, telling her all about the frustrations of his day, which included a very average lunch at a riverside restaurant in Henley that he wouldn't bother taking a client to ever again, and the appalling standard of other people's driving on the M25. Denise um-ed, conveying something that sounded like sympathy but wasn't, while she whacked the heat back on under the pans and shouted for the boys. Simon moved onto the bane of middle-lane hoggers, a familiar pet peeve. He was warming nicely to his theme when she went over to the freezer to fetch a bag of peas. Whether she yanked too hard or the already-cracked drawer was too full, she didn't know, but suddenly there was a loud snapping sound and the contents of the drawer dropped on her foot, including a rock-solid pork loin. The pain was intense. Denise blinked and tried hard not to cry as she surveyed the spray of frozen produce that was now spread across the kitchen tiles.

It was the small tut from Simon that did it.

Like a handclap triggering an avalanche, the frustration and stress of the day teetered, creaked, then split wide open – letting plumes of emotion billow out. While the pan of water for the peas boiled furiously on the hob and the pie burnt to a crisp in the oven, Denise let rip.

She began with the call from Karen.

There had been another incident with Eric. This time a serious one. He'd lost his temper over the choice of TV channel in the communal lounge and the remote had been thrown. Whether Eric's target had been the other resident's head or it had been a lucky/unlucky hit was unclear. The man (Denise's relief that the unfortunate other resident hadn't been female and, therefore, couldn't be Thea's mother, was immense) had been taken to A&E. Stitches had been required. When questioned, Karen confessed that it might have been glue they'd used to seal the wound, but *that really wasn't the point*. An enquiry into the incident was under way and there was going to have to be a reassessment of Eric's care plan, with specific focus on behaviour management. Karen's tone clearly signalled her all-round pissed-offness with the hassle that another safeguarding incident would trigger. All of which was bad enough, but Karen had ended the call by querying whether Cherry Trees was the right 'setting' for Eric any more or whether *somewhere more experienced in managing the increasingly aggressive manifestations of his Alzheimer's* might be worth looking into. The thought of starting all over again to find a new 'home' for her father-in-law had made Denise feel simultaneously exhausted and panicked.

Then... work had been awful. There'd been the usual barrage of major and minor problems, all requiring her to spend hours on the phone cajoling and coercing various people into doing what was basically their job in the first place – a process that had been made harder by Simon not responding to any of her emails. What was the point of having a mobile if you didn't bother to check it, even if you happened to be in the middle of an indifferent risotto?

Then... when she'd got home she'd caught Joe looking at porn on his laptop when he should have been revising.

Simon was going to have to speak to him, again, about his lax approach to college work and his attitude to women.

And... the carpenter had left a message to say that he wasn't coming next Tuesday, despite having promised, faithfully, that he would, after cancelling on them twice already.

The avalanche ran on to shallower, wider slopes and lost some of its momentum.

And... the fridge drawer was now well and truly bust, and you couldn't replace just one drawer; she'd already looked into it and it wasn't possible, the manufacturers didn't sell single replacements, which meant they were going to have buy a whole new fridge-freezer.

And... they were going have to throw all the food away that was currently spread across the kitchen floor defrosting, as there was nowhere else to put it.

The cascade was losing momentum, slowing to a rubble of tumbling ice chunks.

And... the bridge of her foot really hurt. She was worried she might have broken something.

And... the avalanche petered out to a trickle of snow.

And... Thea was going away, which was making Denise feel unreasonably and irrationally down.

She didn't actually voice this last piece of information. She knew if she did, she might actually cry, which was plainly a ridiculous, hormonal overreaction.

Litany of worries vented, Denise sat on the floor, no doubt crushing some rapidly melting peas with her arse, and waited for Simon to say something – anything – to make her feel better. She knew that was a tall order, but wasn't that what a true partner did: dig you out when you got buried alive?

Simon put down his beer and came towards her. He crouched down and studied her. He looked concerned, Denise could tell by the deep crease in his forehead. He patted her, awkwardly but affectionately. She was glad of his touch, though she had to fight the sensation of feeling like a dog.

'Whoa there. That's a lot of stuff to be stressing about at once.'

She sniffed. More canine behaviour. The thought that she might be going mad occurred to Denise. Sitting on the floor, surrounded by rapidly melting vegetables and weaponised frozen meat, she hadn't the energy to discount the possibility.

'What's brought all this on?' Simon asked in a voice that was calm or, more accurately, designed to be calming.

She wanted to explain properly why she was feeling so overwhelmed by things that she normally took in her stride, but instead she heard herself downsizing her struggles. 'It's just been a rubbish day. Then the drawer snapping. That was the last straw.'

Simon twisted round to look at the offending article. It had broken into three big pieces that no amount of Gorilla Glue was ever going to stick back together. 'Don't worry...' He gave her another pat. 'I'm sure we can sort things out.'

The logical part of her brain knew this was true. What she needed to do was stop dragging every responsibility onto her lap and hugging it all so fiercely to herself. The problem was she didn't know how to stop. How could she change behaviour that had become so ingrained in her that it had replaced her actual personality?

121

Simon smiled. He gave her one last pat, then dispensed his words of support and wisdom. 'I'm sure we can still use the shelf in the freezer without the drawer.'

Solution provided, he began clearing away the debris from the avalanche.

Dinner was a muted affair. The others chewed their way through her burnt offerings, then scattered to the four corners of the house, obviously wary of being anywhere near her.

Later, in bed, Simon asked if she was all right. Denise knew he wanted her to say 'yes'. She couldn't. Instead she tried to articulate her concerns, but this time in a level, unemotional tone of voice. She spoke about how onerous she found her visits to the care home, and how the thought of trying to find somewhere new for Eric was making her feel panicky. Simon justifiably pointed out that the home had 'read the riot act' before, when there had been incidents, but they'd always come round in the end – probably concerned about the potential loss of income. He added that although his father could be stubborn, he was 'relatively low-maintenance'. How little he knew!

It was a speech designed to reassure her.

'Will you come with me next time I go? Speak to the manager? See if you can smooth things over?' Denise asked.

'Of course I will.' She felt a tiny easing of tension. 'Just not this weekend. It's the charity tournament, and I really have to be there both days. Any other weekend and you know I would. Sorry.' He switched off his bedside light and shuffled down in the bed, getting himself settled. 'I'll happily ring them, if you want me to, but I'm sure by next week it'll have all calmed down. Night.' Then he rolled away from her.

Item one on the agenda dealt with, he was asleep in under a minute.

The owl must have flown away or gone to sleep, the lucky sod, because the garden was quiet now.

Not so Denise's soul. It was as agitated and restless as ever, the anger in her chest still blocky and uncomfortable.

Denise knew she was living the life she had chosen. She had wanted a husband, children, a job, financial security: the modern version of a successful traditional family. It had been an active, informed choice. Bettering herself – it was what she'd strived for, and believed she'd achieved. Middlesbrough to St Albans. The Co-op to Waitrose. Holidays in a rented caravan in Whitley Bay to premium economy flights to the US. She had got what she'd wanted.

But, of late, her contentment seemed to have gone walkabout.

Life accumulated and grew more complex, she knew that. Her list of responsibilities was neither longer nor more onerous than anyone else's. Elderly parents, three quasi-adult children, an ageing marriage, a growing weariness with a job she'd done for nearly thirty years – she wasn't surprised life wasn't easy.

But did it have to be so difficult?

Her worry was that *she* was the problem. Perhaps it wasn't life that was getter harder, it was that she wasn't coping as well as she used to. With every month that passed she seemed to be losing more and more of her resilience and, with it, her emotional self-control. She knew that her age was a big part of the problem, but there was nothing she could do about that.

The histrionics over the freezer drawer... perhaps it was understandable that Simon was growing increasingly wary of her mood swings.

Something rustled in the rhododendron bushes that grew in a thick line alongside the fence. Her heart skittered. She was running scared in her own garden. Denise knew she needed to do something to sort herself out. No one else could fix her. Maybe Thea was right: maybe drugs were the solution. Denise stood still and listened. There was definitely something moving around in the bushes. She held her breath.

A fox emerged. Nonchalant. Perfectly at home. It moved slowly, sniffing the grass as it went. It was lean, smooth, sinewy. The fox must have caught her scent because it stopped, lifted its head and stared at her. She stared back. They were barely a couple of metres apart. Its eyes were circled with a ring of gold, its whiskers quivering. Seconds passed. Denise was so close she could hear the fox breathing. It seemed curious, but unfazed by her presence. Then, as if remembering something more interesting that it was supposed to be doing, it dropped its gaze and trotted past on its way to the wrought-iron gate at the side of the house. There it stopped, glanced back at her, then slipped fluidly through the metalwork, off on its nocturnal adventures.

Not an epiphany as such, but maybe a sign.

Chapter 17

DENISE HAD so little faith in herself any more that she expected to change her mind in the cold light of day, but it was precisely because Thursday dawned as normal and life ground on as always that she went ahead and rang Thea.

One night away.

It was what she needed.

She said nothing to Simon. She had plenty of opportunity to do so, as they sat only a desk apart. But the topic simply never came up, because she never brought it up. If Simon noticed the change in her mood, he made no comment. Perhaps he was just relieved that the hysterics occasioned by the exploding freezer drawer appeared to have subsided, and that there had been no further mention of the issues with his father.

Anticipation.

Excitement.

Such emotions had been so sadly lacking in Denise's life of late that she felt quite giddy. The coming weekend would not be filled with the usual chores. It would not comprise another awkward visit to Eric's care home, a trip to the shops, getting the house straight and an evening on her own, watching one of her beloved films. It would be filled with... God knows what. Or at least she hoped it would.

She waited until Simon and the boys were out of the house on the Saturday morning before she packed. The simple act of dragging one of the small cases off the top cupboard and carrying it through into the bedroom set her heart beating. She opened her wardrobe and studied her clothes. What the hell did one take on a weekend away when you didn't know where you were going or what you would be doing? She erred, as was her wont, on the side of caution.

Half an hour later she carried her suitcase downstairs and positioned it by the front door, ready for every eventuality.

With time to kill, she wandered nervously around the home she poured so much effort into, and yet from which she couldn't wait to escape. As she prowled she kept a lookout for Thea's distinctive red Mini. Denise felt embarrassed by her excitement. It was only a couple of days away – she was building it up too much. Thea would think her strange if she didn't rein it in a bit, and she really wanted Thea and herself to get on. It was like being a teenager again, stressing about being liked, about doing and saying the right thing. But new friendships did not come along every day, and Denise, in her current state, felt that she needed a new ally, especially one who seemed to be as together and sorted as Thea.

When at last Thea's car pulled up outside, Denise hurried to put on her jacket and went to collect her case.

But there was no knock at the door.

Perhaps Thea had changed her mind. After all, Denise had more or less invited herself along on the trip. Thea's surprise, when she'd phoned to ask if the invitation was still on the table, had been obvious and although she'd recovered quickly – saying it was 'fine if she wanted to tag along' – Denise couldn't be sure she wasn't just being polite. 'Tagging along' was hardly a fulsome invitation. The fluster that Denise was in was ridiculous. Jesus, she was regressing to the old version of herself: socially anxious, and a drag to boot.

She peered out of the lounge window, taking care not to be seen. The Mini was still there, but there was no sign of Thea. She must have called in at Marc's house to see her daughter. Yes, that must be it. She hadn't changed her mind, she was merely saying goodbye. Feeling foolish, but less agitated, Denise took off her jacket and sat back down on the sofa to wait.

Chapter 18

It was a bright, clear sky, Saturday morning. A lovely day. Thea was on her way to see Ella. Her last goodbye.

She was nervous.

She needed to make her peace with her daughter.

She couldn't leave until she did.

Thea had tentatively suggested they meet on neutral territory. She had not, obviously, phrased it like that, but Ella had said she preferred to meet 'at home'. Thea had swallowed that barb without comment. She had to, she had a lot of ground to make up.

The sunshine glanced off the windows, turning them golden. Thea rapped the knocker on the fortress door and waited.

It was Ella who opened it. She didn't look at Thea or say 'hello'. She simply turned and walked away. Thea followed her inside, sheepish, cowed. Ella was wearing shorts and a T-shirt. Her feet were bare, her hair tied back in a messy ponytail – at-home, comfy clothes. The clear signal was that there was no reason to dress up; nothing special was occurring here. She held the door to Marc's study open. Thea stepped inside. Ella pointed at a chair and went to sit in Marc's place on the far side of the desk. This was *not* the way Thea had wanted it to go. If only they could have met in a café or on a park bench, anywhere other than inside Marc and Jenny's lair. A big slab of waxed oak separated them. Ella rested her elbows on the desk and her chin on her hands. A beautifully constructed barrier.

Thea heard herself swallow. 'Thank you for seeing me.'

Ella shrugged. Ambivalence was a such a sharp weapon, when wielded by one's own child. The 'How's school?' question slid into view, but Thea rejected it. Inanities wouldn't do.

'I know I can't take back what I said, Ella – believe me, I would if I could. But I want you to hear me say again, in person, how very sorry I am. It's not a big enough word, I know, but I am truly sorry for hurting you so badly. For handling the whole thing so clumsily. I panicked. That is no excuse. I know that.'

Ella's response was another shrug of her shoulders and a wistful glance towards the garden. An indication that she was pining to be out in the wholesome, poisonous-mother-free fresh air perhaps?

Thea swallowed again. It was important that she use his full title. 'Your dad and I have talked.' That got her attention. 'We've agreed to you using this as your main base during the week.' Ella stiffened. 'And at the weekends, if that's what you want. It's important that you are where you feel most comfortable. But we want to keep it flexible, to suit you. That's why we aren't planning on involving the lawyers.

At least not yet. After all, making sure you're happy is our responsibility, not theirs.' Some lies were genuinely white. Now was not the time for Ella, or Marc, to know about Thea's instructions to her solicitor. It was best to keep things simple – until they had to become complicated.

Ella was now staring at a point somewhere behind Thea, her hands still obscuring her face.

'We hope we can manage it ourselves, like sensible adults.'

The dig at herself got no recognition. Playing for time, and for a thawing in her daughter, Thea glanced around the study. It was festooned with family trophies. A wonky papier-mâché pig with egg-box trotters, loads of framed photos full of smiles and sunshine, a pen pot covered in neon feathers and foam shapes. Upstairs a toilet flushed and there was the heavy thud of toddler footsteps. Thea heard Jenny's voice and Teddy's high-pitched reply. The sense of homeliness was overwhelming.

'Ella?'

'What?'

Thea was reduced to pleading. 'Please. I can't stand leaving, with things this bad between us.'

Finally Ella's composure wobbled and Thea waited, hoping for a reprieve. What she got by way of response was not enough, but it was all she deserved.

'Okay.'

'Okay?' Thea pressed.

Ella finally looked at her properly. 'I said, okay.' She dropped her hands to the desk. 'I forgive you... for what you said.' There were tears in her eyes.

'Thank you.' Thea knew she was lucky her daughter had

a heart with the capacity to hold love and anger within it at the same time. The sodding desk was in the way. Thea stood up, hoping for hug, needing a hug. Ella stood as well and came to her. They embraced. Thea had to choke down tears. Ella was her girl – would always be her girl – no matter what happened. After barely a second or two, Thea felt Ella pull away. She let her go.

'I'll see you when you get back,' Ella said and, just like that, she was gone. Thea's last glimpse of her daughter was of the grubby soles of her bare feet disappearing around the door.

She heard voices, this time closer, the next-door room? Marc checking in with Ella? He'd be wanting to know how it had gone, what had been said, what had been left unsaid. Thea suspected he had been hovering around outside the study all the time, poised to intervene if she failed to behave as instructed. Thea knew that Ella would not ration her affectation for Marc. She would, no doubt, be currently resting her head against his chest, pouring her heart out to him.

On a higher plane, Thea knew she should be glad that their father/daughter relationship had not been damaged by her reckless outburst, but on planet earth, where emotions were complex and far less self-sacrificing, her jealousy was intense. If Marc had stayed, if Marc had loved them enough, none of this heartache would be happening. She looked around the study, searching for a target. A family photo – too obvious; the pig – too innocent; the height chart, with its wax-crayoned markers – too clichéd; the pen pot – too insignificant. But sticking out of the pot was a screwdriver.

Thea picked it out. It was small, but sharp. She pressed the end into the heel of her hand. It left a red mark. Their voices were still audible. Ella was obviously having no problem finding the right words with Marc.

Thea knew she was on the clock. If she didn't emerge soon, Marc would appear in the doorway, eager to escort her safely off the premises. There was no reason for her to linger.

And yet she did.

Oak was such a lovely wood, but so very soft. Thea stood up, walked round the desk and pushed the rather attractive, retro angle poise lamp over to one side. Ella and Marc's conversation muttered on. It sounded like Ella might be crying. Thea tried to block out their voices, deeply ashamed to be relying on her daughter's distress to keep Marc out of the study. The surface of the desk was pristine, not a scratch or a scuff – much like Marc himself.

She set to work with the screwdriver.

It took her five minutes.

The end result was a crude patch of ugliness in a sea of loveliness. She slid the lamp back into place, covering up her efforts. It was time she made herself scarce. But did she really want her handiwork to go undetected? No, she did not. Hence she gouged a very small, but very deep cross into the surface of the desk near the base of the lamp. *X marks the spot.*

Mission complete, Thea brushed the flakes of sawdust onto the carpet and rubbed them in with the sole of her shoe.

One day soon, or perhaps weeks or even months later – it really didn't matter when – Marc would notice the nick in the wood. She imagined his irritation at discovering this previously undiscovered flaw in the surface of his desk. He'd be confused at first; maybe he'd switch on the lamp to get a better look and realise the marks were new, wilful. It warmed her to think of him moving the lamp and discovering the extent of the damage. He would trace his fingers along the raw, exposed edges of the wood and be horrified. How long would it take him, she wondered, to realise that the marks were the letters T and E gouged deep inside a clumsy, misshapen heart?

She put the screwdriver back into the pot, stood up and made her way out of the house under her own steam, glad to have left her mark.

Chapter 19

THEA WANTED to be gone. She wanted to put as many miles as possible between herself and her empty apartment, between herself and the nice man with his false hopes, between herself and Marc; and, as awful as it sounded and was, between herself and her own daughter. She had to get away because staying was hurting too much.

She climbed into her Mini, threw her phone into the gap near the gearstick, switched on the engine and blasted the horn. Flight, it was the only solution.

Nothing.

She waited, impatience pulsing through her. On impulse she retrieved her phone. It was the source of so much pain and anxiety. She switched it off and shoved it in the glove compartment. It was time to cut the cords that bound her.

She hit the horn again. If Denise didn't come out of her house in the next minute, she was going to drive off. Thea banged the horn again, signalling her intent. The noise was loud enough to wake the dead and draw a frown of sniffy displeasure from a woman walking her cockapoo. She flashed the dog walker her most shiny smile. Nothing pissed off pissed-off people more than the pisser-offer looking like they didn't give a damn. And she didn't. Not any more.

Finally, Denise appeared.

She paused to lock up the house. In the process she managed to drop her keys into one of the flower troughs that flanked the front door. She waved an apology and mimed falling over her own feet, then began rooting through the foliage. Despite her agitation, or perhaps because of it, Thea smiled. There was something comforting about Denise. Her utter lack of pretension was refreshing. Keys retrieved, door locked, Denise ran down the drive, wheeling her suitcase behind her. She headed for the rear of the car.

Thea stopped her. 'No! Sling it on the back seat. There's no room in the boot.'

Thankfully Denise did as instructed. She climbed into the passenger seat. 'Sorry. I'm such a klutz.'

'No worries. Are you good to go?' Thea asked.

'I am,' said Denise. Seatbelt fastened. Hands clasped.

'Great,' said Thea. Sunglasses on. Car in gear.

Problems shelved, for the time being, Thea swung the Mini away from the kerb with a satisfying squeal of its tyres and, without so much as a glance in her rear-view mirror, drove off.

PART TWO

Chapter 20

THEA DROVE fast, much faster than Denise was comfortable with, but of course she couldn't say anything because she was Thea's guest, and this was Thea's car, Thea's trip, Thea's idea. They were on the M1 in no time, cruising along in the outside lane at ninety miles per hour. If anyone got in their way, Thea pulled close to their bumper and flashed them impatiently.

'What did Simon say when you told him you were going away?' Thea asked as they shot past a BMW.

'Sorry?' Denise was too distracted to concentrate on much other than the gap between the Mini and the car in front of them.

'I asked if Simon was okay about our little trip?'

Denise stared straight ahead at the rapidly approaching horizon. 'He doesn't know about it – well, not yet.'

Thea twisted round to get a better look at Denise.

Denise wished Thea would keep her eyes on the road, but felt a ripple of satisfaction to see her amused expression. 'He set off early to play golf, so I didn't get chance to talk to him this morning.' Which was true, but that didn't explain why she'd said nothing to him in the days before. 'I left him a note.' She'd propped it up against the microwave:

Got the opportunity to have a night away with Thea. Thought you wouldn't mind, given you're tied up with the tournament. Will text you later. D x.

P.S. There are ready meals in the freezer and beer in the fridge.

P.P.S. I'll be back!

In all honesty, her avoidance of mentioning that she was about to drop everything and run away for a couple of days hadn't purely been down to cowardice. Denise had been looking for a way to throw a spanner into the smooth running of their family life for a while. 'Disruptive creativity' it was called: a way of changing the dynamic in a situation by doing something unexpected or even counter-intuitive. If it worked in marketing, why not in life? That was the real purpose of this trip for Denise – to shake things up, for Simon and the boys, as much as for her. The thought of them coming back from their various activities to find the empty house and her absent made her feel... in control.

Thea smiled. 'Do you think they'll survive without you?'

Denise shrugged. 'We'll see.' The anonymous fields and pylons of Bedfordshire whizzed by. All she knew was they were heading north – that was it; she'd left the hotel booking to Thea. The thought that she was totally in Thea's hands was a little unsettling, but it was exciting as well. 'Where are we staying?'

Thea grinned. 'Wait and see.' She must have detected the tension in Denise's body because she added, 'Don't worry. I think you'll like it.'

Denise nodded, forced a relaxed smile and made herself sit back.

So much for the great escape. Forty-five minutes later they were careering around the narrow lanes somewhere north of Milton Keynes – rural as it was, it was hardly bandit country. As they rounded another bend, Denise held on to the edge of her seat as if her life depended on it, which given Thea's fluid, but very speedy driving, it kind of did. With no satnav or phone in evidence, Thea made a series of seemingly random decisions every time they reached a junction or a fork in the road. As they swooped up and over the brow of another hill, Denise told herself to relax. This was the point of coming away, wasn't it? To be spontaneous, to go with the flow. Her 'plan', in so far as there was one, was to tailgate on the back of Thea's confidence to a weekend of different experiences, to see how the other half of the world lived for a change – the ones who didn't seem to give a fuck. And the only way she was going to do that is if she allowed herself to have some fun.

Thea slowed the car.

Denise loosened her sweaty grip on the seat fabric.

The sign was understated; blink and you'd miss it, unless you were looking for it, which Thea obviously had been. *Staveley Hall Hotel and Spa.* White writing on a duck-egg-blue background. The colours of the Cotswolds in the Buckinghamshire countryside.

The hotel, which was presumably their intended destination, was hidden from view, surrounded by acres of sun-dappled trees and – if the small signs dotted alongside the drive, which Thea was currently bowling down, were an accurate guide – muscular stags at bay. But as they journeyed through the light and shade all Denise saw were a couple of frisky squirrels and a groundsman sitting on a small tractor having a crafty fag. After what felt like a good while, they cleared the woodland. Laid out below them was a grand, mellow sandstone hall, with a modern glass extension attached to its left hip.

Thea slipped off her sunglasses. 'I thought we'd treat ourselves to a bit of luxury. Is that okay with you?'

A liveried porter called Xavier carried their bags up for them, although it was unnecessary – they were both travelling light. Their rooms were on the same floor. He let Denise in first.

It was a large, elegant, streamlined space, with dove-grey walls and crisp white bed linen. There was the obligatory excess of cushions, offset by a slim vase of pale-cream freesias. The bathroom door was ajar. It afforded a glimpse of a bath large enough for a family of four, though absolutely nothing about the room spoke of families. Having murmured his way through the list of facilities, Xavier smoothly withdrew before Denise had time to say thank you or tip him. The door closed softly. Xavier and Thea melted away. The halls were carpeted. Perfect for unobtrusive room service – no request too personal or demanding – at any time of the day or night.

Denise felt like she'd been parachuted into an oasis. It was a shock, but a very nice one. She slipped off her shoes, strolled across the carpet and stood at the foot of the super-king-sized bed. It was strange to be in a room so dedicated to shared pleasure and indulgence – on her own.

It was beautiful.

She laughed. A short out-loud bark of a laugh, which caught her by surprise. It was ludicrous to think that little more than an hour ago she was at home. She laughed again, adding her very ordinary voice to the collection of very beautiful fabrics and the tasteful fittings. She hadn't asked the price of the room, with Thea standing next to her brandishing her Amex card, it hadn't seemed the done thing; but as she looked around she realised that she didn't care what this gorgeous slice of luxury cost. For one night it was hers, hers alone, and she intended to enjoy it. She threw her arms up in the air and collapsed back on the bed, Kevin McCallister-style, and laughed again – at absolutely nothing.

Chapter 21

DENISE LOOKED around the hotel bar with its plush sofas, arty lighting and abstract pictures and felt nicely indulged. When the waiter come over, Thea didn't waste any time dithering. 'I fancy a margarita, how about you?'

Denise nodded. Thea flicked the drinks menu shut, sat back, crossed her legs and surveyed the scene. There was quite a crush in the bar. The clientele was predominantly smart couples having romantic weekends away, but there was also a group of men, in very nice suits, sitting at one of the bigger tables. They were drinking champagne, one bottle already upended in an ice bucket. Denise relaxed into the chilled-out atmosphere. It was Saturday night and, for a change, she was dressed up and was out where the action was.

The waiter brought their margaritas over on a tray. He set down coasters, the drinks and a small bowl of pretzels, with a flourish. Thea smiled. 'Thank you. Can you add these to room two-one-three, please.'

The waiter straightened up. 'No need to, Madam. Compliments of the gentleman over there.' Admirably, he managed not to smirk as he imparted this hackneyed piece of news.

Denise looked over and saw one of the besuited men raise his glass and salute them. Correction, he saluted Thea.

'Should we decline?' Denise asked.

Thea glanced in his direction, gave the tiniest of nods and picked up her drink. 'Hell, no. If he's buying, it would be rude to refuse.'

The margaritas were good: sharp, salty, evocative of holidays and nights that ended in sex. Denise took an arty photo of them and sent it to the boys, with a message telling them how nice the hotel was. Aaron responded straight away with Looks well bougie. Don't get pissed and Lewis replied with a thumbs up a few seconds later. Joe, her youngest, kept his thoughts to himself.

Denise sipped her drink, feeling the muscles in her shoulders, which had already been eased by an afternoon massage, become even more malleable. She'd messaged Simon earlier. Told him where they were. Reassured him she was fine. She had not enquired how things were at home. Or asked how he'd got on at golf because, to be honest, it was nice not to care for a change. Nor had she picked up when he'd called in response to her text, which he'd done, twice, in the space of an hour. She didn't send him the picture of their drinks, she didn't think he'd appreciate it. She took another sip and another. By the time her glass was drained, she'd stopped thinking about Simon and the boys and was laughing at a story Thea was telling about a disastrous trip to Rome when she was in her twenties.

They ordered a second round of margaritas, to be added to

their own bill this time. While they waited for them to arrive, Denise excused herself and went to the fragrant powder room with its individual mini hand towels and gardenia and ylang-ylang hand wash. Even her structurally unsound pelvic floor seemed less of a hassle in an environment this lovely. Money really could buy happiness, at least the shallow, self-indulgent kind.

When she returned to the bar she saw that there was a man sitting in her seat – their cocktail buyer. He was talking, confidently, animatedly, and Thea was listening, her expression pleasantly enigmatic. Denise felt put out. She walked over to them self-consciously; not that she needed to be, as no one was looking at her, least of all the man. His attention was solely on Thea, but when Denise stood next to the chair, he immediately got up.

'My apologies.' He had a deep voice and a trendy, close-trimmed beard. He was tall, good-looking, in a smartened-up Matthew McConaughey kind of way. And he knew it. Denise reclaimed her seat and flicked Thea a questioning glance that bounced right off her. The Matthew lookalike smiled, a full-on charm offensive. He had crinkly eyes, with a mischievous glint in them, that promised fun without threat. 'Well, we're heading back over, ready for round two. Feel free to come and join us later, if you'd like to. I'll keep an eye open for you.' He dipped his head and for a second Denise thought he was going to kiss Thea's hand, but he merely flashed another of his endearing smiles.

Denise waited until he was out of earshot. 'Join him where?'

Thea gathered up her bag and phone. 'They're at a wedding over in the annexe. He thought we might fancy a bop later.' She stood up. 'Our table is ready. Shall we take our drinks through with us?' She seemed totally relaxed. It was as if this sort of proposition came her way on a regular basis.

Over dinner the conversation flowed easily. Thea asked about the business, and Denise told her and heard herself sounding professional and knowledgeable. Then, mellowed by their cocktails and the wine, they talked about their families.

Thea told Denise a little about her marriage and her divorce. She and Marc had got together young, as freshers at university. After graduation they'd both been very career-focused. She had been lucky and had been able to travel a lot with her job. It had been a hectic, full-on period in their lives. Then, in their mid-thirties, they'd had Ella, their only child. Was there a hint there that they'd had trouble conceiving? Denise couldn't be sure. She quickly did the maths – that would mean Thea was forty-nine or fifty. She looked younger. Thea said their family had felt complete. That closed down any speculation, not that Denise had any intention of prying.

Thea finished the last of her wine and carried on speaking, in the same measured tone. She said that over time they'd begun to want different things – she did not elaborate what – and that after a couple years of trying to make it work she and Marc decided to part, rather than plough on and risk damaging their family irrevocably. The divorce, she implied, had been amicable. They had both, she stressed, made sure that Ella's happiness was the priority. She made no mention of her current love life. Denise was impressed at the equanimity with which Thea described the breakdown, as Denise saw it, of her marriage. She was such a strong woman, so emotionally together.

Denise kept her own description short. She sketched a picture of a contented, busy life with Simon and the boys. Then, worried that it sounded smug and twee and, more importantly, boring in comparison to Thea's life, she mentioned *some recently dropped balls when it came to juggling the old work/life balance.* She was about to change the subject when Thea made one of her by now very familiar, no-messing observations.

'You feel guilty a lot of the time, don't you?'

Denise thought about denying it, but didn't. Thea was spot on. Guilt was her factory setting. 'Yes.'

'Why?'

'I don't know. My upbringing, my personality.'

'But you spend your life working or chasing around after other people. From what I can see, you do too much, not too little.'

'Don't most women?' Denise went to take a drink, but found her glass empty.

Thea paused. 'Yeah, I suppose many do.' She spotted Denise's empty wine glass and poured the last of the bottle into it. 'But it's no way to live. Too many women of our age turn themselves into martyrs. It does no one anyone good, not in the long run.'

'But surely it's not a choice. It's just what happens; the responsibilities simply pile up: elderly parents, kids, relationships, work. But...' The wine and Thea's genuine interest were seducing home truths out of Denise, 'I'm finding it harder to cope with it all than I used to. I'm less confident. Less rational. I feel like I'm in a fight with my own body and my emotions a lot of the time.' She was on a roll now, voicing long-silent griefs and frustrations. 'I even hate the description "a middle-aged woman". It's so negative. Like you're being written off. That sense that you're invisible a lot of the time.' It occurred to Denise that although she'd felt like the Cheshire Cat for a while, it was unlikely to be a problem Thea was familiar with. Which was probably why her response was so robust.

'That's bollocks nowadays.'

Denise mentally told herself to calm down. It had felt good to talk and release some of the pressure, but it probably wasn't Thea's idea of fun. She was sure the couples at the other tables weren't having in-depth discussions about the trials and tribulations of the menopause. 'Yeah, you're right. I suppose it all depends on what's happening in your life – what opportunities you have – rather than your actual age. It is what you make of it.' She drained her glass and resolved to be more upbeat.

'Speaking of which,' Thea signalled to the waiter that they were leaving, 'the night is still young.' She stood up, adjusted her skirt and picked up her bag. 'How about half an hour on the dance floor before bed?'

And in a determined move to embrace the spirit of the trip, Denise responded, 'Yeah, why not?'

Chapter 22

It was funny, but no matter how upmarket the venue, how blushing the bride or how handsome the groom, wedding discos were all the same: cheery and cheesy. The DJ was rocking out the classic dance-floor fillers, and through the huge glass roof of the hotel ballroom the night sky looked like it was studded with multicoloured stars. Many of the guests had gone well past the point of self-consciousness. The men had rolled up their shirt sleeves and abandoned their ties, while the women had literally let down their hair and kicked off their shoes, no longer caring that their expensive sheer stockings were getting wrecked.

Thea didn't bother looking for Robert, their margarita charmer. He would no doubt find her, if he was still sober enough to remember flirting with her earlier. She felt the music pulse up her spine. Cheese or no cheese – she wanted to dance. Not talk, not think about age or families, or who she was and what she was doing, just dance. And there was no time like the present. 'Are we going to hit the dance floor then, show 'em how it's done?' She was already swaying to the beat.

Denise hesitated. Thea waited for her to back out of it, but Denise smiled and nodded. They went together, straight onto the floor, not caring what song was playing.

It was years since Thea had danced with a girlfriend, mouthing the lyrics, meeting each other's gaze as the track changed, waiting to see if she recognised it, making space for each other. Denise danced well, in time, but her moves were restrained. On a dance floor, as in life, she seemed determined to take up as little space as possible. Thea felt no such inhibitions. Dua segued into Drake, a favourite of Thea's. Dancing was such a gloriously simple, selfish pleasure. Movement to a beat. Reaction to a sound. No forethought or afterthought. Just dancing and smiling and getting hot and sweaty, and loving it. No before or after. Just now. As she danced, the room receded to a blur of colour and noise. A backdrop. In that moment Thea was happy.

During the opening bars of 'Uptown Funk' she felt a hand on her waist. It was Denise. 'I'm going to sit this one out.' She was bright red in the face. Thea reluctantly offered to leave with her, but Denise shook her head. 'I'll sit down, cool off a bit. I'm fine. You keep dancing.'

Thea did, letting loose, closing her eyes, feeling free – until she sensed someone at her side. It was Robert. He leant in and she had to rein in her moves to avoid breaking his nose.

'I'm glad you came,' he shouted in her ear. She merely nodded, not in the mood for conversation. 'Looks like you're enjoying yourself.' So he had been watching.

'I am,' Thea shouted back, then she moved away from him and went back to her dancing.

He joined in, staying within her orbit, watching her, smiling his appreciation. He had a decent sense of rhythm, but was too stiff in his torso to properly get into it. But credit where it was due, he stuck it out for another two tracks. Then, as she knew he would, he invaded her space again, 'Can I buy you a drink?'

Dragged back to earth, Thea realised she'd left Denise sitting on her own for far too long. One swift, cold drink, then she would go and re-join her and they would leave. 'Yeah, okay.' As she walked off the dance floor, Robert rested his hand in the small of her back. It sent a ripple up her spine. He guided her towards the bar, and on her way through the tables she caught Denise's eye and mimed a drink. Denise shook her head.

'What can I get you?'

'A glass of water, with some ice, please.' He raised an eyebrow. 'What? I'm hot.' She was doing it deliberately, but why not? There was no harm in a little light banter.

Robert ordered. Got a beer for himself. Thea downed her cold water in one. He laughed, ordered her another. This one she sipped, like a lady. He said something she couldn't hear above the noise of the disco. He leant in closer. 'I said, do you fancy a bit of fresh air?'

Thea looked for Denise, couldn't see her. Had she gone to the Ladies again, or given up on her? The former seemed more likely. Denise wouldn't go up to her room without saying goodnight. 'Okay, but just for a few minutes.'

They headed out through the open French doors at the far end of the ballroom.

It was blissfully cool outside. They wandered across the terrace, then took the steps down to the gardens, making small talk as they went. She asked about the happy couple, though she wasn't remotely interested, and Robert told her some funny anecdotes about the groom's family. Beneath their words rippled a question. There was a low wall that ran all the way around the lawn. He sat down. She sat next to him, a space between them. They looked back up at the hotel. A sea of brightly dressed wedding guests bobbed around the ballroom.

Thea knew he'd brought her outside to test the waters, spurred on by the hope that she might go back to his room with him. Her own motives for coming outside were less clear. Had she simply been flattered to be asked? Pleased to be able to attract him, with her looks and her moves? Was she trying to tamp down her fleeting, but recurring memories of the nice man and his patient, old-school courtship? Or had she followed a total stranger out into a dark garden, knowing full well what he was after, due to a belief – which was growing inside her every day that passed – that she had nothing to lose? That any experience was worth pursuing, no matter how risky?

Maybe.

Or perhaps she'd been motivated by something far simpler. The need for some fresh air.

'You really are something special.' His voice signalled his intent.

'Oh, trust me, I'm not.' *I'm any halfway decent-looking woman, in a tight dress, who agreed to have a drink and a dance with you*, she added in her head.

'You really know how to enjoy yourself, don't you?'

'I do.' Let him have his fantasies. She turned to put her

empty glass down on top of the wall. Robert took it as an invitation to reach out and stroke the skin on the nape of her neck. She leant away from his touch. He dropped his hand, but kept his eyes on her. The opening bars of 'Come On Eileen' drifted across the garden.

She stood up.

He did as well. He stepped in front of her, blocking her path back to the ballroom. 'I so want to kiss you.' The plaintive opening riff of the song gave way to the melody. Robert went in for the kiss.

She swayed away from him. Kevin Rowland began imploring Eileen to 'come on'.

'No!' She said it clearly.

Robert looked confused.

'I'm going back inside to find my friend.' She went to step around him. He took hold of her, his hands on her upper arms. That shocked her. She didn't struggle, or shout, or panic. She looked down at his fingers, pressing into her bare skin, then back up at his face. Wordless. Expecting – as was her right – for him get the message and, more importantly, to accept it.

After a split second, during which she felt a sliver of fear, he let go. 'Sorry.'

He sounded it, but there was no harm in reminding him – bought drinks, shaken hips, walks in the shrubbery notwithstanding. 'When a woman says "no", Robert, she means "no".'

'Yes. I'm sorry. Too much champagne. I apologise.'

The song had got into its repetitive stride now, but above its din Thea heard someone shouting her name. Denise was standing on the terrace, clutching her handbag like a weapon. Thea waved.

'Is everything all right?' Denise shouted.

One last glance at Robert, and Thea set off walking. 'Yes. Fine. I just came outside for some fresh air.'

Denise was looking from Robert to Thea, obviously aware that something was going on, but uncertain as to what. Thea didn't enlighten her, but she did want to reassure her. It was kind of Denise to come looking for her, after she'd abandoned her so rudely.

'Denise. Honestly. Everything's fine. I'm sorry I disappeared. Shall we go up now? It's getting late.'

Kevin finally stopped harassing Eileen, and Ike began wooing Tina.

Denise smiled and linked arms with Thea. 'No. I came to find you because I like this one. Let's dance.'

Chapter 23

In the lift they took off their shoes. Without her heels, Thea was close to Denise's height, which was odd because Denise had thought her much taller. They leant against the mirrored walls, their ears thumping with the bass from the party. They were both disco-dishevelled. A wave of delight rippled through Denise. At home she'd have been in her pyjamas, in bed, next to Simon, awake but restless. Instead she was awake and wandering around a luxury hotel in her stockinged feet – tired, but in a good way, having spent a day doing something different, with someone different.

The lift pinged. They stepped out and walked down the corridor. Denise dug out her key card, swiped it, the lock beeped and the light flashed green. She pushed open the door. 'Goodnight.'

'Night. Sleep well. I'll see you in the morning. Remember we need to be down for breakfast by nine a.m. – I want to be away by ten.' Denise nodded, happy to let Thea decide the itinerary. She had no idea what she had planned, and she didn't care. She watched as Thea walked down the corridor to her room, her heels hanging from her fingertips, her pace languid – a hint of Lauren Bacall in her heyday. Way too classy for a Matthew McConaughey lookalike from Milton Keynes.

Denise pulled the door shut behind her.

Someone had been in to 'turn down' the room. The lamps were lit, the cushions removed from the bed and the covers precisely folded back. There were two gold foil-wrapped chocolates strategically placed on the pillows. Denise dropped her shoes and sat on the bed. The phone in her handbag was silent, but that didn't mean she wasn't aware of its weight – it lurked there, a small, slim block of reproach. She extracted and checked it. There was another missed call from Simon. She listened to his message: Denise. It's me. Please call me, when you're free to talk. I'm around all evening.

The sound of his voice made her stomach tense. His tone was hard to read. He had every right to be confused. It was totally out of character for her to up-sticks and leave. Her behaviour must seem inexplicable, provocative even. What was she saying? It *was* inexplicable to him. A note propped up by the microwave, and two short texts reassuring him that she was fine, was hardly communicating. It was understandable that he wanted to talk to her. Or at least he had at 9.20 p.m.

But it was now 12.18 a.m.

Another day.

She reached for one of the chocolates, absent-mindedly unwrapped it and popped it in her mouth. Creamy sweetness trickled between her teeth.

It was too late to ring. He would be asleep. She composed a message instead, the gist of which was that she'd had a good day, no details offered; a nice meal, no menu provided, and a nightcap in the hotel bar. She made no mention of the disco. She signed off saying she would call him in the morning. Fob-off sent, Denise stood up and stripped off her dress, tights and underwear, letting her clothes lie where they fell. A shower. That's what she wanted. A freshen up and a full-body moisturise, time on her skincare regime before she slipped between the pristine Egyptian-cotton sheets.

She was heading for the palatial bathroom when her phone started ringing. She knew without looking that it was Simon. She wished she'd been quicker, made it into the shower, got the water powering down and, as a result, been justifiably deaf to the ringtone, but she had not – she was standing by the bed, naked, looking down as his name lit up on the screen of her phone. There was no ignoring its insistence.

'Hello.'

'Denise?' He breathed a lot of relief into the word. 'I've been waiting for you to call.'

'I didn't want to wake you.'

'Well, I'm obviously still up.' There was dead air. His reproach and her resistance meeting down the line. He cracked first. 'How's the hotel?'

'Really very nice.'

'And you're having a good time?'

'Yes. Lovely. It feels like a proper break.' *From the routine and the responsibilities and the boys ... and you*, she did not add.

'I was a little taken aback when I got home and discovered you'd just gone off, without saying anything.'

Here it came. Denise pulled the silky powder-blue throw off the foot of the bed, wrapped it around herself and perched on the edge of the mattress. 'It was a short-notice thing. Thea asked me along and I thought... why not? You and the boys were due to be out most of the weekend, so I didn't see any reason why I couldn't.' She didn't sound apologetic; the alcohol and the dancing must have upped her assertiveness.

'No. I suppose not.' There was a pause. 'But a conversation at some point would have been nice.'

Yes, wouldn't it? She'd been saying as much herself for months, but work and golf and the boys always seemed to get in the way. Now that Simon finally wanted to talk to her, she found she had nothing to say. 'I knew you'd be playing golf until late, then having a few drinks in the clubhouse' – as he did most weekends, often arriving home in an Uber, sometimes far later than they'd agreed – 'so I thought I wouldn't be missed.'

'I've been home all evening!'

He sounded plaintive, but Denise wasn't in the mood for indulging his lonely little-boy routine. 'And I've been busy.'

'Until gone midnight!'

Was there a hint of anxiety, or even jealousy, mixed with his irritation? Denise was intrigued to find herself pleased that Simon might be concerned about what she'd been getting up to. The novelty of it was stimulating. She never normally 'got up to' anything. 'Yes. We made a night of it.'

'Are you drunk?' It was a swift, hard jab. Totally uncalled for.

Denise counter-punched. 'No. Are you?' She had an image of the drinks cabinet with its selection of rarely touched spirits, a gap where the best Scotch normally sat.

'No.'

Well, this had degenerated quickly!

She was getting chilly. Her luxury bathroom, with its power shower and rail of pure white towels, awaited her presence. 'It's late, Simon.'

His tone when he spoke again was conciliatory. 'Okay. Yes. You're right. It has been a long day. We'll catch up at some point tomorrow?' She wondered if he heard her sigh, because he hurried on, 'I'll miss you tonight. Sleep well.'

'You too.' He always did. She ended the call.

It had been an awkward exchange, but not as bad as she'd been imagining, primarily because she was sitting on a huge comfy bed, swaddled in a silk throw, with a night alone stretching ahead of her and another day of unknown adventures planned. Let him stew. She was not going to worry about him, or anything else.

She stood up and headed for the bathroom. On second thoughts, she retraced her steps across the lush, toe-stroking carpet and grabbed the chocolate off the pillow. There were benefits to sole occupancy.

Chapter 24

'Not tempted?' the man asked.

'No. It's not my sort of thing.' Silverstone, the home of British motor racing, was Thea's idea of a good time, not Denise's.

The man didn't say anything else for a while, he just leant against the rail and watched the cars rip by. Denise kept her eyes peeled for Thea's Ferrari or, more accurately, she kept a lookout for anything red. Another handful of expensive, high-powered metal came into view. Denise spotted a fast-moving smudge of crimson that could be Thea. It was a brief glimpse.

She hadn't realised there would be other drivers on the track at the same time as Thea. But then again, why should she? She didn't normally spend her weekends this close to a bunch of petrolheads fulfilling their obsession with speed. There were brief patches when the track fell empty and a weird peace descended, like a collectively held breath, but within a few seconds another cluster of vehicles would appear, dodging and weaving around each other, before disappearing again over the shimmering concrete horizon. Even from Denise's very safe distance, they seemed to pass awfully close to each other. Wacky races for people with more money than sense; it was an odd way to spend a Sunday lunchtime.

Ten minutes passed. The cars roared monotonously in and out of view. The air tasted of petrol. It was curiously hypnotic, soothing almost. Denise was pleasantly bored.

'Who's driving?' The man again, making small talk.

'My friend, Thea. She's in the red Ferrari.'

They watched for a few more minutes in comfortable silence.

'It's glorious,' he commented.

He was right. The sun was warm on the back of Denise's neck, the sky above the track pure blue. 'It is.' She immediately realised her error. The man wasn't talking about the weather, his attention was on the track. 'You've driven it?' she asked out of politeness.

'Yes. Thousands of times. I work here. I'm one of the instructors.'

'Dream job?'

'Well, that depends. Some of the paying customers – pardon my French – are complete tools. But yes, I've always loved cars, so I can't complain. I've done far worse things for a living.' He turned and smiled at Denise. 'It's really very safe.'

'I'll take your word for it.'

'No, really. You're at less risk of an accident out there than on normal roads.'

'I am, the way my friend drives. She isn't a big fan of braking.'

He laughed. 'This will do her good then. It's all about touch and timing, like most things in life.'

The Ferrari slid back into view. This time they watched it together.

'She's not bad, your friend.' Just as he acknowledged Thea's driving skills, the Ferrari overtook something flat and yellow, then roared away out of sight. He nodded appreciatively. 'Aggressive, but in control.'

'I'm sure Thea would be very happy to have that as her epitaph.'

'Whoa,' he turned towards her, 'I'm not sure we should be talking headstones at a racetrack!'

They both smiled. Was he flirting? Was she? It didn't really matter, it felt good.

He glanced at his watch. 'My first booking isn't for another hour – what do you say?'

Denise felt herself flush. 'No, I couldn't!'

But then he smiled and said, 'You could. I promise, you'd be perfectly safe with me.'

Chapter 25

THE PEOPLE at the next table looked their way again, which only made it worse. Thea's breath was hiccupy, her eyes streaming. God only knew where most of her mascara was – not on her lashes certainly. She hadn't laughed with this edge of hysteria since she'd been a kid. Every time she met Denise's gaze, it set her off again.

Part of it was the adrenaline still coursing through her veins. The track session had more than lived up to her expectations. It had been challenging, of course, a real test of her reactions and of her concentration, but it was a test that she'd not only passed, but nailed. It had helped that her instructor had got the measure of her early on. He'd worked out where Thea's line was and had taken her closer and closer to it with each lap during her first session on the track. After the break, he'd pushed her past it.

It had been exhilarating and, although she'd wanted to keep thrashing around the circuit all afternoon, extremely demanding. The minute she'd climbed out of the Ferrari the tiredness had hit her. She'd sat through her debrief in a kind of daze, focusing just enough to take in and commit to memory her best lap time: 2 minutes and 29 seconds.

On a high, she'd gone in search of Denise.

But Denise was nowhere to be seen.

Literally nowhere.

After wandering around for twenty minutes, Thea gave up. She needed to sit down. She picked a patch of grass in the sun and flopped down on it, soaking up the atmosphere as her ego hummed and glowed.

Half an hour passed. Her phone beeped. It was Denise asking where she was.

After another ten minutes Denise emerged out of the sun – running. This was not normal. She threw herself down on the grass with something that looked like abandon. Close up, she looked different. She was sweaty and flushed, but in a good way rather than in an overheated menopausal way. And she was grinning – not smiling, but actually grinning from ear to ear. 'You'll never guess where I've been?' She patently did not want Thea to speculate, so she didn't. 'Out there!' Denise wheeled her arms around, indicating the track. Her excitement was attracting attention. It was all very un-Denise-like; perhaps having a bop had shaken loose some of her inhibitions.

'You said "over my dead body" when I suggested it.'

'I know.' She dropped her arms and hugged herself, happily. Thea waited, letting her savour her moment. 'I got talking to one of the instructors, Chris.' She paused.

'And?'

'He offered to take me out.'

'Did he now?'

Denise flushed even pinker. 'He did. And I thought,' another pause, 'why not? Seize the day, and all that.'

'And?'

'He was right. It was glorious. Terrifying, but... glorious.'

'What did you go round in?'

Denise cracked another wide grin and repeated, like a well-rehearsed schoolgirl, 'A Porsche Cayenne.'

Thea wolf-whistled. It was one of her talents that was sadly underused. The whistle drew more looks in their direction. 'How fast did you go?'

Another smile of pride, 'Top speed, on the straight, one hundred and forty-eight miles per hour.'

'Get you!'

Denise laughed and stretched. 'It gets the blood pumping, doesn't it?'

'It sure does.'

'Sorry. How was your session?'

'Good.' Thea didn't want to compete with Denise's flushed triumph.

'Just "good"?'

Thea let out a shriek. 'No! It was fucking awesome.' On a whim she grabbed her phone and bum-shuffled across the grass until she was sitting next to Denise. She held her phone aloft and snapped a selfie.

The photo was good. A close-up of their faces, cheek-to-cheek, both of them flushed and grinning. Friends having a good time. She sent it to Denise.

The mildly hysterical mood carried them back to the car, along the country roads to the first pub they spotted that had a beer garden. Thea pulled into the car park as if cornering at Apex. Denise, now the queen of speed, didn't so much as bat an eyelid at the manoeuvre.

Armed with a glass of wine each, they claimed one of the outside tables. 'So, tell me again, what was it about Chris that swung it?'

'He was so reassuring. So experienced.'

Thea cackled. 'So that's all it takes with you, is it? A man with plenty of miles on his clock.'

Denise shrugged, flippant, relaxed. 'That... and a nice smile.'

Thea took a swig of her wine. It was teeth-achingly cold, chilled to the point of utter tastelessness, but the quality was irrelevant. She felt carefree, reckless, glad to be where she was, with who she was, talking nonsense, drinking cold alcohol. She clinked the rim of her glass against Denise's. 'To reassuring men and fast cars.'

The first glass went down quickly, slaking their thirst and quenching any desire to move. The bees in the garden buzzed. The sun slid down the sky slowly. The conversations around them flowed. Thea felt tiredly, happily content. 'Do you fancy another?'

'Should we?' Denise asked, looking at the time. 'Don't we need to be setting off home soon?'

Thea looked around the garden. She didn't want it to end. It had been fun, and she hadn't expected that. Her pulse skittered slightly. She wasn't ready to go it alone. Not yet. 'Do we, though? Really? What's one more night away. They have rooms. It said so on the sign. We could stay here tonight. Get sloshed. Set the alarm early tomorrow. What do you say?'

Denise looked down at her phone. Her anchor – more like her ball and chain. She tapped the screen, thinking, and Thea waited, anticipating the 'no'.

Then she looked up. 'I say... it's my round.'

They ate in the garden – an indifferent burger with good chips. They both cleared their plates, chasing down the last traces of mayo and ketchup with their fingertips. Total barbarians. At dusk the lad working the bar came outside and fumbled around behind the wood store. A second later the apple tree in the centre of the beer garden filled with hundreds of pinpricks of white light. The change in illumination affected the tone of their interaction, mellowing the giddiness into something softer. During a comfortable lull in their conversation Denise disappeared inside. When she returned it was with a tray on which sat a pot of tea, milk, mugs and a bowl of sticky toffee pudding with two spoons.

'My treat. To say thank you for a special day. For a special weekend.'

'It's not over yet.' Thea didn't want to put a damper on the mood. They could talk about their differing travel plans over breakfast.

As Denise poured them each a mug of tea, the ring on her right hand sparkled.

'That's pretty.'

Denise extended her hand. It was a sapphire star, set with an edging of small diamonds. 'It belonged to Simon's mother. A family heirloom. I was surprised when she left it to me in her will. We were never that close.' She rested her hand back down on the table. 'I always thought she secretly disapproved of me. I was sure that, deep down, she believed Simon could have done better than the office junior.' Inside the pub it sounded like there was a darts match going on. The home team appeared to be losing, given the groans and jeers. 'It's funny. You never know what people really think of you, do you? You get an impression and that's it, sometimes for a lifetime.'

'No, I suppose not. But that's probably for the best. I'm not sure I want most people to know what I'm really like.'

Denise picked up a spoon and scooped up a measure of sponge and syrup. 'You want some?'

Thea sipped her tea and realised it was exactly what she wanted, though she drew the line at the pudding, with its deep fringe of spray-on cream. She shook her head. Looking around the garden, she clocked that most of the other customers were couples. But then again, it often felt to Thea that the world was populated by pairs: husbands and wives, mothers and daughters, best friends. She steered away from the thought by asking, 'How did you and Simon meet?'

'Through work. He was a client at a firm I worked for up in Middlesbrough. After we married, I joined Mather's. For a while I was his dad's PA or, more accurately in those days, his secretary.'

'Jesus! I didn't realise you'd been taking crap from your father-in-law for that long!'

Denise licked her spoon, shrugged. 'Eric is my penance.'

'Here we go again with the guilt. Your penance for what exactly?'

Denise shrugged, embarrassed. 'Having such a sweet tooth?' At least she was laughing about it now.

'Do you like working together? You and Simon, I mean. It must be hard to keep the romance alive when you're with each other twenty-four seven.'

Denise, who had been about to put another mound of pudding in her mouth, laid down her spoon. 'We don't spend all our time together. He travels a lot – to suppliers, trade fairs and suchlike. And he has his golf and I have my interests. Besides, we're a good fit. We're quite different, but I always think that works best, in the long run. We complement each other. He's logical. I'm more emotional. He's practical. I'm not. I think we'd probably argue more if we were more similar.' Her speech on the essential yin and yang of marriage trailed off.

'But…?' Thea prompted, wanting her to drop the dutiful-wife script that she seemed so wedded to.

'There is no "but", more a "what next"?'

'Meaning?' Thea cradled the tea in her hands. She was genuinely interested in how other people's marriages survived, what compromises and sacrifices were made to keep the show on the road. She would always, she supposed, be on the lookout for a formula that worked.

Denise picked up her spoon again and fiddled with it. 'I'm just struggling to imagine the next chapter. Up until now there's been a natural momentum. The old pattern of meet, fall in love, marry, have babies, build a business, raise a family, keep the business running. There's been no time to think. But recently I've started to worry that the rest of our lives will simply be a repeat of the same stuff. Kind of a cycle of diminishing returns.' She scraped together the last of the pudding and the fake cream. 'Oh, don't listen to me. I'm being silly.'

Thea winced. How she hated that word, it was so falsely self-deprecating.

'I watch too many films.' Denise clattered the spoon into the bowl.

The last comment threw Thea. 'What has that got to do with anything?'

'Well, compared to *La La Land*, real life is always going to be a pale imitation, isn't it? I have unrealistic expectations.'

'Of?'

'Of everything. Relationships, people, washing powder... Of how much one person can expect to get out of their life.'

'And of Simon?' Thea had disliked Denise's husband on sight, and nothing she'd said over the weeks they'd known each other had changed her negative impression of him. True, she'd only met him for a few minutes, but it was human nature to make instinctive judgements, and her instinct about Simon was not good. She wondered how he'd reacted to the news that Denise was extending her mini break – she'd texted him as soon it had been agreed. Not well, Thea imagined.

Denise pushed the empty bowl away. 'No, he's right. Life isn't ever going to match up to the silver screen. You wouldn't want it to most of time – too much crime and violence.'

'And passion and laughter!' Thea meant it facetiously, but Denise seemed to take her seriously.

'Too true. It's just a phase I'm going through. The boys. Eric. Work. It all seems a bit of a grind at the moment... but I'm sure it'll pass.' She visibly shook herself. 'And this weekend has been a great tonic. It's set me up for nicely the next round.'

Thea laughed. 'Jeez, Denise, you make it sound like a boxing match.'

Denise cracked a smile and raised her mug. 'Perhaps that's the best way to look at life. Cheers! Here's to round three.'

Chapter 26

THERE WAS something about being cooped up in a small room, with side-by-side single beds, that evoked a potent sense of intimacy. The memory of having to share her bedroom with random visiting cousins came back in a rush. The embarrassed wriggling out of clothes, the 'Excuse me's as they edged around each other trying to avoid touching, the deference as to who switched off the light, the consciousness of another person lying only a couple of feet away in the dark – it was familiar and comforting.

Thea could just about make out the shape of Denise's body in the other bed.

'It's been a great day. Thank you.' Denise's voice was syrupy. She sounded totally relaxed and a little drunk. The track day, the salty chips, the lights in the tree casting a warm glow on their conversation – yes, it had been a good day. She yawned. 'Perhaps I should drive fast cars, eat burgers and drink too much more often.'

In the darkness Thea smiled, content for Denise's simple happiness to sit alongside her own, more complicated emotions. 'Perhaps you should.' The pub below them was quiet, the road likewise. They were only fifty miles from home and their old lives. It felt like a lot more. Denise rolled onto her side and the bed creaked under her weight. Her breathing slowed. Within a few minutes she was asleep. Not bad for a woman who normally suffered from insomnia.

Thea lay on her back, motionless, sleepless, slightly bemused by the turn of events that had led her to this faded, £45-a-night room – with breakfast included – above a pub with a woman she barely knew. No, that was lazy thinking. She knew that Denise hadn't simply come along for the ride; she wanted something from this trip, from Thea. That much had been evident from their first awkward meeting, but it had taken their wine-lubricated conversations in the hotel and over sticky toffee pudding for Thea to work out what that something was.

Denise wanted Thea's bravery. That was what her decision to come away had been motivated by; that's what going round Silverstone had been about; that was why she had stayed away from home for an extra night – it was Denise using Thea to kick-start changes in her own life.

It would be flattering, if it wasn't so laughable. If only Denise knew that what she thought was bravery was, in truth, cowardice. What looked like confidence was really bravado.

Thea rolled over to face the wall, her back to Denise.

This was her journey.

Her destination.

Denise was going to have to find her own path through life from here on in.

Chapter 27

DENISE STUFFED her clothes into her overnight bag haphazardly. She knew her disappointment was disproportionate, but that didn't lessen its potency. Over a breakfast of scrambled eggs and coffee, sitting at one of the rough oak tables in the snug, Thea had revealed her plan. It did not include returning with Denise. Her intention was to 'meander' her way up to Edinburgh to visit her brother, stopping off en route to see the sights. She'd apparently taken the week off work. Denise was to be dropped off at Milton Keynes station so that she could catch the train back to St Albans. Correction, two trains. She was going to have to change at Watford Junction.

Denise was going home.

Thea was not.

The weekend was over.

Feeling slightly thrown by this revelation, Denise called Simon. His response to her text saying she was staying away another night had been decidedly cool, but he would be pleased to know she was coming home now. He picked up on the second ring. 'Hi.'

'Hi.'

'Are you on your way back?'

'That's why I'm ringing. I'll be getting into St Albans at ten forty-five. I was wondering if you could pick me up from the station.'

'Why are you coming back by train?'

'Thea is travelling on.'

'Oh.' There was a pause. 'Where are you now?'

'Still at the pub. We're leaving in five.'

'What pub? I thought you were in the hotel.'

'It's where we stayed last night.'

'What?'

'Look, it doesn't really matter. I was only ringing to let you know when I'll be home.'

'So this was the plan all along, was it? You travelling back on your own?' The bad connection did little to muffle the judgement in his voice.

'There wasn't a plan, as such.' Denise felt herself tense. 'That's the definition of "spontaneity", Simon: doing things without forethought, acting on a whim.' There would be no such spontaneity once she got home. Her disappointment tipped into sadness. 'Simon, please don't start.'

'I'm not starting. I just think she could've told you that you'd have to go through the hassle of getting yourself home. It seems a little selfish to me.'

Denise couldn't bear him criticising Thea, though she wanted to herself. It made her defensive. 'Are we talking about her or me now? I've had a couple of days away, Simon, that's all.'

'Which, as I've already said, I'm absolutely fine with.'

There was silence for a few seconds. 'I'm honestly pleased you've had a nice time.' He cleared his throat, refilled it with better intentions. 'What did you get up to yesterday?'

She knew he wasn't really interested and was simply trying to head off an argument, but suddenly she wasn't in an avoiding mood. 'I had a fantastic time.'

There was another pause. 'I'm glad to hear it.'

She went on, knowing she was trying to provoke a reaction. 'After we left the hotel on Sunday morning we drove up to Silverstone. They had a race day on.'

'Really?'

'Yes. I went round the track. It was glorious.'

'But you hate anything involving speed.'

'So I thought. But I loved it. It was exhilarating. It helped that I was in safe hands.' She chose not to mention Chris. Another small, meaningless, but cherished secret. 'I was on a high for hours afterwards.' Her mood started to lift again at the memory of screaming around the circuit, the tarmac rising up towards her, then dropping away without warning as Chris explained about power and control. 'We...'

Simon's phone beeped, another call. He put her on hold with a hurried, 'Shit, it's Lawler's. I'd better take this.'

Denise was forced to wait, her phone pressed to her ear, reliving yesterday, dreading the day ahead and all the days to follow. She would go home and it would be the same as it always was: work, Eric, shop, cook, clean, burn up, not sleep – repeat. Getting older but no wiser. Living life as one of Thea's despised martyrs.

The other call went on and on, underlining where Simon's priorities lay. As she waited, Denise made a deal with herself.

If he was kinder when he came back on the line, if he was genuinely interested in how her night had gone, if he said anything about looking forward to seeing her soon – she would go home and pick up where they had left off, but with a more positive attitude and with more time for herself carved into her schedule.

And if he didn't?

He was back.

He launched into a detailed breakdown of the problem that Lawler's had been phoning about. He spoke for more than a minute, not once asking for her input or opinion, despite Denise having a closer relationship with Damien, the main contact. Eventually he ran out of indignant steam. 'When did you say you're due in? Ten-fifteen?'

'No. Ten forty-five. Will you pick me up?'

There was a pause, during which she imagined him mentally resisting the need to rejig his diary – for an hour at most. 'Can't you get a taxi?'

Those five small words tipped the balance.

'I could.'

He was no longer listening. 'Okay. I'll see you about eleven then.' He was assuming she would head straight into the office. 'Bye.'

By the time the connection was severed, his assumption was incorrect.

Chapter 28

THEY WERE standing in the pub car park, bags at their feet, departure imminent. Denise was talking, a rush of words. From what Thea could deduce, Simon had said something that had upset her and they'd had an argument that had escalated to the point of no return – more specifically, Denise's no return.

'I was wondering if you'd mind if I tagged along for a bit longer?' Denise must have picked up Thea's hesitation because she hastily added, 'I'll pay my way – petrol money, accommodation costs, stuff like that. And I wouldn't come all the way up to Scotland with you, obviously.' Her hand went to her throat, which was blotchy. 'But if you've nothing concrete organised for the next few days, I thought we could, maybe, do nothing concrete together. It might be fun.'

Thea felt conflicted. Having Denise around had been nice, she'd been good company and a very welcome distraction – for the weekend – but the rest of the trip was something she needed to be brave enough do on her own. Having a friend along for the ride was a complication she could, and must, do without. 'I do have a plan, actually.' Denise's expression became watchful. Thea felt trapped, not wanting to upset her, but not wanting to be emotionally pressurised into saying 'yes', either.

The list would decide the matter, one way or the other. Despite Denise's flirtation with speed at Silverstone, Thea didn't imagine she'd have the stomach for the rest of the week's activities.

She clicked on the Notes section of her phone and passed it over. Denise scanned the series of saved links. You really didn't need to read through them all, it was easy enough to get the gist: tattoo parlours, tandem skydives, wild animal encounters, the best bungee jump in the UK – apparently it was off the transporter bridge in Middlesbrough. 'It's my "fuck it" list,' Thea explained. 'I stumbled across a blog a while ago by a woman called Hannah Jay. She put together a list of things she wanted to do before she turned fifty, stuff she'd never had the time or the guts to attempt before. She gave herself a year to do them all. She ticked everything off within six months, so she started adding things, getting more ambitious and inventive.' She was rambling. She reined herself in. She wasn't supposed to be selling it to Denise. 'I don't have the time for anything nearly as ambitious, but I thought trying some new experiences for a week or so might liven things up a bit.'

Denise stood completely still, Thea's phone in her hand, looking uncertain. 'It sounds like the type of thing people do when they're dying?'

'For God's sake, Denise,' Thea snapped. Denise really could be infuriating. 'It's the exact opposite. The clue's in the name. It's a fuck-it list, not a bucket list!'

Denise blinked, chastened. 'So when's your birthday?'

Thea selected a date that made more sense in terms of the timing of her trip. 'The third of August.'

'Your fiftieth?'

Thea nodded.

Denise went back to scrolling through the list. 'Hence Silverstone?'

Thea nodded again. 'Number one on my list.' She waited, expecting Denise to begin revising the severity of her argument with Simon, rationalising that it might – in hindsight – be best to head home and face her husband's hissy fit than throw herself out of a plane or get inked in some back-street tattoo parlour.

One minute became two, turned into three. The occasional car passed on the road, the birds sang and Thea waited for Denise to hand her back her phone and climb into the car, ready to be dropped off at the station.

It was time for them to go their separate ways.

Finally Denise looked up and announced, 'I quite like the sound of the axe-throwing.'

Chapter 29

WATFORD. IT was hardly the most glamorous of destinations.

Thea parked in one of the many city-centre car parks. 'The place we're heading to is just behind the main shopping centre.' Denise accepted this without question. She seemed determined to be the perfect travelling companion, to earn her place at Thea's side. As they made their way down the less-than-fragrant stairwell Thea reflected on the curious chain of events that had led them to this point – a chance encounter in a Ladies toilet, the coincidence of Denise living across the road from Marc's new house, their connection via Cherry Trees – if she believed in Fate, she would have to credit it with bringing the two of them together.

The shopping mall was busy. There were knots of teenagers milling about, laughing and making their presence felt. Thea caught Denise staring at a noisy group sitting outside a café. She was, no doubt, thinking about her own sons. She talked about them a lot. From the stories she told, it sounded like it would do them good to be left to fend for themselves for a change. To live in a house surrounded by men! Thea understood why Denise might feel the need to escape. Thoughts of her own far smaller, much more fractious family intruded. Communication between herself and Ella was still at a bare minimum. The punishment continued. She understood why, and accepted it, but the self-discipline it was taking not to call her daughter was huge. She was managing – but only just. That didn't stop her thinking about Ella a lot. She wondered if she was getting used to the earlier starts and her new routine. Was Marc being super-relaxed about her hanging around in Starbucks after school or was she being whisked home on the dot of 3.30 .m. by the ever-available Jenny? Was she eating properly? How was her hockey going? Was Jenny buying her the right shampoo and cleanser, tampons and cereal bars? Was she happier? Thea suspected and feared the answer to that question was 'yes'.

Whether Ella would ever get to discover, never mind appreciate, today's planned gesture, Thea couldn't know for sure, but that didn't lessen its significance. This was for her daughter. The thought gave her some comfort.

Once they'd made it through the crowds to one of the exits, Thea double-checked the location on her phone. Her appointment was in ten minutes. She didn't want to be late. Sure enough, Google Maps was accurate, and in 257 metres they came upon Skin Deep. It was larger than Thea had envisaged, from looking at their website, and apparently it had been open since 2015 – or so the shop frontage proudly proclaimed in fancy gold lettering.

Thea had done her research. The reviews for Skin Deep were good. Their hygiene rating was excellent, which, as a nervous ink-virgin, was nice to know. The interior was decked out like an old-style barber's, all leather seats and dark paint, but instead of photos of haircuts, the big plate windows were adorned with shots of amazingly complicated sleeves and chest plates: tattoos that must have cost hundreds, if not thousands, of pounds and taken months to complete. Thea became conscious of Denise standing beside her. 'It's on my list!' She grinned. 'You don't have to come in with me if you're not comfortable around needles.'

Denise shrugged. 'It's fine. It's not me they'll be sticking them into!'

The door tinkled comfortingly upon entry, enhancing the olde-worlde vibe. The girl at the counter looked up and smiled. 'Hi there. Can I help?'

'Yes. I've an appointment at twelve.'

The girl glanced down at the leather-bound ledger in front of her. Another nice, traditional touch. 'Hi, Thea.' She extended her intricately tattooed arm. 'I'm Kirsty. It's me you've been emailing.' They shook hands. 'I'm glad you were happy with the design. We'll have another look at it before we get going, in case there's anything you want to me to tweak.'

Something about this slight Scottish girl made Thea feel relaxed. She followed her over to one of the heavy old chairs and climbed into it. She felt like a child at the dentist's. Denise took a seat on an old crushed-velvet sofa and looked around, curious. Two chairs along, a man in his twenties was having a section of his forearm worked on. He was chatting with the bald, pierced and heavily inked man wielding the needle.

Kirsty produced a folder and flipped through it. 'Here we are.' She passed it to Thea. Compared to the preponderance of skulls, buxom women, strange hieroglyphics and exotic wildlife, Thea's design was modest. A delicate little tree frog. It was beautifully drawn in fine black pen, with a touch of iridescent blue on its back and on the ends of its suckered toes. Kirsty had caught the essence of a real, clinging, tree-climbing wild creature and had transformed it into something mythical by the addition of a series of intricate patterns on its back and legs.

'Is there anything you want me to change?'

Thea shook her head. 'No, it's wonderful. Thank you.'

Kirsty pulled a fresh pair of gloves out of the box and snapped them on. 'Is this your first tattoo?'

'Yes. Is it that obvious?'

Kirsty laughed. 'You'll be fine. I promise to be gentle with you. The main thing is to relax and keep as still as possible. If you need to take a break, just let me know. You don't have to sit like a statue for the whole thing. Ready?' She pulled her chair alongside Thea's.

Thea nodded. She allowed Kirsty to take hold of her arm and position it, underside up, on the metal rest. The inside of her forearm was pale, untouched by the sun. The girl scrubbed vigorously at her skin with a sterile wipe, picked up the tool of her trade and set to work.

An hour and a half later they were sitting in a nearby café, job done. Despite the muzak and the indifferent sandwiches, Thea was on a high.

She'd found the whole process surprisingly enjoyable –

she could see why people got addicted. The buzz of the ink gun, the dip and sway of Kirsty's head as she worked on the design, the coolness as she rhythmically wiped away the excess ink, even the sensation of the needle puncturing the skin over and over again had been curiously pleasurable. The fascination of watching the little frog emerge from the muddy mess of ink had been a powerful analgesic. Thea would happily have sat in the chair for ever, but eventually Kirsty had sat back and turned off the machine.

'All done.'

Thea had looked down at her arm and felt too moved to say anything. It had taken her a few seconds to realise that her silence was causing concern. Kirsty had looked mortified, and the ever-watchful Denise deeply worried.

'Are you okay?' Kirsty had asked.

'Yes.' Thea got herself back on a leash. 'Sorry. I love it.'

'Really? If you're not happy, I can have another pass at it.'

'No!' The thought of messing with the little frog had been upsetting to Thea. It was hers now. She wanted no one else touching it. 'It's perfect as it is. Absolutely perfect.'

The girl had relaxed back into her smiley demeanour. 'Good. You had me going there for a minute. It does look great, if I say so myself. It'll look even better in a few weeks' time.' She'd given Thea's arm one last wipe, wrapped it in clingfilm and, after paying, she and Denise were good to go.

Now, sitting in the café, Thea could feel the sting of the little creature on her flesh, almost as if it were real. The needle points where the ink had been forced into her skin felt like its toes clinging onto her arm. It was a disconcerting, but comforting sensation. The film was tight and wrapped in so many layers that the tattoo was invisible. Thea started to pick at the edge of it with her nail.

'Shouldn't you keep that on?' Denise really couldn't stop being a mum.

Thea ignored her. She worked an end free, unwound the rest of the film and deposited it in a gelatinous mess on her saucer. And there it was: a delicate, indelible homage to her daughter, resting on her reddened skin. Thea twisted her arm in the light, watching the colours shift and shine. It was beautiful and painful, a perfect metaphor for her relationship with Ella.

'Why a frog?' Denise asked.

'Ella likes them.' Thea pivoted to a happy memory. 'We used to go to London Zoo a lot when she was younger. For some reason she absolutely loved the Reptile House. She was fascinated by the tree frogs – how tiny they were, how beautiful. She used to tell me she wanted to steal one and take it home to keep as a pet. Her cunning plan was to get it to cling onto the lapel of my coat like a brooch. Foolproof.'

Denise smiled. 'Better than her wanting to take a snake home, I suppose.'

'Indeed.' Thea tentatively stroked the frog, foolishly worried that she might smudge the colours – which was, of course, nonsense; the whole point of a tattoo was that it was permanent. She smiled, growing accustomed to her new companion. 'You weren't tempted then?'

'Me?' Denise snorted. 'No!'

'Why not?'

'Some people suit tattoos, other people don't. I definitely fall into the latter category.'

'I don't see why?'

'Well, my age, for starters.'

'That didn't stop me.'

'No. But you know what I mean. That,' she pointed at the little frog, 'looks right on you, like it's supposed to be there. On me, a tattoo would look ridiculous.'

'God, not this "age is a barrier" rubbish again, Denise. A tattoo is personal – who gives a stuff what other people think?'

Denise shrugged. 'I'm just not an inked-skin kind of person.'

Thea let it go. She liked Denise, but they had very different approaches to life. It was, at times, hard to believe that Denise was the younger of the two of them. Thea, who never contemplated growing old, gracefully or otherwise, found Denise's compliance with such outdated social conventions odd.

She turned her arm over – returning Ella's frog to the shade – picked up her phone, clicked on the itinerary. The next appointment was the following day, but not until lunchtime. They had time to kill. 'We can stay around here for the rest of today if you want to, do some shopping, do a bit of sightseeing.' They both glanced around. There appeared to be few sights worth seeing

'Or...? Denise asked.

'We head north. Nottingham is the next stop.'

Denise finished her drink. 'North it is, then?'

As they walked back to the car, it struck Thea how contradictory Denise was. Too staid to contemplate a tattoo, but more than happy to get back in the car and drive to God knew where, to do God knew what with Thea. Whether her nonchalance was feigned or not was hard to tell. Whatever the truth, Denise now seemed fully committed to their trip. Maybe they were both having their own crises. Both in search of some answers, or at least some solutions. Perhaps that's what had drawn them to each other in the first place.

Either way, as they climbed the smelly stairwell back up to the car, their adventure still had legs and, for the time being, they were striding out together.

Chapter 30

On the drive up the M1 Denise googled the top ten things to do in Nottingham. It transpired that the key attraction was a network of underground caves that extended for miles beneath the city. Thea was not enthusiastic about taking one of the tours – too touristy and tame for her taste – but by the time they arrived the clouds that had been gathering on the journey up had darkened and a persistent rain was falling.

They spent the next couple of hours with a suitably characterful guide in the warren of underground gloom, being regaled by a factually dubious, but colourful version of Nottingham's *Horrible Histories*. It was really quite entertaining, or at least Denise thought it was.

There was another advantage to being underground, apart from staying dry – down in the bowels of the city there was no phone signal. But as soon as she and Thea emerged from the caves, via a narrow stone stairwell that came out behind Primark, of all places, Denise's phone started vibrating with notifications. Thea must have heard it as well because she raised a questioning eyebrow. 'Simon?'

'I'm guessing so.'

'What did you tell him?'

'Just that I wasn't going to be back as planned.'

'Was he pissed off?'

'I imagine so.'

'But you're about to find out for sure.'

'I am.'

Thea wandered a short distance away, giving Denise some privacy. Should she go for his texts or his voicemail first? She went for voicemail. Best get it over with: 'Denise. You need to call me.'

His text messages were the same in tenor, though, judging by the increase in his exclamatory punctuation across the four messages he'd sent, there seemed to have been an obvious escalation in his irritation. Denise looked at his anger, expressed so succinctly, and felt curiously detached. It helped that she was miles away, in a city she didn't know, with a woman who felt like a friend, but who was really a comparative stranger, doing something that was completely alien to her – namely, precisely what she wanted or, at least, mostly what Thea wanted. It was an act of rebellion that, no matter how small and insignificant in the grand scale of world events, was huge for Denise. Being away from home had freed her mind and, it surprised her to discover, also her conscience. She refused to feel guilty, or at least she was trying not to. The boys were fine – too busy, she suspected, to be missing her. And if they were missing her, well, good. It might bring them closer together when she got home. And Simon was around. They did have two parents, after all

191

With true Hollywood blockbuster timing, at that very moment there was a break in the grey clouds and a weak shaft of sunlight fell upon Denise. She lifted her face and felt the warmth on her skin. Even the sound of a lorry reversing into the loading bay behind her did nothing to dent her mood. She texted quickly and honestly. No deliberating, for a change: I'm going to take another couple of days. I feel it's doing me good. I hope everything is okay at home. I've been in touch with the boys to let them know. If there is anything you can't sort out with work, let me know. D

She did not add the usual kiss. She thought that small x might tip Simon over the edge. She switched her phone to Silent, dropped it back into her bag and walked over to Thea, who asked, 'Everything okay?'

'Yes, fine.' Denise replied. 'But I could do with a drink.'

Arms linked, they wandered around the damp city centre until they found a little French restaurant down a side street, where they drank cheap red wine and stuffed themselves with cassoulet and apple-and-cranberry galettes with vanilla ice cream. The maître d' flirted equally with both of them, performing a routine that had obviously been honed over many decades of flamboyantly ushering *ladies* to their tables. On the way to the hotel, Denise dashed into a Tesco Metro and scored them a couple of cocktails in a can. It was hardly *Sex and the City*, but it would do. Their hotel was very much not up to Carrie's standards, either, though as with all Premier Inns it was clean and purplishly reassuring. They accepted the offer of a twin room without debate. Denise was pleased about that; it seemed to mark a shift in their friendship. Shoes discarded, jeans off, they sprawled on their respective beds, talking crap.

Denise, who was already feeling buzzy from the wine with dinner, took a slug from her Peach on the Beach – when in Nottingham, and all that. '*Je ne regrette rien*.'

'How very French of you.'

'No,' Denise shook her head, 'that got lost in translation. What I mean is... I regret not having more regrets.'

Thea was lying on her bed, in her knickers and a T-shirt, balancing her can on her stomach as if it were a table. Oh, for a belly that flat. 'No, come on,' she said, 'there must be some good stuff locked away in your dim and distant past. What about the wild years, before you turned into a paragon of wifely duty?'

Denise went into the filing system inside her head and found the drawer marked 'Personal'. She opened it and withdrew a slim buff-coloured folder. Inside was a single sheet of paper on which were three bullet points. Three regrets. How pathetic was that!

'Okay. But be prepared, this confession includes scenes that some viewers might find distressing.' She took another swig from the can. God, it was sweet. 'I hit a girl called Carol Burton in the face, in the dinner queue, at junior school when I was seven.'

'This is better. So you have a tendency for sudden, unprovoked acts of violence.'

Denise lay down on her, bed mirroring Thea. 'It wasn't unprovoked. She said I was fat.'

'You did say you were in the dinner queue. Had you pushed in?' Thea's mockery made Denise feel good. A joke shared.

193

'Very funny! No. She was always taunting me about my weight. One day I'd had enough. I smacked her right on her nose. It bled quite spectacularly. To her credit, she didn't dob me in to the dinner ladies.' Nor had she made snuffly-pig noises any more when Denise walked past. Thea raised her can, saluting her.

Denise moved on to the second bullet point. 'Then, when I was ten, I killed a rabbit.'

'What the fuck? I'm sharing a room with a psychopath.'

Denise ignored her. 'I was being paid to look after it while our neighbours went away on holiday. Blackpool – to see the illuminations. He was a single dad with three kids. I was supposed to put new straw in the hutch, give the rabbit its food and change the water in the feeding bottle. But it looked so soft and fluffy that I wanted to stroke it. I took it out of its cage. Big mistake. It got spooked and scrambled free. I got scratched all over my arms. I had to keep my jumper sleeves down for weeks. Anyway, I digress. I chased the rabbit around the yard for ages, but the poor thing was so scared it wouldn't let me pick it up, it just kept running around. Then it escaped through a gap in their gate. I followed it, but it kept on hopping. In the end it hopped into the road and—'

'An ice-cream van? A dustbin lorry!'

'No.' Denise paused for dramatic effect and realised, as she did so, that it was the first time she'd told the story out loud, for comic effect, rather than rerunning it pointlessly and miserably in her head. The retelling took away a lot of the shame. 'It was the local vicar in his Ford Fiesta.'

Thea drummed her feet on the bed in delight. 'So you implicated a member of the clergy in your crime.'

'What made it worse was that he was lovely about it. Really kind. He helped me dig a hole. We buried its furry corpse in the flower bed in their front garden.'

'Please tell me he said a few words.'

'He did. I let him think it was my rabbit.'

Thea was rolling around with laughter.

'Do you know the worst bit?'

'Pray tell.'

'When he was doing "the service" he asked me what the rabbit was called. I was so panicked that I couldn't remember, so I made something up.'

'Go on.'

'Snowy.'

'My God, Denise. Pet homicide and a total failure of imagination.'

'It wasn't even a white rabbit.' By now Denise was laughing as well, her crime purged of guilt. 'I had to lie, when the family came back from Blackpool. I said it died of natural causes.'

'Were the kids devastated?'

'No. The little sods didn't seem the slightest bit bothered.'

Thea's shrieking slowly subsided. 'And?'

'And what?'

'That can't be it? One childhood right hook and a flat-tened rabbit that got a good send-off.' Thea was smiling, her cheeks streaked with mascara, her hair a tousled mess. She looked lovely.

Denise thought about her short list of shame. The temptation to share was strong, but the events outlined in the final bullet point were unlikely to end in giggles.

They would end in humiliation. 'No, that's it.' She mentally shoved the sheet of paper into the file, and the file away in the drawer. 'See what I mean – I'm a total lightweight when it comes to dastardly deeds. Anyway, less about me. What about you?'

Thea stared at the ceiling. 'Like I said, my misdemeanours are too numerous to mention.'

'Oh no. You don't get out of it that easily. You always do that: steer the conversation away from yourself. Not tonight. Come on, spill!'

Thea sighed. 'If you insist.' She pushed herself into a sitting position. 'You've seen enough of me to know I don't suffer fools gladly, and that I'm not good at biting my tongue, so I guess I can upset people, though it's not always intentional.'

'That's way too vague. Come on. I gave you the juicy details. I want specific examples of misdeeds and bad behaviour.'

Thea pretended to have to think. She sipped as she did so. 'Okay. Confession time – off the top of my head. I never tip my hairdresser because he's already extortionately expensive... even though I always worry that he's secretly going to take it out on me every time he cuts my hair, so the anxiety's not really worth the gesture. I lied on my application to the Civil Service – which, in hindsight, was quite ballsy of me. I totally made up a two-month work-experience placement in New York. Afterwards they said it was my international experience that had swung it for me. And so my illustrious career began with a fat fib.

'I re-gift nearly all of my brother's Christmas presents. They're always very tasteful and expensive, but they're never what I want, and I resent him being in Edinburgh and thereby avoiding any responsibility for my mother. Though now, as I'm saying it, I can hear how petty that sounds. Is that enough for you?' Denise shook her head. 'Okay, there's plenty more where that came from. I'm really not a very nice person, you know. I didn't vote last time round. I know, I know! A thousand suffragettes will be spinning in their graves. I refuse to feel guilty about using fabric conditioner or bubble bath or bleach, on my teeth or down the toilet – I defend my right to smell nice and achieve pure-white radiance, over the fate of fishes. Oh, and I broke my ex-husband's...' She paused.

Denise ad-libbed, 'Spirit? Arm? Heart?'

'I wish. No, I broke his favourite decanter. On purpose.'

'Why?'

'Because he *had* a favourite decanter. Do I need another reason?'

'No. Far be it from me to interfere in someone else's love life.'

'Or total lack of one! Oh, and I regularly flirt to get out of parking fines.'

'You're such a badass!'

'You ain't seen nothing yet.' Thea grinned.

'Well, here's to something that neither of us is ever gonna regret.' Denise raised her nearly-empty cocktail in a can and Thea raised hers. 'To running away.'

'And never coming back,' Thea added.

They stretched across the gap between the beds and clinked cans.

Chapter 31

DENISE WOKE with a start. The room was far too hot. Her throat was dry and her bladder full. She glanced across at the other bed and saw Thea's slim back and her swathe of dark hair. The room was bright, despite the lowered blinds. Denise's watch told her it was 6.20 a.m. She slid carefully out of bed and crept into the small bathroom, where she gulped water from the tap and splashed it on her face and neck, rehydrating as best she could. Her face bore the hallmarks of the previous night's drinking and the lack of skincare. There were black smudges of mascara under her eyes and her lids were puffy and red, but even under the harsh glare of the bathroom light and her own judgement, she was surprised to discover that she looked good. Or perhaps it was more that, despite the threat of a hangover, she felt good, glad to be alive.

She swallowed another handful of water before gently opening the door. She went over to the bedroom window and was pleased to find that she could open it. Only a crack, but it was something. The noise of the latch must have disturbed Thea, because she rolled onto her back and pushed the duvet down her body. She must have stripped off her T-shirt during the night. Denise watched, waiting to see if she would wake. It was an invasion of Thea's privacy, but it was a chance for Denise to glimpse another woman in the flesh and, much as she knew it would depress her, she simply couldn't let that opportunity pass.

Thea's body was, as Denise had suspected, perfectly proportioned, her skin tanned. She looked healthily sexy, a glowing advert for a woman – apart from a scar on her stomach. The scar ran from just above her navel down to the line of her briefs. Not a C-section or, if it was, it was unlike any Denise had seen before. She found herself transfixed by the dark strip of raised skin with the long line of indentations on either side. These dark marks were presumably where the stitches or clips had once held the flesh together as it healed. It looked like an old wound, but the sight of it was still shocking – a flaw in something that was otherwise flawless. Denise didn't know why she was so surprised, or so fascinated. Why had she assumed Thea had got through life unscathed? Few people did.

A door banged in the corridor outside, and Thea stirred again. She rolled away, taking the duvet with her this time.

The movement broke Denise's trance. She climbed back into her own bed, lay down and closed her eyes, but the image of Thea's repaired abdomen remained. What injury or illness did the scar represent? Why had Thea not spoken about it? Again the sense that she was holding back more than she was sharing assailed Denise. They were getting on so well, or so Denise thought, and yet there was still so much Thea seemed unwilling, or unable, to talk about.

The sounds of the city waking up filtered into the room. Denise opened her eyes and looked across at her new friend, wondering when, if ever, Thea would trust her enough to truly open up.

Chapter 32

THEA LOCKED the bathroom door with a touch of relief. It was surprisingly tiring having a good time with someone else – all that talking and listening and sharing – she was obviously out of practice. It was almost like having a partner again.

She twisted the shower on, but didn't get in. Instead she dropped the toilet lid and sat down on it. Perched just so, she said 'good morning' to her other travelling companion. The little tree frog looked beautiful, despite the swelling around the edges. She gently stroked it, admiring how the green Kirsty had used was exactly the same vibrant shade that she remembered from their visits to the Reptile House. As marks on her skin went, this new addition was definitely her favourite.

Her toilet bag was on the shelf under the mirror. She reached for it reluctantly. Inside was her phone. She switched it on. Waited as it woke up. When her apps appeared she very nearly switched it off again. As expected, there were hundreds of notifications. You could ignore messages, but it didn't stop them building up, like fat in the drains.

Out of habit, she flitted down the long list of emails in her in-box first. She'd been CC'd into the usual barrage of sense and nonsense, despite her out-of-office being on. She ignored it all. None of it was her responsibility any more. The thought sat strangely with her. She was so used to her job taking up the lion's share of her time and attention that the lack of that pressure made her feel shapeless. She didn't bother with any of her social media. She'd posted nothing from her trip, not wanting to leave a digital trail. Her friends might find her lack of posts a little odd, but as this wasn't one of her envy-inducing overseas trips, they probably wouldn't worry. They might not even notice. Likewise, she ignored her newsfeed. The world had shrunk to one day at a time. No past. No future.

WhatsApp, her daughter's preferred platform for communication, was next up. Thea hesitated. She traced her fingertips across the smooth surface of the little frog again, but it had no magic powers. There was nothing from Ella. The deafening absence of so much as a photo or a single emoji was a clear, brutally efficient reminder that some bridges, once burnt, took a long time and a lot of energy to rebuild.

But what were you supposed to do if you had neither?

That left text and voicemail.

She scrolled rapidly through her messages, wanting to get it over with. The nice man was there, whispering to her from the edge of her old life. As she read his tender, teasing, perfectly punctuated messages she felt sad for what might have been. She knew she should block him, for his sake and hers, but she was only human, after all.

That left her voicemail.

Thea took the precaution of turning down the volume on her phone. She flexed her neck and her shoulders. Then dialled 121. The metallic voice informed her that she had two new messages.

The first call was from Cherry Trees. Thea felt her stomach swoop, but it was only the nurse confirming that an appointment had been made for her mother to see the optician the next time he visited the home.

That left one message from a now-familiar number.

Even above the sound of the shower, Mr Tennant had no problem being heard. 'Thea. This is getting serious. You must have received and opened some of the correspondence from us by now, and picked up our numerous messages. This simply will not do. You are an intelligent woman. You know this isn't going to go away on its own. Think about your family. Your daughter.' That was low. 'You need to call me as soon as you get this. Delaying really is no longer an option. I shall await your call.'

She deleted his message.

She didn't need him to remind her that time was running out; she knew that only too well. It was why she was so determined to keep going.

Chapter 33

'Is it outdoor or indoor?' Denise asked.

'Indoor.'

'Is it dangerous?'

Thea shook her head. 'No. I don't think so. Not unless you get really carried away.'

'Good.' Denise smiled.

Thea didn't want Denise to get too complacent. 'But you will have to wear some protective gear to do it.'

Denise seemed to be enjoying not knowing what the next activity on the list was. That didn't, however, stop her trying to guess as they crawled through the congested streets of Nottingham. 'Is it something involving paint?' Thea shook her head again. 'Or clay? Are we going to do pottery?'

'No, there's no painting. But pottery? Well, after a fashion.'

'So something creative?'

At that, Thea laughed out loud. 'No. It's most definitely not creative. In fact I'd say it's the exact opposite.'

Knowsley, their destination, turned out to be a small village. If Thea hadn't double-checked the postcode before they'd set off, she would have had her doubts that they were in the right place. It was in the middle of nowhere, surrounded by fields of what looked like potatoes. The village was made up of an unlovely collection of pebble-dashed 1960s houses, a short parade of shops and a pub. Even the voice on the satnav sounded bored as it guided them into a small car park in front of a disused church. The only other vehicle was a dirty white transit van, the type that was always being PNC-checked in police dramas. The church itself was made of solid red brick, no stained glass – Methodist plainness taken to the extreme. The only indication of the church's change in use was the black-and-red sign above the door, on which was painted a maniacal figure wielding an axe.

'Is this it?'

'It is.' Thea applied the handbrake, underlining that they had arrived. 'I rang before we set off. They've booked you in for the session before me.'

'To do what exactly?'

Thea was already getting out of the car. 'Get rid of some of the pent-up violence that lurks inside your soul. Now that I know you're a bitch-slapping bunny-killer, it seems even more appropriate. Come on.'

The Rage Rooms, Knowsley, Nottinghamshire, NG15 2RD, were the brainchild of Mr Kevin P. Harrop, according to the black-and-red-themed website through which Thea had booked. Or, more accurately, The Rage Rooms were a copy of other 'smash and go' rooms, as advertised on Facebook. For £35 per head on weekdays and £45 at weekends, the cheaply bought and converted old Methodist chapel could be hired for thirty-minute sessions of cathartic, safe destruction.

It was Kevin himself who responded to their knock at the door. 'Hello, there. Welcome to Rage,' he boomed. His bonhomie seemed ill-suited to the chapel's pious past, but Thea and Denise returned his greeting warmly. Kevin explained that he was both the director and only full-time employee of Rage Rooms Ltd, but that Leanora, his niece, came in to help when she could, in and around her college work and her stints at the village chippy. All of which was information they really didn't want or need, but Kevin seemed determined to impart it as he ushered them inside.

The interior of the church had been gutted and haphazardly divided up with a series of chipboard partitions. It was dark, confusing and smelt of sawdust. A series of doors had been set into the new walls. Kevin opened the door labelled *The Selection Room* with a flourish and led them inside.

The Selection Room was, to all intents and purposes, a transported charity shop. There was shelf upon shelf of second-hand items lining the walls and filling the huge industrial bins in the centre of the room. Kevin proudly told them that everything they were looking at had been destined for landfill – until liberated by him. 'Here at The Rage Rooms we pride ourselves on our green credentials. It's one of our missions. Even the post-smash scrap goes off to be recycled.' He didn't say into what. He went on to explain that they were free to choose anything with a green sticker, up to a maximum of twenty items. The yellow and red stickered items were also available, at an additional charge of £2 or £5 respectively, although the deal they were booked on included one red and one yellow-stickered item in the price.

'So it's up to you. Knock yourselves out, Ladies. A word from the wise: don't underestimate the crockery. The teapots are especially good. They proper explode, if you catch them right.' He seemed about to leave, but couldn't resist one more piece of advice. 'And in terms of the tech,' he waved his arm in the direction of some big metal cages at the end of the room that were full of monitors, wires and keyboards, 'go for whatever grinds your gears. There are plenty of PCs and laptops – oh, and everybody's favourite, printers!' At the doorway he stopped again. 'The boxes in the corner on the left are full of old mobile phones. I'll leave you to browse.'

Thea threw Denise a look that signalled that she wished he would. He didn't. Perhaps he was lonely.

'Your slot doesn't start for another half hour, but there's no one booked in before you, so give me a shout when you're good to go and we'll get cracking.' Finally he left. They were about to take their first steps into the cave of crap when he reappeared in the doorway. 'Sorry. I meant to say there are trolleys and baskets over there to put your stuff in.' There obviously were. 'But if there's anything you need any help lifting, just give me a shout. That's what I'm here for.' Thea could have sworn he actually winked.

They waited until they were sure he'd gone for good before they started to explore.

It was like the biggest house clearance ever. Everything was crammed onto the shelves without regard: the old and the newish, the once cherished and the never wanted, the everyday and the totally unidentifiable. Food processors sat next to alarm clocks, mugs and cloudy tumblers next to eggcups in the shape of chickens. There was a shelf of toasters surrounded by a sea of old breadcrumbs. Another shelf dedicated to kettles. It was bewilderingly familiar and at the same time deeply strange.

'So, basically, we pick stuff and smash it up?' Denise asked.

'That's the idea.'

'Why?'

'Why, what?'

'Why do people want to do it?'

'It's supposed to be therapeutic. Hannah Jay – the list woman I told you about – went to one in New York. She raved about it. Swore that it was one of the best half hours of her life.'

Denise looked doubtful, but that didn't stop her going to retrieve a trolley. She started adding things to it with surprising decisiveness. Thea stood back and let her make her choices. She was shocked and slightly disappointed when she saw Denise lift an old record player down and add it to her growing stash. How could anyone want to smash up something musical? A sudden pulse of desire to be back at Cherry Trees, dancing with her mother, assailed Thea. She braced and absorbed it.

A big, ugly, heavy casserole dish went into Denise's trolley next, followed by a selection of rather dainty cups and saucers. Domestic section scoured, she moved over to the boxes of mobile phones. A Nokia, followed by what looked like a Samsung, then an early-iteration iPhone with a smashed screen. Denise turned to Thea and grinned. 'My work phones in historical order, or near as damn it. God, some of this stuff makes me feel ancient. As does that.' She pointed at a bulky desktop computer. 'I think I'll have that as well. Kevin can do the honours. It's like the one I used to have when I was Eric's secretary.'

Thea noticed that Denise avoided anything that looked too personal. She moved swiftly with averted eyes past the shelves wedged full of primary-coloured toys, as if the thought of smashing up some child's plaything was sacrilege. Her trolley full, she asked, 'What about you?'

Thea shrugged. 'No, it's all right. I'll get mine later.'

Thankfully, Kevin reappeared at that moment to take Denise through. He was trailed by a thin teenage girl who wordlessly took hold of the handles of the trolley and wheeled it away down the corridor. The squeak of the wheels as it went added a touch of hysterical comedy to the moment, but both Thea and Denise managed not to laugh.

Kevin suddenly seemed serious, as if the impending session had some religious significance. Perhaps the old chapel still exerted some power. 'Leonora will get everything set up for you. Now, if you'd like to follow me, I'll take you through the safety briefing.'

Kevin's briefing was nothing like the one at Silverstone, except for the part where they each had to sign a waiver form, which stated that they were prepared to *accept personal liability for any injuries that might result from their participation in the activity*. All that remained was for Denise to struggle into her heavy-duty boiler suit. Thea looked away as she inched it up over her hips and bust. It was obviously designed for a male physique. Kevin then handed her some thick gloves and a pair of goggles. He checked the goggles were a tight fit – he didn't *want anyone blinded by flying glass on his watch* – and adjusted her helmet.

'Right, Denise. You're good to go. I'll be just next door, if you need me. The weapons are all laid out on the side. It's your choice entirely, but from experience, I recommend the crowbar for the bigger items. It's destructive, but a lot lighter than the lump hammer. And let's be honest, how often do you get tooled up with a crowbar these days? Have fun.'

He opened another chipboard door into The Destruction Room. As Denise stepped through, he couldn't resist one last piece of Kevin wisdom.

'Remember, Ladies... what happens in The Rage Rooms stays in The Rage Rooms!'

Chapter 34

THEA FOLLOWED Kevin into the adjacent room. She was surprised that in such a shoddy, DIY venue he had gone to the expense of putting in a two-way mirror. Though, on reflection, watching other people go ape-shit was probably one of the selling points of the experience, especially for works dos.

On the other side of the glass, Denise seemed at a loss. She was standing, stock still, in a room within which everything had been painted black: the walls, the floor, the ceiling, the furniture, even the window. Pushed to one side was an old metalwork bench on which sat the *implements of destruction*, as the sign pinned to the wall announced in a dripping blood-red font. In the middle of the room was some kind of platform on which were arranged Denise's selected items, including, in pride of place, the old computer. The cups she'd chosen were hung from hooks that had been embedded in the walls at varying heights, and the mobile phones were propped up on a shelf – spotlit for effect.

These decorative touches were another surprise. Leanora might be sullen and poorly paid, but she did have an eye for merchandising.

For what felt like ages Denise didn't move, except for her head, which turned slowly back and forth in its oversized helmet as she surveyed the room.

Kevin scratched his beard and nodded. 'Yep. I thought she'd be a burner.'

'Sorry, what?'

'The world divides into people who can't wait to get going – we call them bursters – and them that take a bit to get going – burners. Your friend, here, looks like a burner.' Another scratch. 'Mind, they often do the most damage, in the long run.'

Almost as if she'd heard them, Denise moved over to the bench and began studying the weapons. It was curiously fascinating to watch. Her first implement of choice turned out to be a golf club. Thea watched as Denise lined herself up near the cups – a tee-off stance, if she wasn't mistaken. She waggled her hips, took a few practice swings, set her head at the correct angle, then set to work, whacking each cup with power and remarkable accuracy. As pointless violence went, Denise brought a peculiarly hypnotic grace to the exercise. The lack of noise in the viewing room added to the dislocating sense of weirdness at what they were witnessing.

Kevin seemed impressed. 'Your friend' – they were the only two customers and he still couldn't remember their names – 'has got game.'

Now in her stride, there seemed to be no holding Denise back.

The PC was obliterated with a hammer: methodically, rhythmically, ferociously. When Denise struck the screen, it exploded into an arc of glass that, even without the sound effects, was impressive.

'You can't hear a thing, can you?' Thea marvelled.

'No. I spent a lot of money on the soundproofing. Had to. We had complaints from the neighbours. It wasn't the noise of the destruction so much – rather, the swearing that was the issue.'

'I can imagine.'

Denise was moving around the room with confidence now, smashing things at will. No rest for the destructive. It was a demonstration of silent, efficient decimation. Soon the room was littered with a confetti of glass, lumps of shattered plastic and small, sharp pieces of crockery. The mobile phones were dealt with one by one, by the hammer. Smash! A bounce of bits. Gone. The record player met a similar fate; this time the tool of choice was the baseball bat – Denise was using the full range of weaponry at her disposal. And Kevin was right, the teapots were spectacular, they exploded like fireworks in spray of coloured porcelain.

Pretty quickly, the only item left intact was the casserole dish. Denise positioned it on the centre of the platform and re-selected the golf club. Memories of Simon, perhaps. Without hesitation, she went in for the kill. She took a huge swing – Thea could see the weight visibly driving down through her body into her arms. But the club merely glanced off the rose-patterned surface. Denise reset and tried again, bringing the club down with real force, but to no effect. She paused, adjusted her helmet and reached for the crowbar. She tried again. This time a few chips flew off. She went at it repeatedly and methodically, but the heavy old pot resisted all her attempts at destruction. Denise's frustration grew. She had a go with one of the big hammers, but it too dinged off the surface, making little or no impact. Her agitation was becoming almost cartoon-like.

'Do you think I should intervene?' Kevin's voice startled Thea. She'd been mesmerised.

'No. Let her keep going. It's her rage, after all.'

'Okay.' Kevin seemed slightly put out, 'but I don't want her damaging that hammer. It's a good one. Had it since we opened.'

Through the glass Thea studied Denise. She was breathing so heavily that her goggles had steamed up. She rubbed at them with her gloved fingers. She studied the pot, then turned and surveyed the remaining weapons. Mind made up, she reached for the lump hammer. It was so heavy that she struggled to lift it off the workbench. Undeterred, she manhandled it down and dragged it across the concrete floor to the platform. Thea felt Kevin wince alongside her. He was obviously a man who loved his tools. Denise set her feet in a wide stance. Braced. Then, using every ounce of her strength, she hoisted the hammer as high as she could and brought it down on the pot. It was like watching someone tackling the strongman challenge at the fair.

The result was not spectacular, but it was effective.

For a second or two it looked like the beast of a casserole had survived, but then a crack appeared and the pot fell apart. Four big, thick chunks, like a flower opening.

Kevin laughed.

Thea clapped.

And in the black, debris-strewn room, Denise danced a jig.

Chapter 35

DENISE WAS wet through to her underwear, her arms ached and her fingertips were red raw inside her gloves, but she felt triumphant. The casserole had not defeated her. She had prevailed against that pretty, rose-sprigged, shockingly robust symbol of domesticity. In a fog she let Kevin lead her from the room. He left her to get changed. His parting shot of, 'Way to go with the lump hammer!' made Denise glow with pride as well as sweat.

As she sat, dazed and spent, the boiler suit pulled down around her waist to let in some air, she felt a sense of peace settle in her.

Who knew she had so much rage inside her?

Who knew that letting it out could be so satisfying?

She heard someone thumping around in The Destruction Room. The thought of the mess she'd made briefly induced a flicker of shame, but the price of a session must include the cost of cleaning up, surely. Yes, it was definitely someone with a broom. Leanora, earning her minimum wage. Denise decided that before she left she would leave the girl a tip – a big one – to say thank you.

But not now. For now she sat, cooling and calm, in her plywood box, inside an old church, somewhere in the flatlands of Nottinghamshire, spent but happy. There seemed no good reason to move. She had no emails to answer, no calls to make, no clothes to wash, no meals to cook, no one's mess to clear up. She had nothing to do but savour having gone mad and feeling so much better for it.

After a while she heard voices out in the corridor. Kevin and Thea.

It was enough to motivate Denise to stand up, peel off the remainder of the clammy boiler suit and get dressed. Now it was Thea's turn. This she didn't want to miss.

But when she emerged from the changing room she couldn't see either of them. The front door to the old chapel was wide open, letting some much-needed natural light into the gloomy interior. Kevin appeared on the steps, carrying a plastic crate. He smiled as he passed her. 'Just getting your mate's stuff in, ready to set up for her.'

Denise was puzzled. She headed outside. Thea was over by the Mini. She slammed the boot shut. On the ground near her feet was another grey plastic crate, identical to the one Kevin had been carrying. No wonder there'd been no space for their luggage in the boot. 'Hi,' she said.

Thea smiled. 'Hi. That was impressive. I didn't know you could play golf.'

Denise gave a mock bow. 'I thank you.' She was still on a high. 'I've honestly never swung a club in anger before today. That was great. All you have to do is let yourself go. Do you need a hand?'

'No. I'm fine.' Thea bent down, picked up the crate, which appeared heavy, and carried it inside. Denise followed her.

Though she tried to peek, she couldn't see the contents. They were covered by a towel.

'Give it here.' Kevin reappeared. He was like Mr Benn, popping up exactly when he was needed. He took the box from Thea. 'You go and get suited up. Leanora's getting on with the set-up. Denise, you wait here. I'll take you through to the viewing room in a sec.'

In an instant Denise found herself alone in the dark centre of the church, momentarily confused as to which door led where. Maybe allowing the rage to roam free switched off your common sense. But then Kevin was back, beckoning her to follow him. Round a corner into a different room with a viewing window. On the other side of the glass was the black room, the workbench, the 'tools', and spread around the room was Thea's stuff – stuff that hadn't come from The Selection Room, but from the boot of Thea's car.

Denise could make out a number of sleek silver frames, complete with photos; what looked like a full dining set – good-quality, a lovely midnight-blue glaze; some pictures – modern, arty in style; an expensive-looking coffee maker; and some trophies – for what Denise couldn't make out. It was nice stuff, from a nice home. From Thea's? It all looked very wrong in The Rage Rooms.

Thea entered. Even in a baggy navy boiler suit, gloves, goggles and helmet, it was still very obviously her. The angle of the head, the set of the shoulders, the height, the grace – despite the cumbersome get-up. She didn't hesitate. She picked up a hammer: not the lump hammer that had ended the casserole pot, but one of the standard yellow-handled ones with the claw head. She weighed it in her hands for a second or two, then set to work.

It was a whirl. One body, one weapon, one line of attack. Lift, hit, smash to smithereens, move on. Glass and crockery and wood flew into the air, hitting the glass wall like hail.

Kevin clucked his appreciation.

Thea worked around the room like a demonic Disney character. She even used her feet to stomp on the growing pile of detritus on the concrete floor. Her energy was impressive, her technique clinical. Within ten minutes everything was reduced to rubble. She checked her work. Satisfied that nothing had survived, she replaced the hammer neatly in its space on the bench and walked out.

Kevin went through to meet her.

But Denise lingered. She stepped closer to the glass and let her eyes range over the decimated fragments. Shards of ice-white fractured glass, the dark-blue enamel remnants of the dinner set, the splintered wood, the lumps of polished chrome: all lying scattered in the dust. Only the photos remained – a hammer, ironically, being unable to do much damage to glossy paper. Denise saw a series of stylish holiday prints: a stroll on a beach at sunset, a hike amidst snow-capped peaks, a smudgy silhouette of a couple in a close embrace and a formal wedding pose – the arc of a relationship, captured across time, discarded amongst the destruction.

She was shocked, and absolutely certain that Thea had just spent ten minutes smashing up her own life.

Chapter 36

THEA WANTED to get away: from Kevin, from his depressed-looking niece and, most of all, from the bitterness in her gut, but Denise had gone walkabout, again – something to do with *giving the girl a tip*. Thea stretched and flexed her fingers, arched her back, as much as she could in the confined space of the Mini. The jolts from the hammer blows were still ringing in her joints. It was painful. Everything about her felt shaken and out of sync.

At bloody last! Denise appeared, escorted by Kevin, who was still chatting away. They said their goodbyes like relatives who wouldn't be seeing each other again for ages. Finally she got in. Thea was already pulling out of the car park before Denise had even reached for her seatbelt. Thea's last view in the mirror was of Kevin, standing on the steps of the chapel, waving them off.

As they roared out of Knowsley a silence descended that was distinctly uncomfortable. Denise was saying nothing, which was very unlike her, and Thea was in no mood to make conversation. Instead she drove, fast, skimming along the country roads, her foot flicking between the accelerator and the brake. Speed. It was as good a solution as any. Thea saw Denise's hand reach for the dashboard as they rounded a bend. That was totally unnecessary – she was in complete control. So much for Denise the Brave.

Thea increased her mph on a straight stretch. Almost immediately she spotted her nemesis up ahead. A caravan. A huge beige obstruction. She drove up behind it, watching as the brake lights flickered indecisively on and off. So much nervous caution. Some people really shouldn't be allowed out on the roads, they were a danger to themselves and other people. She felt Denise tense. Thea dropped off the back of the caravan's rear, not out of respect for Denise's jitters, but so that she could get a better view of the road ahead. There was a bend coming up, but not for another 200 metres. Foot down, she pulled out into the opposite lane. Denise sucked in a breath. They were parallel with the wallowing whale of the caravan, which vibrated dangerously as they passed. A van appeared on the crest of the hill, coming towards them. The driver flashed his headlights. Thea pressed her foot down harder on the accelerator. They cleared the caravan and she pulled the Mini back in.

The van driver gave her a decidedly rude gesture as he whipped past. It was fine. Tighter than she'd thought perhaps, but fine. In the mirror she could just about make out the stricken face of the old guy towing the caravan. White hair, white face. But he receded from view quickly. Thea stared ahead, refusing to engage with Denise.

'Please don't do that again.'

So she did speak.

'Do what?'

'That. Drive so recklessly.'

'It was fine.'

'It wasn't.'

'It was!'

'Thea!' Thea had never heard Denise shout. Never heard her so much as raise her voice. 'I want you to find somewhere to stop.'

'Why?'

'Just do it!'

Despite her inner compulsion to keep going, Thea started looking for somewhere to pull over, because suddenly, inexplicably, she appeared to be having a panic attack. Which made no sense because she didn't panic, ever – she'd learnt there was no point. But the sensation of some giant invisible hand squeezing her ribcage to breaking point would seem to indicate otherwise.

She drove on, with no decrease in the speed of the car or in the severity of her symptoms – who was Denise to tell her how to drive? – until she saw a layby. She braked hard. If Denise wanted to be so dramatic about nothing, then she could have some drama. Gravel peppered the bodywork as the Mini came to an abrupt stop. Thea yanked on the handbrake and turned off the engine, but the inside of the car didn't fall silent, it was too full of the sound of her ragged breathing.

Chapter 37

'GIVE ME the keys.'

'What?'

'I said, give me the keys.' Thea's breathing was all over the place and her colour was awful. There was no way Denise was going to let her drive them anywhere in her current state.

Thea threw the keys into Denise's lap. A petulant gesture. Denise picked them up, got out of the car and walked round to the driver's side. The traffic ripped past, creating a draught that tugged at her clothes – a salutary reminder, should she need one, of how close they'd come to being casualties of such speed.

Thea stared ahead. Denise rapped on the glass. This was getting ridiculous, and dangerous. She pointed at the passenger seat. Reluctantly, Thea climbed out and walked slowly round to the other side of the car. Denise was relieved to get back inside, away from the lorries. Once in the driver's seat, she refused to be pressurised by Thea's black mood. One of them had to remain calm. She took her time repositioning the seat and the mirrors, making sure she felt comfortable. She could tell that her caution was infuriating Thea, but Denise absorbed her shimmering anger. Whatever was eating at Thea, she needed to get it under control herself. Engine on. Indicator on, she was ready to move off.

She waited until she was sure it was absolutely safe, before pulling out into the traffic.

Denise drove carefully, wary of the unfamiliar controls. The Mini had far more sensitive acceleration and braking than the VW. It felt twitchy under her nervous control. The dual carriageway eventually fed onto the motorway. The satnav told her which lane to stay in and she obeyed it, religiously. Her hands were sticky with sweat on the steering wheel, but at least concentrating on her driving as if their lives depended on it took her mind off Thea's extreme behaviour. The one relief was that Thea's breathing seemed to have settled, though she was still not speaking.

At the first sign for the services Denise took the exit, with relief. She parked in an empty space a good distance away from the main buildings. Engine off. Keys out of the ignition. It was a deeply awkward silence that ensued. She toughed it out for a few moments, then said, 'I think we should go in. Get a drink.'

Thea finally spoke. 'Whatever you say. It appears you're making the decisions at the moment.'

Denise ignored her. She reached for her bag and got out of the car. She could plainly see Thea through the windscreen, still refusing to look at her. Denise started walking away.

She didn't get far before she heard the car door thunk. She clicked the key fob without looking round.

The presence of other people helped to calm Denise's rattled nerves. She directed Thea to find a table and went off to join the queue. Tea, two bottles of water and, on a whim, at the till, two bars of chocolate. Good for stress. Armed with their provisions, she stood and scanned the busy food court. Thea was nowhere to be seen. Denise felt a flash of irritation, followed by concern. The day had turned bad, suddenly and spectacularly. A brush with death would do that, she supposed, but she suspected Thea's behaviour was more a by-product of their visit to The Rage Rooms than of the incident with the caravan. Something had been unleashed within Thea by her experience in Kevin's cheap and tacky chapel of destruction – something dark.

As Denise walked around the tables looking for her friend, she reflected on how little she really knew about Thea. She had some basic biography and a few entertaining anecdotes, but not much else. Thea's sanguine rendition of her divorce on their first night away had obviously been a load of bull. Who smashed up their own memories? And yet here was Denise hitching her life – and, in the process, the fate of her marriage – to a woman who, to all intents and purposes, was a stranger.

There was still no sign of her. Frustrated, Denise put down the tray and was about the reach for her phone to call her, but then didn't, because she knew Thea was unlikely to answer. That was another peculiarity: Thea's phone detox. Who, in this day and age – especially a mother – set aside their phone for whole days at a time? Motivated by mental well-being or not, it was a perverse thing to do.

Denise made a second circuit of the food court, her feelings oscillating between frustration and concern. Her search eventually revealed an outdoor seating area at the rear of the services. Through the plate glass, Denise saw Thea. She was sitting at one of the picnic benches, her back to the building. Denise took a deep breath, dropped her shoulders, adopted a neutral expression and stepped through the doors.

Chapter 38

THEA STARED at the landscaping. A natural oasis was a
tall order just off a motorway. Threadbare grass, a large
man-made pond or miniature lake – depending on your
perspective – and, God help them, a handful of shipped-in,
depressed-looking ducks. But it was better than being inside
the food court, with the boisterous families stuffing down
their sandwiches and talking over one another. Her heart was
still clattering around inside her chest so hard it felt like it had
become untethered. She willed it to settle, but it refused. She
recognised the feeling and hated it. Overcome with emotion
– it was such a hackneyed phrase, but it was accurate.

Fab-at-Fifty Hannah had been talking bollocks when
she said raging was cathartic. The visit to The Rage Rooms
had not left Thea feeling *energised and unencumbered*.
Smashing up the expensive framed wedding photo, the
ugly cut-glass vase that Marc's mother had bought them
for their first anniversary, the set of plates they'd painted –
badly – on their first visit to Center Parcs had not helped.
Or at least not in the way she'd hoped. Yes, there was now

far less clutter for Ella deal with, when she went back to the apartment; and, yes, she and Denise would now be able to put their bags in the boot of the car, like normal people; but in terms of catharsis, the experience had been a disaster.

She did not feel cleansed.

She felt battered.

The emotion stirred up had not been release, but regret. When she'd looked round the room and seen the carnage she'd wrought on the possessions she'd once taken pleasure and pride in, she'd felt ashamed. It was a shame that was as old as the hills, one rooted in her inability to hang on to her marriage, her husband and now her child. She'd hoped that the destruction would rid her of that sense of failure, free her from the jealousy and the bitterness. She'd wanted to hammer the past into the past, once and for all, and make it stay there. Marc had done damage and so, tit-for-tat, she should be allowed to destroy something. The process was supposed to have balanced the scales.

But it was a ridiculous, reductive equation. Possessions might represent emotions and relationships, but they weren't substitutes for them. You couldn't break a feeling – that was its peculiar power.

The thought of having to work her way through the rest of her list now seemed pointless, the trip a stupid attempt at distraction. Why throw yourself off a bridge or out of a plane? What would it prove? No one was watching anyway.

She didn't have any more *fuck it* left to give.

She would stop messing around.

Drive straight up to Scotland. Tomorrow.

Be done with it.

Denise put the tray down without a word. More tea. It was her solution to everything. She unwrapped one of the chocolate bars, snapped it into two chunks and offered Thea a piece. Thea took it, wanting to acknowledge the gesture, but was unable to stomach the chocolate. Denise drank some of her tea and ate three pieces. They watched the ducks drifting disconsolately around on the scummy water. A good ten minutes passed. It was strange to have someone prepared to sit alongside her turmoil so peacefully. Thea appreciated it. 'Sorry.'

Denise took another drink. 'That's okay.' The ducks went to war over a burger bun thrown by a man old enough to know better. It was a short-lived skirmish. The drakes came out on top. 'Are you all right?'

'Yes.'

'You're not, though, are you?' Bread consumed, the ducks went back to bobbing about like decoys. 'Why did you bring all that stuff with you all the way from Harpenden?'

'What do you mean?'

'The stuff you smashed up in The Rage Rooms.'

'I had a clear-out. I thought it might as well be put to good use. The website said you could bring anything you needed to get rid of.'

'I know. So you said, before.' There was a pause. 'But I can't imagine many people do.'

There was silence for a few seconds.

It was obvious that Denise had recognised the significance of the items. Why hide the truth? 'You know very well what it was. It was stuff from my marriage. Things I should have got rid of years ago.'

'Um.' There was another lengthy pause. Thea did not feel inclined to fill it. 'How did it feel, taking a hammer to your past?'

Denise surprised Thea at times. Venturing into murky waters willingly was an act of bravery of sorts, even if you did it tentatively. Thea looked at her. Denise seemed more interested in the ducks than in their conversation. Thea knew it was a ruse, but it helped. 'To be honest, not great. It felt kind of meaningless, like I was trying prove something, to myself. Something that I didn't believe anyway.' She raised her arms and wiggled her fingers. 'And that hammer was frigging heavy.'

Denise continued to stare out across the lake, the epitome of calm. 'In the past, whenever I saw stories about wronged women cutting up their partner's suits and junking their golf clubs, I used to cheer them on – for their balls, and their bravado. But I've always wondered whether it really makes you feel any better. It must be hard to switch from loving someone to hating them. Are you still angry with Marc?'

Thea considered Denise's question. Her default setting with Marc was anger. It was an emotion so deeply ingrained that she rarely stopped to question it any more.

She was angry that he'd left her.

Angry at the pain he caused her.

Angry that he'd fallen in love with Jenny.

Angry at his steadfast refusal to admit that he had been unfaithful.

She was angry that he was happy with Jenny.

And she was bitterly and heartbrokenly angry that he'd gone on to father two more children with her. A whole new family – which he had claimed he didn't want or need. A family that Ella was now part of.

Thea yawned and felt tears form in her eyes and her throat. 'Yes, I'm still mad at him. We're all mad with each other. That's how we operate as a family now. We prove we care by being incensed with each other all the time. It's very unhealthy.' She was wading dangerously deep in the truth now. 'But worst of all, I'm furious with myself.'

'Why?'

It was now or never. An opportunity to confess. There weren't going to be many more. 'For not being strong enough.' At that, Denise did turn round, ready to defend Thea against her own accusations? But it was time for Denise to realise that the person she'd put on a pedestal had feet of clay. 'I'm not the person you think I am.'

Chapter 39

THEA STARTED crying, heavy tears that dripped off her chin into her lap. She made no attempt to wipe them away. Denise had never seen her like this, unravelling. She dug around in her handbag for some tissues. She knew there was a pack in there somewhere – underneath her fan and her phone and her make-up bag. She dumped some of her crap on the table and located the pack. She handed it to Thea, who withdrew a couple of tissues and held them against her face as if her cheeks hurt.

Denise was at a loss as to what to say. True or untrue, Thea's statement revealed a Shakespearean-scale mess. As Denise sat quietly beside Thea, her hand resting on her back, letting her cry, she glanced at her phone. Three missed calls in the past half hour. Not from Simon – from Joe. Joe never rang her, none of her boys did, not unless he had absolutely no other choice. A trickle of anxiety ran down her spine.

Distressed as she was, Thea must have seen her check her phone because she said, 'It's okay if you need to call him back.'

Denise was torn. She wanted to be there for Thea, but her maternal instinct was screaming at her that something was wrong, and twenty-odd years of conditioning were impossible to ignore. Joe's last text had been normal enough. What could have occurred in the space of two hours to trigger this sudden urgent need to speak to her? Her family over Thea – sadly, that was the hierarchy. 'Sorry. One quick call. I just want to check that nothing's happened at home.' She stood up and walked over to the edge of the lake.

Joe answered her call immediately. 'Mum?' It was only four days since anyone had called her Mum, but it felt a lot longer. Perhaps that was because she hadn't been living like a mum. Her youngest son's voice sounded as monotone and languid as normal, which was reassuring, but Denise knew from experience that teenage inflexion was often an inaccurate indicator of teenage emotions. She went in with no preamble. 'Is everything okay?'

'Yeah.'

'You rang me. Three times.'

'Yeah. I know.' He sounded reluctant to admit it. 'I just wanted to say hi.'

'That's nice.' It was, but it couldn't possibly be the real motivation for him calling her. Could it? His tone was off. Was there something bothering him? Had something happened with his brothers? Their humour was often cruel, and they made no allowances for Joe being the youngest. Could he be worried about things between her and Simon? She sought to reassure him. 'Joe. Like I told you, everything is okay. I simply needed a bit of a break.'

'Cool.' There was such a long pause that Denise wondered if he'd fallen asleep. But then he roused himself again. 'Are you having a good time? The track day looked good.' So polite, all of a sudden.

'Yes, I am. Thank you. And it was.' She didn't go into details. She would tell him all about it when she got home.

There was another long pause, this one filled with some crackling and what vaguely sounded like another voice. Then he asked, 'When are you coming home?'

'I'm going to take another day, maybe two. I'll be back by the end of the week. You're not starving, are you?'

'No. Dad's been cooking.'

'And Aaron and Lewis are okay? Not being total pains?'

'No more than normal.'

'Well, give them my love.' It was as painful for him as it was for her. She was missing them. She glanced over at Thea. She had stopped crying and was sitting staring at nothing.

This time she definitely heard another voice. Then Joe said, 'Dad wants a word.' There was a rustle as the phone was handed over. The realisation dawned that Simon had got Joe to call her, to get her on the line. She'd been ambushed.

'Denise.' After Joe's reticence, Simon's briskness was a shock.

'Yes.' There was obviously something happening at the other end because, for a second of two, there was a muttered conversation and what sounded like a door banging. Joe fleeing, or being excluded from the scene?

Simon came back on the line, loud and clear. 'Look. I don't want to be difficult, Denise, but can you please tell me what the hell is going on?'

Denise swallowed down air and some, but not all, of her irritation before she answered. 'I've told you. I need some time away from work and the house, and your father.' Eric needed to be added to the list.

'For an undefined period, doing whatever takes your fancy, with a woman you barely know.'

'Yes.'

'Why?' It was a valid question, but one that she didn't have an adequate answer for or, more accurately, not one that she could articulate quickly and on demand, so she said nothing. Simon picked up the slack. 'This is about us, isn't it?'

Denise was beginning to realise that it was and it wasn't. 'In part.'

'I don't know what that means, Denise.'

She understood his frustration, but she couldn't assuage it. 'I know this can't be easy for you. I do appreciate that. I'm not doing it to be difficult, I'm really not. But getting away has made me realise that I need some space. I'm sorry, but I just do. And for some reason it has to be now. It's important. I am thinking about us – about you – but I'm also thinking about myself.'

'Well, that's good to hear.' His sarcasm was justified, but it hurt. It left no room for any love or affection. 'And have you reached any conclusions?'

'Not yet.'

'Any idea when you might?'

'Simon. Please. I'm asking you to give me some time. Just a few more days.' She glanced around. The picnic table was empty. Thea had gone. 'I can't talk to you now.'

'Oh. Sorry. Am I interfering with your busy schedule? I'll hold the fort here while you run around with this Thea woman, shall I? I don't even know where you are.' He was angry. He had every right to be, but she couldn't deal with his anger now.

'I'm sorry, Simon, but I really have to go. I'll call you back later, I promise.'

'Denise, don't hang up on me. I'm—'

She ended the call, feeling clear, in that moment, where her priorities lay.

As she scoured the crowd, she felt like an anxious parent who had let her child out of her sight. Somehow Thea had gone from being her inspiration to being her responsibility, all in the space of a few hours.

Denise searched the lake area and the food court, but Thea was nowhere to be seen. Next she headed into the refuge for all women, the Ladies. And thankfully there she was, leaning over a washbasin, reapplying her mascara. Their eyes met in the mirror. 'Sorry about that. Meltdown over. Normal service resumed. I won't be a minute.'

Denise indicted that she was in no rush. Some lip balm and a fluff of her hair, and Thea declared herself good to go. But as they walked out to the car, Denise laid her hand on her friend's arm, slowing her to a stop. 'Thea, wait. Where are we going?' She meant more than simply which direction.

Thea looked across the rows of cars, all paused midway en route to somewhere. 'I don't know,' she admitted.

The rumble of the traffic was constant. Endless momentum. For a moment they were outside it.

They had a decision to make.

Onwards or backwards?

Thea's plan or something else?

Thea seemed all out of suggestions.

Denise still had the car keys. She fished them out of her bag and set off walking again. 'Why not let me decide, for a change?'

Chapter 40

THEA WOKE up as they passed Alnwick, having slept for most of the drive north, which could have been a sign of her new faith in Denise's driving or simply an indication of how worn-out she was. Despite her fresh mascara and her sleep, she still didn't look well. Her eyes had a hollow look about them. Some long walks and lots of fresh air would hopefully lift her spirits.

She looked out at the Northumbrian countryside. 'It's very pretty.'

'Trust me. You ain't seen nothing yet.'

Denise drove into Bamburgh. It was still full of day-trippers despite it being nearly six o'clock. She turned down a narrow street. The houses lining either side were wedged in like books crammed haphazardly on a shelf. There was nowhere to park, so they had to circle back round. Denise eventually spotted a gap three streets over, near the pub. She managed to parallel-park the Mini fairly tidily at the first attempt, of which she was proud.

'So why are we here?' Thea asked.

Denise got out of the car. Thea joined her. Although they were on a very everyday-looking side street, the air was different – sharper, clearer. 'We're going to visit my mother.'

'Oh.' Thea looked slightly disappointed.

'What were you expecting?' Denise asked.

Thea grinned, briefly, a flash of her old self. She swiped her hair off her face, though the breeze immediately whipped it back. 'I don't know. An old flame? A secret love child?'

Denise laughed. 'And people say I have an overactive imagination.' They collected their bags from the boot. Thea didn't ask for the car keys back after Denise had locked the car. That was not a good sign – the Mini was an extension of Thea's personality, and handing it over to Denise was very out of character. Denise set off walking and Thea fell in beside her. The dynamic between them had definitely shifted.

'You've never mentioned your mum before.'

'No.' Guilt bubbled up in Denise's chest. She seemed to have an endless supply of the damn stuff.

'So, spill!'

'There's not much to *spill*.'

Thea then surprised Denise even more by linking arms with her. 'Mothers and daughters, there's always something.'

They'd reached the end of her mother's road, but Denise didn't turn down it; instead she continued on towards the beach. Time for Bamburgh's big reveal!

As predicted, Thea stopped in her tracks. 'Wow!'

'Yep.'

They stood side-by-side, taking in the view. There was no denying that the sweep of the bay, dominated by the castle, was impressive. On a clear blue-sky day like today it was breathtaking. The grandeur of nature and history, perfectly balanced.

'Did you grow up here?'

Denise laughed. 'No. Not all the North-East looks like this. Mum moved here after Dad died. She sold up, used what she got for the house, plus Dad's life insurance, to buy the cottage. Never looked back. And before you say it: yes, I know I could learn a few things from my mother in terms of being decisive. She's very much of the same opinion. In fact I'm sure you two will get on like a house on fire. Just do me a favour, will you?'

'What?'

'Please don't encourage her.' Thea had jumped down onto the beach and taken off her sandals. Denise joined her. They stumbled along the soft sand, the sea breeze hitting their faces. It was impossible not to feel more awake and, somehow, better with sand between your toes. 'What I mean is... I don't really want her to know that Simon and I are...' What were they? She honestly had no idea. 'Aren't in a great place at the moment.'

'Of course.'

'She'll only make more of it than there is.'

'Okay.' Thea actually held her hands up in submission.

Further along the bay two people were kite-surfing. Thea and Denise stopped and watched. It looked terrifying. It involved skimming along the surface of the waves at a ridiculous speed on a surfboard attached to a huge semicircular kite. When the wind, the kite and the surfer were aligned 'just so', the surfer abruptly lifted up into the air and hung suspended for a long-held breath. For a few glorious seconds they looked like they were flying. Then, just as abruptly, they dropped back down to earth. Denise was transfixed. 'Before you get any ideas, I am not attempting that!'

Thea smiled and gave a slight shake of her head. Denise felt a touch of sadness that Thea's appetite for adventure seemed to have deserted her – it did look exhilarating. Or at least it did until one of the surfers lost control. Still attached to the line, he flipped through the air like a thrown doll, then plummeted down into the sea in a whirl of limbs. It felt like a very long wait until his head re-emerged from the waves and he began the laborious process of reuniting himself with his board. Once they knew he was safe, they both instinctively turned away.

Another few of minutes of trudging brought them back up the beach onto the swathe of green that encircled the footprint of the castle, heading for her mother's cottage.

'This is where she lives?'

'It is. She went for a house with a view.' Denise unlatched the gate and they stepped into her mother's postage-stamp back garden. 'They used to belong to the fishermen.'

'I can see why she wanted to move here.'

The cottage backed onto the grass, with the castle to the left and the beach to the right. The perfect location. For a brief moment Denise wondered what her mother's cute little cottage, with its peerless views and olde-worlde charm, would be worth on the overheated second-home market. The very act of having such a thought horrified her. It revealed a side of herself that she disliked: the bookkeeper who knew the price of everything, but the value of nothing. This was her mother's home, not an asset.

She knocked on the peeling paint of the back door. Nothing. She had phoned and left a message to forewarn her mother that they were coming – hopefully she hadn't forgotten. Denise knocked again, loudly. It was only a four-and-a-half-roomed house, she couldn't not have heard them. What if something had happened to her? Denise had a sudden, very clear image of her mother in a small heap at the foot of the very narrow, very steep stairs. Perhaps she'd tripped in her rush to answer a ringing phone and been lying there for hours. But then her mother appeared, intact, hands in her cardigan pockets, glasses on her head when they needed to be on her face. She stopped in the middle of the tiny kitchen and peered through the glass panels in the back door.

'Mum. It's me!' Denise shouted.

Her mother nodded and turned away. Denise watched with loving frustration as Lilian searched through various pots and bowls on the old dresser that took up half the room, hunting for the door key, before realising it was already in the door.

At last she let them in. 'I was expecting you round the front.' Like visitors, not family or friends. Denise had only herself to blame. Lilian kissed Denise on the cheek, then held her at arm's length, examining her – an old habit that dated back to their days of living in a home without a full-length mirror. Until she was fourteen the only assessment that had mattered to Denise had been her mother's. At the time she'd hated it, but in hindsight she could see its advantages.

It had been a world without endless self-examination and dissatisfaction. Lilian made no comment on Denise's current crumpled appearance; in fact she nodded, as if satisfied with what she was seeing, which was praise indeed. 'Come in, come in. I'll get the kettle on. This is a nice surprise.'

Denise was about to introduce Thea, but her mother got in first.

'You must be Theo.' Lilian was not up on her Greek goddesses. 'Come in. I'm Lilian.' Thea was kissed as well, but was spared the physical examination.

With all three of them in the kitchen, it immediately became uncomfortable. After some shuffling around, Denise and Thea made it to the doorway. They squeezed through it, past a stack of logs, into the tiny sitting room.

'Shouldn't we offer to help?' Thea asked.

'No. Mum wouldn't thank you. She's very independent.'

'How old is she?'

'Eighty-three.'

Thea was surveying the interior of the cottage with blatant curiosity. She had to stoop to look through the window out onto the street – a stylish giant in Lilliput. Denise watched, musing on her decision to bring Thea here, to her mother's tiny house. It was a place that had never been her home. Indeed, when the freshly widowed Lilian had announced that she was selling up and moving to the seaside, Denise had been shocked and, if she was honest, put out. Why couldn't her mother stay and guard the family home like a cherished relic, keeping it there for Denise to visit when she so desired? Why this sudden assertion of an opinion? This slightly shocking appetite to start afresh?

But what Denise had realised, as she and Thea had stood aimlessly in that depressing motorway-service car park, was that Bamburgh did represent something important in her life. It represented safety.

When things were tough, home was where your mum was.

There was a lot of crashing about going on in the kitchen. Denise listened and smiled.

'Is this you?' Thea was craning to look at a small photo on the wall near the fire. It was so old it looked sepia, though close up, a little Kodak colour still tinted the cheeks of the chubby little girl in the picture and the T-shirt of the little boy sitting next to her. Denise hadn't seen the photo for years, but perhaps that was only because she hadn't been looking.

'Yes.'

'Weren't you cute?'

'You mean fat.'

'Who's fat?' Lilian carried the rattling tray into the room. Denise held back on offering to help. Her mother passed round the mugs. Lilian was not a teapot and milk jug kind of person.

'Who's that with you?'

Denise smiled. 'My brother, Shaun.'

'He's a good-looking little dude.'

'Yes, he was,' Lilian said. And that was it, in terms of information on her son.

'Your cottage is in an amazing position, Lilian.' Thea seemed to have been revived by her walk on the beach.

Her mother straightened up in response to the praise.

'That's why I bought it. To be near the sea. I couldnae get much closer.'

'Did you grow up at the seaside?' Thea settled back in her seat and sipped her drink. Denise was impressed that she managed to cover up her shock at the strength of her tea. Lilian believed that any beverage worth drinking should be strong enough to indelibly stain your internal organs.

'Oh, good heavens, no. I didnae see the sea until I was ten. I was so frightened when I did that I wouldnae go in. Not even to paddle.'

And so they were off.

Anecdotes emerged from Lilian like doves out of a magician's sleeves. It was the most animated, chatty and funny that Denise had seen her mother in years. She learnt more about her mother's childhood and working life in the following hour than she had in the previous fifty years. It was illuminating, entertaining and touching.

And sad.

Because as the performance went on, unwelcome memories of previous visits up to the little cottage crept into the edges of Denise's consciousness – the sense of claustrophobia, the memories of her mother's voice being drowned out by the boys' incessant demands and of her own deafness to anything other than their needs and wants. Had her mother stopped talking because her daughter ceased listening? And was this really all it took – the absence of the demands of her own family – to reignite her relationship with her mother?

It seemed so.

'You'll stay here tonight, won't you? There's room, if you don't mind sharing.' Denise was delighted to be asked, but she hesitated. She looked at Thea, expecting some small, polite indication that staying in her mother's tiny cottage was the last thing she wanted – Thea was, after all, used to en-suite bathrooms and walk-in showers. But Thea looked totally at home. Still Denise wavered. 'We don't want to put you out, Mum. They'll probably have a room free at The Bell, or we can drive out to The Nook.'

'It's nae bother.' Lilian paused. Suddenly the momentum of the past hour stuttered. 'Unless you'd prefer a hotel.' Denise had in the past, again citing the boys' needs.

'We'd love to stay,' Denise speedily reassured her. Thea smiled her agreement.

Her mother nodded and recovered her briskness. 'That's settled then. I'll go and make up the beds.'

And so it was agreed. Their odyssey was on pause, for the time being.

Chapter 41

THEA WAS woken by footsteps. She was momentarily confused; all the angles and patterns seemed wrong, they were far too acute and busy. But of course they were at Lilian's cottage, in Bamburgh – the land that time forgot.

Denise was already awake. 'Sorry, she's an early riser.'

Thea stretched, as much as her narrow single bed would allow. Despite its confines she had slept surprisingly well. 'What time is it?'

'Six-thirty.'

'Wow.'

'Yeah.'

They lay in their respective beds, looking at the ceiling.

'Shall we go down and say hello?' Thea had warmed to Denise's mother. Lilian had an energy and humour remarkable for her age; plus getting up and going downstairs would have the added benefit of preventing her and Denise having an in-depth conversation. Denise hadn't brought up Thea's emotional breakdown the day before, but it was unlikely to be forgotten or, more accurately, left alone. She was programmed to empathise, and there was no way that Thea's performance in the car and at the services would be interpreted as anything other than a cry for help. That was the problem with Denise: she disabled Thea's pretences.

'If you want to,' Denise said, although she didn't move, 'but I warn you, there'll be consequences.'

Thea climbed out of bed, taking care to duck her head – the sloped ceiling in the bedroom was low – and started getting dressed. More time with Lilian or with her own thoughts? She knew which she preferred.

Which was how, twenty minutes later, they found themselves wrapped in a couple of threadbare towels crossing the cricket pitch behind the cottage, being watched by a thin old man and a heavyset black Labrador, joining Lilian in her early-morning swim.

Thea had borrowed one of Lilian's old swimming costumes. It was more than a little snug. Too short in the torso and tight across the chest. Lilian had cheerfully described it as having a 'hungry bum'. It was a phrase Thea had never heard before, but it accurately described how the fabric kept disappearing up between her butt cheeks. Denise was sporting a hideous rose-pink, cap-sleeved T-shirt and a pair of leggings, again courtesy of her mother. Lilian herself was resplendent in a red-and-white polka-dot one-piece that fitted her perfectly, and a black swim cap. No wonder the old man and his dog were agog.

It was a beautiful late-June day. Full sun. A gentle breeze. Perfect swimming conditions. How cold could it be?

Lilian eased off her sensible shoes, did three vigorous arm swings, then walked straight into the sea as if she was making her way down the high street. Thea was deeply impressed, but she wasn't surprised. Denise's mother was obviously made of stern stuff. There was no screaming or wincing or carrying on – no histrionics of any kind. She simply walked straight ahead, an unwavering, unflinching line of pure determination. The water rose up her body until only her thin neck and her black cap were visible. Then she was off, away through the choppy waves. No word of goodbye, just an old lady swimming out to sea – nothing to see here.

As they stood watching her, putting off their own dip, Thea asked, 'How long has she been doing this?'

'Since the day she arrived.' Denise seemed to be eyeing the water with more trepidation than anticipation.

'What, she goes in every day?'

'The only things that have stopped her have been a broken hip in 2018 and a couple of bouts of flu.' The pride in Denise's voice was obvious.

The gentle breeze, which was far stronger down by the shoreline, whistled around Thea's exposed buttocks. 'That's impressive.'

'Yeah.' Denise was jiggling from side to side.

'How long will she stay in?'

They watched Lilian's head appearing and disappearing in the waves. 'I don't know. She used to do ten "back-and-forths", but I'm not sure any more. I've not actually seen her swim for years.' Thea hadn't meant anything by her comment, but, as ever, Denise seemed to feel the need to elaborate defensively. 'She usually prefers to go in on her own.'

Thea watched Lilian cutting a slow and steady line through the waves. She was really quite far out. It made Thea feel anxious, which was ridiculous. Lilian knew exactly what she was doing. She might be eighty-three, but she was obviously strong and fit, and totally in control of all her faculties. It was she and Denise who were a danger to themselves.

But they were here now. The sea awaited. And it was another experience to add to the list, this time a spontaneous one.

Thea dropped her towel and dug her swimming costume out of her butt crack. One last treat for the old guy. 'Come on then; if we're really doing this, let's get on with it! One, two...!' On the count of three, they launched themselves into the sea.

Their screaming lifted every single seagull off the beach.

The first five minutes were hideous. The water was so cold it felt like each wave was being personally vindictive. Every mouthful of brine was a tangy reminder that the North Sea was not her natural element. Thea's eyes and throat stung, her muscles contracted and her sense of orientation completely deserted her. But after the initial shock receded, things slowly started to improve. As she acclimatised, she started to uncoil. She stopped fighting the cold and tried instead to absorb it. It was all in the mind, or so she told herself. Once her body accepted the madness of what she was doing, her heart rate steadied and, much to her surprise, she began to derive a weird, masochistic pleasure from her salt-water baptism. Although there was more inelegant flailing-around going on than flawless front crawl, she didn't care. This was not about exercise, it was about stoicism, and solidarity with Lilian. Thea spotted Denise over to her left, doing her own frenetic version of breaststroke. As always, Thea found her presence reassuring.

Finally accustomed to the cold, and no longer intimidated by the vast expanse of water, Thea rolled onto her back and let the waves support her body. She glanced at her arm. Her little frog looked like it was swimming as well. Kirsty had advised Thea to keep the area around the tattoo as dry as possible to avoid infection, but she reckoned the anaesthetising cold was enough to offset the risk. Could tree frogs even swim? Ella would know. The swell tugged Thea this way and that. It felt good to let go and become just another piece of flotsam. The sea threaded its salty fingers through her hair, pulling her head down into the waves and her eyes up to the sky. The blue canopy above her head was wide, high and calmly indifferent. Thea closed her eyes. The sun on her face, the chill at her back, she let herself drift – empty of thought and intention.

Denise's shouts eventually pulled her back.

Reluctantly Thea righted herself. She was further out than she'd thought. She looked around, scanning for anchor points: the castle, the distant row of cottages, their Reggie Perrin-style pile of towels on the beach. They were all still there. Denise was a good distance away, her features unclear. Thea waved and Denise waved back, then started swimming towards her.

They were both out of breath by the time they met in the middle, two slick-haired heads bobbing like seals in the choppy water. Denise's face, washed clean by the waves and framed by a border of wet hair, looked young. 'It's freezing, isn't it!' Her teeth were chattering, but she was smiling. 'Have you had enough?'

'Yeah.' Thea suddenly had. She felt the need for firm ground under her feet, not unfathomable depths, and she'd started worrying about Lilian again. They shouldn't have let her go off on her own. They should have shown more care. 'Where's your mother?' Thea scanned the bay, but Lilian's black swim cap was nowhere to be seen.

'She got out. She's gone back up to the house to put the kettle on for us. More rib-sticking tea coming up.' Denise grinned.

They headed back in, swimming breaststroke side-by-side.

The hardest bit was getting out. There was much stumbling and inelegance as they emerged from the waves. Botticelli's Venus they were not. There again, they didn't have a huge scallop shell to ride on, or a handmaiden holding aloft a rich brocade cloak. Thin, sandy towels and an appreciative woof from the black Lab were all the welcome they got, but it was enough.

Chapter 42

LILIAN WAS dressed and ready for them when they returned, two mugs of steaming tea on the kitchen table. 'I've run the bath for you. Let me have your wet stuff, and any other washing you have, and I'll put a load on.'

Denise was about to tell her mum there was no need. But there was. She'd packed for a weekend away, not a week, and despite the emergency M&S knickers and T-shirts she'd bought in Watford, she was running low on clean clothes. So instead she thanked her mother. They clattered up to narrow stairs, taking their tea with them.

'You go first,' Denise insisted. Thea's lips had gone a worrying grey colour. She started to object out of politeness, but Denise cut her off. 'Honestly. You're turning blue, I think your need is greater than mine.' There were benefits to having more padding.

Thea didn't wait to be asked twice. She dashed across the landing into the tiny bathroom and banged the door shut. Left alone in the bedroom, Denise stripped off her sandy, wet leggings, T-shirt and knickers, gathered up her dirty clothes and stuffed them all into a plastic bag. Then she swaddled herself in an old dressing gown that she found hanging on the hook on the back of the bedroom door. It was scratchy against her skin, but comfortingly heavyweight. Inside its tartan shabbiness, the chill in her limbs receded. She cradled her tea, cherishing the warmth while she listened to Thea slosh around in the bath. It wasn't nosiness, it was simply impossible not to listen, given the modest scale of her mother's house. Thea started humming to herself. It was a contented sound. Denise was relieved to hear it. Her decision to come to Bamburgh had been a good one.

'There's no need to rush,' Denise shouted, 'I'm fine with my tea.'

'Thanks.' Thea yelled. 'I won't lie – it's bliss. But I won't be long. I don't want you getting hypothermia.'

Denise felt a small, perfect burst of happiness. Here she was, sitting in her mother's house, wrapped in an old dressing gown, with a wincingly strong cup of tea clasped in her seawater-wrinkled hands, shouting through the bathroom door to a friend. She absent-mindedly started playing with the tassel on the end of the rope belt, enjoying the slip and slide of the silky threads through her fingers. As she heard the splash of the water when Thea stood up in the bath, it came to Denise that the dressing gown had belonged to her father. Who else's could it have been? Denise was surprised that her mother had brought it with her to Bamburgh. She'd seemed coolly unemotional about Denise's father's possessions after his death. They had all – what few items there were – gone straight into bin bags, destined for the tip or the charity shop. Lilian had clearly and unequivocally wanted out of North Ormesby with all its old associations, friends and memories. And yet here was her dad's dressing gown, the most mundane and yet personal of belongings, hanging in the spare room of her cottage. Perhaps all marriages, happy and unhappy, were never truly laid to rest.

Denise's reverie was disturbed by the bathroom door opening. Thea emerged, wrapped in yet another of her mother's thin, washed-within-an inch-of-its-life towels. All the linen in Lilian's house was well past its best. 'Thank you. I can feel my extremities again.' Denise heard the water in the tub gurgling away. She was too embarrassed to rush into the bathroom and save the draining bath water. Lilian's old boiler was only good for one bath. Denise let it go. If a flannel-wash in the sink was good enough for her mother, then it was good enough for her.

'Sorry.'

'For what?' Thea asked.

Denise gestured at the threadbare towel that was barely big enough to cover Thea's modesty. 'Mum doesn't believe in bath sheets. She thinks they're a step too far. Like coffee-makers and the wheel.'

Thea laughed. 'It's fine.' But then there was an awkward pause. 'I've finished, if you want to use the bathroom.'

Denise took another swallow of her tea. 'I will in a minute.'

'Okay.' Thea sat down on the bed, clutching the towel to her. It took Denise a second to realise that Thea was waiting for her to leave before she got dried and dressed. It took her another couple of seconds to remember why – the scar on her stomach.

Denise grabbed her shorts and remaining clean T-shirt and allowed Thea her privacy.

In the bathroom, as she watched the sink fill, Denise reflected on her friend's personality. Initially it had been Thea's confidence that had drawn Denise to her. Denise – like the man at the hotel – had been attracted by Thea's surface shine. But as brightly as she glittered and sparkled, it was a distracting illusion. The past forty-eight hours had revealed that, like everyone else, Thea had her fragilities. It was these struggles that fascinated Denise. If the process of revelation required patience, so be it, she was prepared to bide her time. Because, silly as it sounded, even inside her own head, Denise believed that getting to the bottom of the mystery of Thea was somehow the key to understanding herself. They were *meant* to meet and make friends.

Denise shut off the tap and fetched the soap from its niche by the bath. It was a solid amber block of Pears. It was almost as if her mother was deliberately leaving triggers around the house. But that was plainly nonsense; it was simply a sign that Lilian had stayed loyal to her chosen brand of soap for more than sixty years. The bathroom was fuggy from Thea's bath. Denise shrugged off the dressing gown and let it fall to the floor. She pushed it aside with her foot. Her own confidence reboot had to start somewhere. What better place than in her mother's tiny, steamy bathroom?

She picked up the bar of soap and worked up a lather, enjoying the familiar feel of the oval shape between her fingers. The fragrance was a direct shortcut to her childhood and adolescence. Above the sink was a small mirror, big enough to reflect her face and nothing more. She began to wash, methodically. Face, neck, shoulders, armpits, arms, torso. Soap and soft flesh beneath her fingertips, lifting the salt from her skin. She reached her belly. It was not flat like Thea's, not taut, not tanned – not scarred. She moved down her legs, then did the best she could with her back. She emptied the sink and filled it with fresh water, took the flannel and proceeded to wipe away the lather.

Once clean, she rewrapped herself in the old dressing gown. She pulled out the plug and watched the sudsy water drain away, thinking not about her own imperfections, for a change, but about someone else's.

Chapter 43

THEY HAD spent the day walking and talking, and eating cake and sitting and looking at the view, and now they were back. It had been a day well spent, doing very little. Denise moved around her mother's tiny kitchen totally at ease in her baggy shorts and creased T-shirt. The stone flags under her bare feet were cool. The back door was wedged open with an old flat iron and the breeze coming off the sea was delicious.

To her surprise, she and Thea had learnt to fold themselves into the tiny, cluttered spaces of Lilian's cottage remarkably quickly. It wasn't that difficult really, you just had to take smaller steps and keep gesticulations to a minimum. Denise had, however, struggled to know where to put the supplies they'd bought for supper. A chicken, a mountain of fresh veg, the ingredients for a crumble, two bottles of wine, bacon for breakfast in the morning. Lilian's small kitchen simply did not have enough workspace to accommodate such abundance. But despite the cramped conditions, the blunt knives and the paucity of pans, Denise was happy. She wanted to cook for her mum – food as love, it was another inheritance that she'd been wilfully blind to.

The longer she spent in this tiny cottage by the sea, the more Denise felt at peace – with herself, with Thea, and with her mother. It was good to have time to reflect on what they had in common, as opposed to what set them apart. Denise was embarrassed that she couldn't remember the last time she'd made a meal for Lilian. That was shameful. As she scrubbed potatoes and chopped carrots, she vowed that she would make the effort to come up to Bamburgh more regularly, on her own, without the distractions she normally brought with her. Her time was in limited supply, but she needed to make sure that she spent some of it with her mum – before it was too late.

As she worked she listened to Thea and her mother talking in the garden. They had carried a pair of deckchairs outside to make the most of the glorious weather. All Denise could see was the outline of their bodies through the faded canvas and the backs of their heads – Lilian's chalk-white, Thea's glossy chestnut. Beyond them the washing flapped on the line. It was like an image of an old postcard. *Having a great time. Wish you were here.* Though, in truth, Denise had no wish for anyone else to be there, other than the three of them. Every now and again one of them would laugh at something the other said. Denise felt she had done a good thing by bringing them all together.

Veg prepped, she cleared a space on the cluttered work surface. Time to make a start on the crumble. As she began to rub the cold butter into the flour, she heard her mother ask, 'So how long have you been divorced?' Denise paused, her fingers claggy, interested in what Thea's reply might be. They had not returned to their conversation at the services, and Denise, with a patience born of having time, had not brought it up. She knew Thea well enough now to know that she would speak when she was ready, and not before.

'Four years.'

'And you're on your own now?'

'Yes.' Denise detected a slight change in Thea's tone, then a concerted, perhaps strained effort at humour. 'No one will have me.'

'Oh, I don't believe that for a second. I'm guessing you could have your pick, if you wanted to.'

Denise saw Thea shift in her deckchair. 'I don't think I'll ever have another relationship.'

'What makes you say that?'

'The evidence. One proposal, one marriage, one child, one divorce – I'm obviously a once, and once-only, kind of girl.' Again Denise marvelled at Thea's ability to appear open and honest whilst at the same time revealing so little of herself.

Her mother, perhaps sensing Thea's resistance, moved the conversation on to what she assumed would be safer ground. 'Denise mentioned you have a daughter.' It was like she was inadvertently pinballing off all of Thea's vulnerable points.

'Yes. Ella. She's fifteen. She's with her father at the moment.'

There was lull in their conversation. Thea volunteered nothing more. Thankfully, Lilian didn't ask for any further explanation. But it was she who broke the silence. 'It's a difficult age. But trust me, it gets easier – for them, and for you. You just have to hang on in there while they're working out who they want to be.'

Denise saw her mother lean forward awkwardly in her deckchair and pat Thea's arm: understanding from one mother of a teenage daughter to another, the huge time-lapse reduced to nothing by empathy. The gesture snagged at Denise's conscience. She'd never before reflected on how difficult her mother might have found being the parent of an unhappy teenager. The solipsism of youth. It reminded her of her own boys. They loved her, but they were, as yet, incapable of imagining what it was like to *be* her. And perhaps that was as it should be. Lilian and Thea settled back in their chairs, facing the view rather than each other, united in their best-kept secrets. The crumb was crumbled. Denise topped the apples with it and sprinkled over a dusting of sugar. Meal prep done.

She heard the creaking of joints – the deckchair's and her mother's. Lilian rose. 'Well. It's been lovely chatting to you, but I really must be making a move. If I don't, I'll nae get out of this chair again. And I said I'd drop the paper round to a friend. I won't be long.'

On her way into the house, Denise saw her mother pause and look back at Thea as if puzzled by their conversation. She recognised the feeling. When Lilian turned and saw Denise at the kitchen window, she smiled.

Having cleared a mountain of stuff off it first, they ate their evening meal together crammed around Lilian's small dining-room table. Roast chicken, roast and mashed potatoes, veg and gravy. Full plates for Thea and Denise, a half portion for Lilian. 'It's another benefit of old age,' she smiled, 'your stomach finally shrinks!' She did, however, accept the offer of a glass of wine, then a second after the remnants of the meal had been cleared away.

'Thank you. That was lovely.'

Thea raised her chunky beaker. 'Yes. Compliments to the chef!'

Lilian did not possess wine glasses, just a random assortment of glassware, some of it dating back to Denise's childhood. The goblet Thea was currently holding up to the overhead light was ancient. It came from a garage forecourt and had been acquired by collecting Green Shield Stamps. Denise remembered the thrill of going to trade in their full card for all sorts of household items – she and her brother taking it in strict turns to carry the precious fold of cardboard with its wonky rows of stamps. The memory slipped easily and cleanly into focus. The repeat pattern of the stamps; the awareness, even as a young child, that the card was valuable and must be guarded against the wind and rain; and – greatest of all fears – the horror of it being dropped down a grate. Denise felt another surge of affection for her mother and her childhood. This was what she'd been missing out on: the stimulus of being around her own past. It wasn't only the making of new memories that was important, it was also triggering and treasuring old ones.

'My pleasure.' Denise raised her own glass in acknowledgement. It was nice to have her efforts appreciated.

Just as a peaceful, drowsy silence settled, Denise's phone started ringing. She had to scramble around to find her bag.

It was on the floor in the hall, abandoned and forgotten. The ringing went on and on. The caller was not giving up. She knew who it would be. With her mother and Thea looking on, she checked the ID and declined the call, peace quickly restored. Denise was fully aware that she was storing up trouble; Simon's increasingly impatient messages were a testament to that, but she was determined not to let thoughts of home intrude, not now. Fully complicit, neither her mother nor Thea asked who the call was from. Instead her ever-active mother changed up the mood by going in search of her games box and a pack of matches.

The rest of the evening passed in a rattle of dominoes and a stream of gentle mickey-taking. Once Thea had mastered the basics, there was no stopping her, but after a series of high-stakes games it was Lilian who finally emerged triumphant – a matchstick millionaire. Satisfied with having so thoroughly taken Thea and Denise to the cleaners, she announced that she was going to head up to bed. She stooped to kiss each of them, paused, then retraced her steps at the last moment in order to stroke Denise's cheek. The gesture was the perfect, fleeting seal on a pretty good day.

Chapter 44

AFTER LILIAN had gone to bed, Thea and Denise moved quietly around the house tidying away the last bits and pieces, then they followed her upstairs. It was only 10.30 p.m., but Denise was tired. The novelty of it was not lost on her.

In bed, they sat propped up against their respective chipped headboards.

'Your mother is amazing.'

Denise had heard it before. Lilian was incredibly feisty and fit for her eighty-three years, and counting. She was as good a role model for old age as you could find. Independent, active, sharp, accepting, but not cowed by her advancing years. But as a mother: *amazing?* In the past Denise hadn't been too sure about that. Lilian was from the school of tough love and, when Denise had been younger, she had found that hard. There had been little room in the Sawyer household for uncertainty or anxiety – traits that Denise had inherited in spades, from somewhere. Or perhaps she'd developed her twitchy approach to life of her own, wilful accord. Growing up, Lilian's mantra had always had been:

accept your lot and if you really can't stomach it, change it.
Indecision was an alien concept to her. Although, thinking
back to the overheard conversation between her mother
and Thea earlier in the day, perhaps Lilian had been more
aware of, and worried about, Denise's struggles when she
was younger than she'd realised.

'Yeah. She is. For her age.'

'At any age!' Denise wondered if Thea was making a
comparison between Lilian's robustness and her own
mother's frailty, though from what little she'd seen, Thea
and her mother had a strong connection despite the ravages
of dementia.

'What was your dad like?' Thea asked.

Denise glanced at his dressing gown hanging on the hook
on the back of the door. 'Hard-working. Always made sure
there was bread on the table. A man of few words. A good
dad.'

'There's a *but*.'

'Oh, I don't know. I don't think it does any good to go
back over stuff, applying today's standards to the past.' Thea
made a non-committal noise. 'Okay. In retrospect he could
be a little bit overbearing. I'm sure he didn't mean to be,
but there was no doubting who was head of the house. And
there was no challenging him. It was all very regimented.
Meals at set times, washing on certain days, family chores,
expectations that you pulled your weight, not a lot of praise
or affection. We were always well looked after, but there was
never much fun. I don't remember either him or my mother
having much fun.'

'She laughs now.'

'That's true.' It was. 'She's much happier now, living up here, on her own. After all those years of fitting around everyone else's needs, it must be a relief to live as she chooses. It just goes to show that there's life after kids and marriage.' Denise's thoughts inexorably turned to Simon, but it was too complex and big a topic to unpick, so she slammed shut that door as hard as she could. 'What about your parents?'

Thea paused, then spoke in a whisper, mindful no doubt of Lilian on the other side of the bedroom wall. 'My parents were in love for the whole thirty-nine years of their marriage.' She must have seen Denise pull a sceptical expression. 'Yeah, I know. It's unusual, isn't it? After all that time, you'd think you'd discover something about your partner that truly ticked you off.'

Denise did not rise to nibble the bait in relation to Simon. She wasn't ready to 'share' that much. Thea pulled her covers up around herself. Her head stuck out of the top like the nut on the top of a Walnut Whip, but in the dim thirty-watt light of the small bedside table lamp she still looked beautiful. Lilian had lent them both nighties to tide them over until their own clothes were dry. It made them look like extras in a 1970s sitcom.

'My father courted her all their married life. It was as if he was still trying to win her over, even though he'd already got her. And in return she genuinely thought he was *the best of men*. They had a pride in each other. I heard it whenever they spoke to someone else about each other. It wasn't an act. Egotistical perhaps, but not fake. I can vouch for that. Because I saw them when they were alone, when there wasn't an audience. If anything, it was more intense between them when they were on their own. Even after they'd been married for all those years, they still needed to be together to be happy.' Thea sounded wistful.

Denise felt wistful. 'It sounds idyllic.'

'I think it was – for them.'

'But not so much fun for you?'

Thea backtracked. 'No, it was lovely in many ways. I grew up knowing what being in love looked like.'

'But lonely to live with?' Denise pushed gently at the door, wanting, as ever, for Thea to open it and reveal more of herself.

Thea lay back against the headboard. 'Maybe a little,' she conceded. 'I suppose I always suspected, even from being quite young, that they loved each other more than they loved me or my brother.'

At least the boys would never have to deal with that, but even as Denise was thinking it, she realised that she regretted it. The boys knew that, first and foremost, she and Simon were parents rather than partners. Frustrated with herself for letting thoughts of her own husband intrude, Denise refocused on Thea's family. 'Does he feel the same way?'

'I've no idea. It's not something we've ever talked about. You don't, do you? Not normally. I suspect he'd say I was over-analysing it.'

Denise was pleased that Thea was beginning to confide in her. 'What's your relationship with your mother like now?' she asked.

Thea hesitated before she answered. 'Simpler.'

'How?' Two could play at Thea's game.

'She's in her own world most of the time.' Thea batted Denise's anticipated sympathy away. 'No. Really. It's not so bad. Not at the moment, anyway. She's retreated to a place where she's happy. Well, if not exactly happy, then at least content. It's the calmest she's ever been.'

'Does she still recognise you?'

'I'm not sure she knows I'm her daughter any more, but she's always delighted to see me. She has always liked having company.'

'It's odd to think I saw you with her at the home before we met at the do at The Grosvenor.'

'When?'

'Oh, a couple of months ago. I caught a glimpse of you dancing together. I knew instantly that you were mother and daughter.'

'How?'

'The way you both carry yourselves. You both have a real sense of style. The shape of your heads. And the obvious affection.'

They fell silent for a second. It was odd to think that 300 miles away Eric would be pacing around his room, chuntering to himself about the state of the world, while Nancy swayed around hers, imagining herself in the arms of her long-dead husband. Two very different people, making their own very different ways through the maze of old age. Denise was ashamed to feel nothing but relief to be so far away from her father-in-law. She wondered what Thea felt about not seeing her mother, but didn't ask.

At the thought of Eric, a wave of heat began. Chest, neck,

face, top of her head. Denise shoved down the bedcovers. Thea glanced over, understood and said nothing. Denise picked up a magazine that was on the small bedside table and began wafting herself.

Thea asked, 'Why do you visit Eric so often, given what a pain in the arse he is?'

'Because someone has to.'

'But you hate visiting him, don't you?'

'Yes.' It was awful, but it was true.

'Then don't do it. Or at least don't go as frequently.'

'Like I said, someone has to.'

'Why can't that someone be his own son?'

Why not Simon, indeed? The heat intensified. Denise wiped sweat off her lip.

But instead of continuing to chide Denise for her lack of backbone, Thea softened her tone. 'It's a bugger being a woman, isn't it?'

Whether she meant night sweats or the responsibility for elderly relatives, or the complexity of family dynamics, wasn't clear. Denise laughed, despite her discomfort. 'Yes.' Simply having someone acknowledge the things she was finding so difficult seemed to make them better. She was still on fire, but she didn't feel embarrassed or stressed about it, like she did at home, because she wasn't on her own.

She looked over at Thea, sitting so elegant and composed in her narrow bed in her frilly nightie, and felt a wave of affection. She didn't want Thea to be alone with her struggles, either. 'Thea?'

'Yeah?'

'What's the scar on your stomach from?'

Thea didn't flinch. Reassuringly, she also didn't hesitate in answering. 'I had a hysterectomy.'

'When?'

'Seven years ago.'

'Why?' Who knew being this direct was so easy?

'I had cancer.' Her voice was calm.

'Do you want to talk about it?'

Thea wriggled down under the bedcovers and lay on her back. 'Not specially. It's not that riveting a tale.' She paused. 'But I don't mind you knowing. I'd had problems for ages, before and after Ella was born – pain, excessive bleeding. They kept saying it was "just fibroids", but I knew there was something wrong. They should have done further explorations, but of course they didn't, and I kind of gave up chasing it. It was a new nurse at my doctor's who picked it up and pursued it, but by then it was too late. Much too late. Once I knew it was cancer, the surgery couldn't happen soon enough for me. I was on a weird high when they eventually wheeled me down to have it done. When I came round and they said they'd had to perform a total hysterectomy, I was relieved. To my mind, the more they'd scooped out, the better. For a long time afterwards I'd lie awake at night thinking about my reproductive bits slopping around in a metal dish. Big chunks of me, gone, incinerated – and, with them, the cancer. That brought me comfort. Then I started on the treatment.'

She fell silent. Again Denise waited. It was Thea's story to tell as she chose – gore and all.

'The treatment was bad. I bloated up. Bits of me stopped working. My body failed me. I was a patient, not a person, for a long time. It was far worse than the surgery. I went into sudden-onset menopause overnight, but in the midst of everything else that was going on, I didn't even register it or what it meant. They gave me HRT. More tablets. I swallowed them, along with the hundreds of other pills I was taking every day.' She barely paused. 'Long story short: I recovered. Got fit again. Went back to work. I got my life on track. Rebooted. Moved on.' She stopped talking.

Denise badly wanted to show Thea some sympathy. 'It sounds a dreadful experience to have to go through.' Thea turned her head on the pillow. They had both heard it, the return of Denise's old voice, the tinny tone of a well-worn platitude. Denise panicked. 'Sorry. That was a such a silly thing to say.' Her panic worsened. Her neck prickled. The sense of losing something important – namely, Thea's respect – rendered her speechless. The silence was agonising. Despite their beds being only centimetres apart, Denise felt as if she was stranded on an island, looking across the water at Thea marooned on her own tiny dot of land.

Then Thea laughed. A proper loud, reassuring bark of laughter that broke the tension. 'Whoa there, *compadre*. Take a breath.' Denise did as instructed. 'It's okay not to know what to say. I don't normally talk about it, but given that you obviously got an eyeful, I thought I'd better explain.'

Cancer. A hysterectomy. Treatment. Recovery. Early menopause. Divorce. Denise's admiration for Thea rose. She felt shy in the presence of such resilience, and weak in comparison.

Then Thea yawned. 'Enough of this. I'm boring myself, and I'm knackered. Let's get some sleep. God knows what your mother has in store for us tomorrow.' And with that, she rolled onto her side, her back to Denise, signalling the end of their confidences.

It took a long time before either of them fell asleep.

Chapter 45

LILIAN WAS fully aware that she was set in her ways, though who could blame her? What was the point of getting this old if you couldn't, finally, do what the hell you liked? Having Denise and her friend to stay was disruptive, but it had been nice to have company for a change. They'd brought laughter and conversation into the house and Lilian had enjoyed that enormously. She was, however, beginning to wonder when the next leg of their round-Britain trip was going to happen. Thea was supposed to be heading up to Edinburgh to see her brother. What Denise was planning was unclear, which was very unlike her. Normally her life was extremely tightly scheduled. But for now neither of them seemed in any great rush to move on.

Lilian had been surprised when Denise called to say she was 'in the area' and 'was wondering if it might be okay to call in'. If her daughter felt to need to pretend the visit was a spur-of-the-moment thing, then so be it. Lilian had long since accepted, but still failed to understand, Denise's convoluted motivations for the things she did and said. She made life so much more complicated than it needed to be. She always had done. It sprang from her concern about what people might be thinking of her. It pained Lilian that, even now, Denise still second-guessed herself so much. It was a consequence of her childhood, no doubt; everything was nowadays. But there was nothing to be done about that – nobody's upbringing was perfect. You couldn't unravel the past and knit it into a new garment, however much you might want to.

Denise's friend Thea was a breath of fresh air.

Indeed, the fact that Denise was travelling with a friend at all was something of a surprise. She'd never, in all the time Lilian had been in Bamburgh, come to visit without either Simon and/or the boys in tow. Good heavens, the noise and the mess they made – still did, even now they were no longer children. It had been much better without them around. Lilian knew that she should love her grandchildren, should cherish every rare moment, but in truth she dreaded them descending on her little cottage. 'Doting', how she hated the word. Why should she dote on them? Their visits were always so awkward. Despite the beach and the castle, her grandsons were invariably bored and restless, hankering after their city lives and entertainments, whilst she always felt under pressure to be something she wasn't. It was sad, really, that they felt like virtual strangers rather than family.

And Simon?

She'd never really warmed to Simon. He seemed to love Denise and treat her well enough, but he was too full of himself for Lilian's tastes. Or perhaps he was just too different from everything Lilian knew and trusted. Forever the boss's son – slick, polished, confident. She knew, the minute she met him, that Denise would fold herself around Simon's certainty. Which was precisely what she'd done.

But there was trouble in paradise. Denise had barely mentioned her family or her work, and that was not usual; normally they were all she talked about. The odd thing was that she didn't seem overly concerned by whatever was going on at home. Look at her ignoring her phone the other evening – that was very out of character. In fact it was more than a lack of concern. Denise seemed to be revelling in being away from them all. She was altogether less uptight, more relaxed. It was a pleasure to see, and a pleasure to be around.

The obvious conclusion was that Denise's happiness was due, at least in part, to her friendship with Thea. Watching them together, Lilian speculated. They seemed so close and yet, from memory – and Lilian prided herself on her memory – Denise had never mentioned Thea before. She seemed to have crash-landed in her daughter's life out of nowhere, bringing with her something that was having a very positive effect on Denise. They were chalk and cheese, but somehow the combination worked.

Lilian asked Denise about their friendship when they were washing up a few bits left over from lunch. Thea had headed down to the beach with a borrowed book. Lilian had been surprised when she opted for a romance – a bestseller that someone had mistakenly given Lilian for Christmas. But when it came to personal tastes in books, as in so much else, it was very much a case of *each to their own*. Lilian's own preference was for autobiographies. She liked to see how the other half lived.

275

Knowing how prickly Denise could be about personal matters, Lilian took care to ease into the question with a compliment: 'You seem different.' She did – barefoot, bare-faced, humming to herself.

'Do I?'

'Yes. You seem happier.'

Denise shrugged. 'I think it's done me good, having a break.'

Lilian nodded. Left it a beat or two. 'Thea seems nice.'

Denise laughed. 'I'm not sure "nice" is quite the right word, but I'm glad you like her.'

'I do. I think she's good for you.'

Denise bristled slightly. 'I think we're good for each other.'

Lilian was pleased that she'd pushed back; it wasn't only Denise's happiness that had increased; her spine seemed to be gaining strength as well. 'She's a bonny girl.'

'She's hardly a girl, Mam.' Denise hadn't said 'Mam' for years. Its reappearance in her vocabulary over the past few days had been another small joy for Lilian. Twenty-four years of marriage, living down south for all that time, and yet some of Denise's past life obviously still lingered.

'No, exactly, she's not.' Lilian dried the butter knife slowly. 'Are you and her...?' Lilian inclined her head, indicating a relationship that was more than close friends.

Denise paused, her hands submerged in the suds. 'What do you mean?'

'I mean, are you and Thea more than just friends?'

The look on Denise's face was priceless. 'No! Of course not.'

'Oh, don't be such a prude. I merely thought the two of you seem so well suited. And close.' Lilian wasn't sure whether it was the thought of her elderly mother discussing a relationship between two women or that her question begged another, bigger one – namely, what was going on between her and Simon – that had so shocked Denise. Normally Lilian would have respected her daughter's privacy, but their time together over the past few days had bolstered her confidence. She was Denise's mother, after all. 'Are things okay at home?'

Denise slotted the last plate into the rack, dried her hands and seemed about to speak, but nothing came out of her mouth. Lilian watched her daughter's face. She looked perplexed rather than upset. As a child, she used to scratch her right eyebrow when she was thinking, and sure enough her hand now rose to her brow. Lilian felt a blast of love for this fully grown, slightly confused woman standing in her kitchen.

'Yes. In that they're the same as they always are.'

'But?'

'But the problem is… I'm not.'

Lilian gave her comment some thought and couldn't for the life of her think of anything to say that was helpful. Being a wife, a mother and working full time was a heavy load, especially if it wasn't being shared – Lilian knew that all too well; nor had she forgotten the fear and the confusion that came with making a change. But this was Denise's life, not hers. History did not have to be repeated. So instead of offering any advice she prompted, 'Is that a bad thing?'

Denise stopped worrying away at her eyebrow. 'In all honesty, Mam, I don't know.'

Lilian smiled. 'Well, for what it's worth, I'd say that nae knowing what happens next doesnae seem to be doing you any harm at the moment.'

Denise's frown disappeared. She put her arms around Lilian and hugged her.

The feel of her daughter's warm hands on Lilian's back was lovely.

Chapter 46

Lying on the sand, with the sun beaming down on her, Thea felt untethered. Denise had chosen well; Bamburgh was a good place to rest and recoup. After years of defying her body, she was now letting it dictate the rhythm of her days. The book she'd borrowed lay unopened on the towel next to her. She'd grabbed the first thing that came to hand off Lilian's cluttered shelves. It had turned out to be a romance – plenty of irony there, should you be looking for it. She had no intention of reading it. No intention of doing anything other than lie on her back and breathe.

Living in Lilian's tiny cottage was comforting.

Walking on the beach was calming.

Floating in the icy waves was relaxing.

Lying here in the sun was seductive.

It was an existence of simple routines and pleasures, with very few decisions to be made, other than whether to have another cup of tea or not. She was well and truly off-grid. Other than Denise and Lilian, no one knew where she was.

As a result, her real life and the threats to it were nullified. She was safe.

She closed her eyes and let the sound of the waves fill her head. Her life, like the kite-surfers, was suspended mid-flight. It was glorious and liberating.

While it lasted.

Chapter 47

IT HAD been barely forty-eight hours and already they were living like old women. They rose early. They wandered along the coastline, stopping frequently to admire the views. They swam in the icy waves. And they spent many long, hypnotic minutes watching the kettle come to the boil on Lilian's popping gas stove.

Thus their days fell into a rhythm that seemed to be exactly what they needed.

Not content with adopting Lilian's habits, Denise and Thea also took to supplementing their limited clothing supply with items borrowed from her drawers. From a distance it would have been difficult tell them apart.

Thus the pace of life slowed to a delicious, leisurely crawl.

On Thursday evening Thea announced that she wanted to buy them all fish and chips, a thank-you for Lilian's continued hospitality. Denise volunteered to pick up the food on the way back from her evening stroll. Time on her own. It was another blessing of this trip. For the first time in years she did not have to explain or account for her whereabouts, she was a free agent. They each went their own ways, coming back together as and when they wanted to. Together in spirit, but content to be apart. It was a freedom that Denise hadn't realised she'd been craving. Armed with one of Lilian's many cardigans, in case it was cool down by the shoreline, Denise set off, leaving Thea and her mother pottering about in the garden. As she passed through the gate she heard Lilian explaining which herbs were best suited to the extreme conditions that coastal gardening presented. The *Macbeth*'s witches' overtones were strong.

When Denise returned to the cottage with their meal an hour later there was an ancient bottle of malt vinegar and a drum of salt standing ready and waiting on the table. Sadly, the fish and chips no longer came wrapped in newsprint bundles, but regardless of the packaging, the smell was tempting. It summoned Thea and Lilian from their rooms instantly.

They ate in the kitchen with the back door wedged open. For five minutes there was no conversation, just the smack of lips as they munched their way through their respective mountains of dripping-dipped food.

It was Lilian who spoke first. She'd wisely opted for a child's portion and so was perhaps less over-faced with food. 'You missed Shaun. He rang while you out.'

'How is he?' Denise asked.

'Ach, fine, really. But you know what he's like. He's getting himself in a right tizz about his birthday.'

Denise should have been alert to the dangers and steered the conversation onto a different topic, but she was distracted by the challenge presented by her enormous battered haddock. 'Is he having a party?'

'No. He and Rick are going away for a few days.'

'Somewhere nice?'

'I'd imagine so. You're not fifty every day.'

It was barely perceptible, but Denise saw Thea register the comment. She instinctively glanced towards the front room where the photo of the two of them hung. Denise and her little brother. Her little brother, who was turning fifty. Which made Denise a flat liar.

'No, that's true,' she commented lamely, before turning her attention back to hacking away at the thick layer of batter on her fish.

After they'd eaten, Denise and Thea went and sat on the garden wall, their stomachs pressing against their waistbands. Thea pinched a sprig of rosemary off a bush and crushed it between her finger. 'It's a pity you missed speaking to your brother.' She'd been bound to bring it up.

'That's okay. I'll ring him when I get home.'

The tangy fragrance of the rosemary was pungent on the evening air.

'I'm glad he's okay.' It was such an odd thing to say that Denise twisted round to look at Thea. She flushed. 'And alive.'

'What?'

Thea grimaced. 'I got the wrong end of the stick. That photo of the two of you as kids. When I commented on it, you and your mother both went quiet. I thought the worst.'

'You thought he'd died!'

'Yes. Well, there didn't seem to be any other photos of

him – you know, as a teenager or an adult. So I assumed something bad had happened.'

Denise snorted. 'No, you daft sod. He's in LA.'

'What?'

'He's been there for the past twenty years. I'm sure Mum has some photos of him somewhere in the house. She's just not big on family portraits, and Shaun is one hundred per cent digital these days.'

'How come he's in the US?'

'Because he's a lucky bastard.' Denise qualified her statement. 'No, that's unfair. It was always his ambition to work in the film industry.'

'You're kidding me! You have a brother who works in Hollywood and you're only mentioning it now.'

'He's not an actor, he's a techie. You know the kind of thing... creating thousands of CGI soldiers for battle scenes, removing any signs of modern life from the backgrounds in historical films, stuff like that. Not that I understand properly what he does.'

'You've been out to visit him?'

'Once. He got us onto the lot, gave us a tour, but he really spends most of his time in an air-conditioned room staring at his computer. We've not been over since we've had the boys. It simply isn't practical. He comes here every eighteen months or so to see Mum, and me.'

'How did he end up working in the movies? God, I'm so shallow. I just like saying the words.'

'Hard work, lots of self-belief, the relentless pursuit of a dream and, like me, a desire to get as far away from Middlesbrough as possible. Though of course, being Shaun, he took it to extremes. It was our thing when we were growing up: going to the cinema. I used to take him to a Saturday kids' club at our local fleapit.' Denise let her memory glide over the intervening years and the thousands of miles that separated her from her little, now nearly fifty-year-old brother. 'It's the only time I've ever seen anyone fall in love right in front of my eyes. He was transfixed. He got obsessed with how it all worked – how they did the special effects, how the sound fitted with the pictures. He wanted to take apart the magic and see the mechanism, while I merely sat there soaking up the atmosphere, getting lost in the stories. I spent a lot of my teenage years taking him to see films. My last useful purpose as his big sister was getting him into eighteen-rated movies. Once he looked old enough, I was done. It was a habit that survived into adulthood, for both of us, but whereas my passion became a hobby, he turned his into a career.'

'Hence all your DVDs.'

Thea held the rosemary to her nose and took a deep breath. She was obviously not going to refer to the anomaly of Shaun – Denise's younger brother – turning fifty while Denise herself was allegedly only forty-seven. But Thea had shared her painful secrets with Denise, so it only seemed right to reciprocate. 'Thea. I'm sorry, there's something I've been lying to you about.'

'What?'

'My age.'

'It's a woman's prerogative.' She seemed indifferent.

'But it's ridiculous.' Suddenly it was.

Thea twirled the stem of rosemary between her fingers. 'Denise. It really doesn't matter.'

'It does. Because it's not something I've just started doing as I've got older. I've been lying about my age for years, to everyone.'

Thea dropped the rosemary sprig and, as ever, cut to the chase. 'Why?'

'It's complicated.'

Thea folded her arms. 'I've got time.' Her eyes skimmed across the view. The one thing Bamburgh had in spades was space and that, in turn, seemed to stretch seconds into minutes, and minutes into hours. 'If you want to tell me.'

Denise did. She wanted the release, and she was prepared to endure the embarrassment to achieve it. She was done with pretending. It was exhausting and pointless. 'It's going to test your patience, and you're definitely going to think I'm mad.'

'Try me.' Thea shuffled around on the wall getting comfortable, signalling her willingness to listen.

'Okay. It goes back to when I was growing up. I was very shy as a teenager. I found taking my O levels quite stressful. I was predicted to do well. I didn't. Not really. Certainly not as well as everyone was expecting. The pressure got to me. I did even worse in my A levels. I lost confidence in myself. It all became a bit of a vicious cycle.' She could still summon up the sense of shame. The star pupil falling so spectacularly from on high, twice. 'I was unemployed for a long time after college. I was probably unemployable. I was at home, a lot, not earning, not really doing much of anything. Not a recipe for self-worth or family harmony. My mum and dad found it hard to understand what was wrong with me. It was in the days before people had much sympathy with things like that. It caused a lot of tension.'

The anticipated flush started, an uncomfortable echo of how trapped she'd felt in her late teens and early twenties. Denise let the heat ripple through her and went on with her story.

'I got temp work, but every time I settled anywhere, they seemed to want me to do more, have contact with the public, or with customers. I struggled with that, big-time. And I was never very comfortable around colleagues. I think they thought I was stuck up. Anyway, Mum was working in the staff canteen at a place called Carrington's. They made sugar products for the catering industry. She heard on the grapevine that they were looking for an office junior. I was unemployed, again. Mum thought I should apply, but by then I was twenty-three, hardly a junior. But my dad insisted on it. He said I had to contribute something to the family finances. I filled in the application. It was Dad who suggested I lie about my age.'

Thea impressively kept any thoughts she might be having to herself.

'I looked young for my age, and with no make-up on, I looked even younger. It wasn't that much of a stretch to think I might be seventeen. I never thought I'd get offered the job. If I hadn't, my life would have been very different, in lots of ways... But I did. I couldn't turn it down. Dad wouldn't hear of it, and Mum, well, I think she thought it would be good for me. And it went from there. The woman who ran the office was nice. Old-school, firm but fair. She liked that I was quiet, diligent. We got on. It was just the two of us. She trained me up. When she retired a few years later, I took over her role. I was twenty-six by then, but they thought I was still only in my early twenties. I remember how, in my reviews, they always used to comment on my maturity. It made me squirm.' Denise paused.

Thea smiled. 'Surely there's a moratorium on these kinds of things. You weren't doing any real harm. And let's not forget, I got my first job by lying... The placement in New York, remember? That's a total whopper, compared to you knocking a few years off your age.'

Denise couldn't, and didn't, agree. 'Perhaps... if that's where it had ended. But it didn't.' She gathered herself up for the next instalment. 'I was running the admin side of the business when we were approached by a potential new client, Mather's.' Thea stilled, listening more closely. 'Simon came up on a site visit. All part of their due diligence before they started buying from us. We had quite a lot of dealings with each other over the following few weeks, getting the details of the contract agreed. On the day it was signed, he asked me out. To this day I don't know what he saw in me. We started a long-distance relationship – with him making all the running, and most of the effort. He drove up to Middlesbrough most weekends. It was romantic. Like something in the movies. He made me feel special, less like myself. When he proposed, I said "yes". I loved him, and it was a way out of my job, out of my life, out of my parents' house – out of everything that I thought was making me unhappy.'

'And?'

'And I never told him the truth.'

'Oh.'

'Yes… Oh. Simon thinks I'm forty-seven. I'm not. I'm fifty-three.' It was the first time she'd owned up to her age, out loud, in decades.

'Hence your little brother's impossible fiftieth birthday.'

'Exactly.' The heat in Denise's face started to lessen. The sea breeze felt cool against her skin. 'I should have told you before.'

'Denise! It's fine.'

Thea looked neither shocked nor horrified, just perplexed. But why wouldn't she be bemused? It was a mad thing to do: to lie so consistently and thoroughly about something that – Denise now realised, with absolute clarity – simply did not matter.

'But how does it work? Surely Simon must have seen your passport, or had to fill in a form or something with your actual age.'

It was a reasonable question – if you looked at it sanely. 'It's taken a lot of hard work and effort to keep it from him, and from everyone else. I think it's the reason why I'm such a control freak.' Denise paused, then went for full disclosure of her madness. 'I have a spreadsheet of which agreements, accounts and arrangements are in my real age and which are in my fake age. And I have to keep a lot of things out of Simon's sight… which has been possible because, from the very beginning of our marriage, I've done most of the admin. It is, after all, what I'm best at. I am, and always have been, little more than a glorified office manager.' She ignored Thea's supportive tut of disagreement. 'But sometimes I forget, or I make mistakes. Then I panic. It's a minefield that gets more and more difficult to navigate as time goes by.'

'It sounds bloody exhausting.'

'It is.'

'Is this why you've been trying to hide that you're going through the menopause?'

Denise nodded. Her temperature was back to normal now, which only added to the relief of finally speaking about the bizarre charade she'd be performing for so long. 'Yes. But that's proving virtually impossible now. I've started to drop hints to Simon and he hasn't asked too much, which helps.' But it hurt.

Thea shook her head, but again Denise detected more bemusement than scorn, possibly even a touch of respect. 'You are a dark horse. So much for your confessions. The bunny-murdering tale pales into insignificance compared to this. You're like one of those Hollywood stars who lie about their age for years, so that no one really knows how old they are in the end.'

Denise knew Thea was trying to make her feel better, but her levity wasn't helping. Having Thea laugh only served to make the scale of her absurdity even more apparent. What must she think of Denise's ridiculous self-inflicted predicament, compared to what she'd gone through herself? An overwhelming feeling of inadequacy crashed over Denise. She really was a silly, delusional woman.

Thea must have seen her distress because she switched tack. 'Hey. It's not my place to judge, but it sounds like a complete ball-ache.'

'It is.'

'Then why not just tell him the truth?'

Denise raised her eyes to the view. 'Because Simon already thinks I'm having some sort of mental breakdown.

This trip has confirmed it for him. If I told him that his wife of twenty-four years is actually six years older than he thought she was, he'll think I've gone completely crazy. Perhaps I have.'

Thea reached out and took hold of Denise's hand and clasped it tight in her own. 'Oh, you're not crazy, Denise. I think this is probably the sanest you've ever been.'

Chapter 48

DENISE WOKE with her heart bashing against her ribs. Sharp, staccato raps. The knocking continued, but it wasn't really her heart bursting inside her ribcage, there was someone at the door, at 6.15 a.m. on Friday morning. What the hell! She scrambled out of bed and shrugged on her dad's dressing gown. Cloaked in her tweedy armour, she hurried down the narrow stairs. The knocking was more insistent now, signalling some sort of emergency – though there was no smoke, flames or blue flashing lights that she could see.

Denise fumbled the door open.

Simon was standing on the doorstep.

They stared at each other. Her shock was quickly replaced by self-consciousness. It was as if she hadn't seen him in years – she was reminded of Brad Pitt rocking up at the family ranch in *Legends of the Fall*, but without the flowing locks. The first word out of his mouth was 'Sorry'. Next came a rush of explanation. 'I drove up overnight. I got a couple of hours' sleep in the car when I got here.' He touched the shadow of stubble on his chin, as if evidencing his claim. 'I didn't know what else to do. I know it's early, but I couldn't wait any longer.' He seemed to take her silence as a bad omen. 'Denise, please, we need to talk. We need to fix this.'

She nodded, because he was right: they did need to talk. He made a move, but the thought of him coming into her mother's home seemed too big a step, too soon. The cottage was not the right setting for this conversation. 'Mum and Thea are still asleep. I don't want to disturb them.' Though his knocking might well already have done that. Even more reason to get Simon off the premises. 'Let me get dressed and I'll meet you...' she racked her brain, 'on the benches outside the pub.'

He looked crestfallen, but nodded. 'The Ship?'

'Yeah, The Ship. I'll be along in five minutes.' And with that, she closed the door.

Simon was in Bamburgh.

He'd made a grand gesture. Romantic, impulsive and out of character. Or perhaps not, perhaps this was an echo of his former self. He'd driven more than 300 miles through the night to be with her. He wanted to talk. He wanted to fix things. She was touched.

Simon was in Bamburgh.

He had caught up with her. He'd come to convince her that what she was doing was foolish, selfish and pointless. He'd come to fetch her home. Take her away from her mother and Thea. Drag her back to her life. Her adventure was at end. She wasn't sure she was ready for that.

She climbed the stairs slowly, her head down, not realising that her mother was standing on the landing, watching. Lilian was fully dressed.

'It was Simon,' Denise volunteered.

'So I gathered. What did he want?'

'Me. I suppose.' But it wasn't as simple as that, and that was what Denise was dreading. 'And I guess he wants an explanation.'

A gleam entered her mother's short-sighted blue eyes. 'For your trip away with your new best friend?'

Denise nodded. 'And for why I've been behaving the way I have recently. It wasn't good between us, even before I upped and left him holding the ball.'

This news did not seem to come as a shock to Lilian. 'And what are you going to tell him?'

'I honestly don't know.'

Lilian patted her arm. 'Don't let him pressurise you into going back, hen. Not if you're nae ready to. You, and Thea, can stay as long as you like, as far as I'm concerned. 'She smiled, impishly. 'Well, within reason.'

'Thank you, Mam, that means a lot, but I can't keep running away from my responsibilities for ever.'

Lilian studied her. 'When exactly did you leave home?'

'Last Saturday.'

'So you've been away for less than a week?' Denise nodded. It felt longer, but then they had travelled a long way. 'And how many years have you and Simon been married?'

'It would be twenty-five years this autumn.' *Will be.*

Lilian gave another fleeting, conspiratorial smile. 'I think you're owed a few more days of freedom, if you want them.' She smiled. 'I hope it goes okay.'

Four minutes later Denise pulled the front door shut behind her and set off towards the pub. Thankfully, Thea had rolled over and gone back to sleep, so Denise had managed to avoid an inquisition about what she was planning to say and do. Although as she headed along the still-sleeping street, she wondered whether a practice run might not have been helpful. She'd left St Albans on a pissed-off whim, but the impetus to run away had, she now realised, been building for years.

It was a weekend that had become a week. A short break that had become a deep fracture. And it was going to take more than an awkward conversation, on a pub bench, with a nice view of a big castle, for her to explain why she'd chosen to abandon Simon, the boys, the business and her myriad other responsibilities in order to run away with a woman she'd only just met.

As soon as Denise rounded the corner she spotted him. Simon cut a lonely figure sitting outside a shut pub in the hazy morning sunlight. Or had she added the 'lonely' descriptor because that was the emotion she wanted him to be feeling? Had this whole trip been about wanting to make him feel her absence in a way he never seemed to feel her presence? For a second she thought he was on his phone, but as she drew closer she saw he was simply sitting, staring at his hands. It was a pose she rarely saw him in – reflective. He must have sensed her approach because he looked up, and smiled. It was a hesitant, tired smile that lacked the confidence that normally underpinned his expressions. Given the escalating ill temper of their exchanges across the past week, she'd been expecting reproach, anger even, but everything about him seemed subdued.

He rose to his feet as she approached and she suddenly felt uncertain of the etiquette. Should she kiss him? Embrace him? It was odd to feel so uneasy in the presence of the man she'd spent most of her adult life with. He leant towards her and awkwardly kissed her on the left cheek. It reminded her of their first date – the nervous formality was very similar. Despite his long trip he smelt good. Had he thought to bring his aftershave with him for her?

She walked around the picnic table and sat opposite him.

Across the street a delivery van reversed into a space in front of the shop. They both watched it as if it was the most fascinating manoeuvre they'd ever seen.

'I had to come.'

He hadn't – which made the gesture all the more significant. He'd just driven a very long way through the night with no guarantee of a friendly welcome: from Denise, or her mother. Lilian and Simon had always had a cool relationship. They had nothing in common except her and the boys, and very little effort had been made, by either of them, to get beyond that important, but ultimately slim connection. There had been years of polite ambivalence on both sides. So while Bamburgh had felt to Denise like a good place to stop, take stock and recharge, it was definitely not Simon's natural habitat. To travel so far, overnight, to a place he had no affinity with, in such a dramatic fashion, spoke of an awareness that something serious was going on, and of a desire to face it. That gave her hope.

'Are the boys okay?' Denise had been thinking about

them, a lot, but not worrying, or at least not in her usual way, which was sweating the small stuff. What she'd been trying to work out was what they really needed from her. She was the mother of men now, not boys. She would have liked to talk to Simon about it, but they had more pressing matters to deal with.

'They're fine. A bit confused about what's going on.'

'That's understandable,' she conceded. 'I've spoken to them.' She let his successful attempt to entrap her hang between them.

He ducked under it. 'Yes. I know.' He turned his hand over and picked at a ridge of hard skin in the centre of his palm. The battle scar from his three-wood. 'We've been getting on okay. I haven't poisoned them, yet. But they're used to having you around. I'm used to having you around. The house feels very different without you.' Did he mean they were missing her cooking and the daily laundry service, or her?

'But you've coped?' She could hear the sprinkle of grit in her voice.

He obviously heard it, too. 'Yes, of course we've coped, but it was a bit of a shock. You leaving like that.'

'I imagine it was.' Were they going to argue or talk?

She watched the delivery driver slide a tray of fresh bread out of the back of his van. The smell was tempting, perhaps she would call in and buy a crusty loaf and a pack of salted butter after she'd finished talking to Simon.

'Denise. What's going on?'

She felt ashamed. She should be focusing on him, not breakfast. He was owed an explanation, she knew that, but where to begin? Wilfully or honestly, she wasn't sure. She opted for the basics. 'Thea decided to take a trip. She asked me along. I declined, at first. Then I decided to go. It wasn't premeditated.' A word associated with a crime.

'But that's the weird part of all this.' He waved his arm about, as if blaming the sleepy beauty of Bamburgh for her disappearance. 'You just left. No warning, no conversation, no plan in place for how we'd manage in your absence. You simply walked out.'

'I left a note.'

He took an audible breath, seeking patience. 'You did.' She could tell by Simon's expression that he had not seen the humour in it. 'I'll be back' scribbled on one of Eric's precious Post-it notes and stuck to the door of the microwave – an attempt at channelling Arnie's famous nonchalance. In hindsight, it was in poor taste. 'We've had no idea what you've been doing. You've ignored many of my calls. Not responded to my texts for hours on end. We've... *I've* been worried about you.'

Denise looked in his face and knew that what he was saying was true. But he was exaggerating. She *had* been in touch, but on her terms, which meant that what she hadn't done was respond immediately to his increasingly querulous messages demanding to know exactly *where she was, where she was going, when she would be back and... what she thought she was playing at*. And whatever Denise was doing, she was certainly no longer playing. She'd never been more serious in her life. 'I told you I was fine, that there was no need to worry.'

'"Fine!" How can you say you're fine? This isn't fine. We're apart. I have no idea what you're planning, what you're thinking.' The catch in his throat sounded painful. 'Are you leaving me?'

The driver pulled down the roller at the back of his van, hopped in the front and drove away, leaving behind an empty space.

Simon looked more distressed than she'd seen him in years. What she was doing was hurting him. It was important that she try and explain. 'The routine we'd got ourselves into, it was suffocating me.'

She saw him wince at her use of 'suffocating'. 'I'm sorry, Denise, but I don't know what you're talking about.'

She finally looked him fully in the face. 'I know you don't, and that's the problem.'

'So tell me! Please.'

'Okay.' She scratched at her right eyebrow. This mattered. This was her marriage. *Their* marriage. 'What I mean is... I felt trapped. I felt invisible. And I was lonely. I realised that the only way I could get you to notice me was to not be around.'

He shook his head in despair and frustration. 'You should have said something.'

'I did.'

'When?'

The words were gathering momentum now. 'Every time I nagged about no one ever emptying the kitchen bin; when I said I didn't really want to go to some event or other; when I asked for a hug; when I came back from visiting your father and asked if you were planning on calling in to see him with me; when I drank wine on a midweek evening, hoping it would help me sleep when...'

He looked horrified and frightened. It was his fear that stopped her saying any more. It was as if she'd just exploded the bridge that connected them, and they were both staring down at the chasm between them.

Simon reached across the table and took her hands in his. Two hand-holds twelve hours apart, one offering something, the other asking something. Denise felt conflicted. He gripped her fingers tightly, imploring. 'I love you. I know how much work you put into the business, into the family. I'm sorry that I don't say "thank you" more often, that I don't say "I love you" anywhere near enough. You have to believe me: we've been lost without you this past week. Truly we have! We need you to come back. You're the one who holds it all together. I promise things will be better. Please, Denise, come home, with me.'

She searched his face. It told her what she already knew – namely, that what he was saying was true. He squeezed her hands, his fingers crushing her knuckles. She saw his desperation and she knew what she had to do.

Chapter 49

THEA HEARD a door bang, in her sleep or in reality, she wasn't sure. She'd had a disturbed night, vivid dreams followed by long patches of wakefulness. She and Denise seemed to be trading places, in terms of their nocturnal habits. The room was stuffy despite the window having been left open overnight. She rolled over, expecting to see Denise in the next bed, but it was empty, the covers shoved back, the pillow dented where her head had lain. She was probably in the bathroom, as she so often was. Thea glanced at the old alarm clock that sat on the bedside table: 6.34 a.m. She swung her legs over the side of the bed, stood up, raised her arms above her head and stretched, trying to ease the kinks out of her spine. The ceiling was so low that she could lay her palms flat against it and push. She knew she wouldn't go back to sleep, so she pulled on her shorts and a T-shirt and went out onto the small landing.

The bathroom was empty, no sign of Denise. Thea used the loo, splashed water on her face. She felt the need for air. The call of the beach was strong. Having lived her whole life happily landlocked, she was surprised by how much pleasure she was getting from having the sea on her doorstep. She crept downstairs, not wanting to wake Lilian.

She needn't have worried because Lilian was in the kitchen, standing at the sink, looking out of the window. She didn't turn round at Thea's approach, although she'd obviously heard her. 'Morning, dear. Did you sleep well?'

'Morning, Lilian. Yes. Thank you.' It was simpler, and more polite, to feign.

'The sunrise was stunning this morning.' What time had she got up?

Thea walked over and stood behind her – it was impossible to stand next to her, the kitchen was too narrow. The main event was over, but the encore wasn't quite finished. They both watched as the final streaks of pink faded into the pale-blue canopy of the sky. When the very last wisp of rose had evaporated, Lilian said, 'You want a cuppa?'

'No. Thank you. I was going to take a walk before breakfast. If that's okay?'

Her daybreak reverie over, Lilian busied herself with the kettle. 'You don't have to ask my permission, love.' She lifted down a mug and fished a teabag out of the box.

'Do you know where Denise is?'

'She headed out.' Thea waited for Lilian to elaborate. She didn't.

'Did she say where?'

'Nae.'

Lilian was the most laconic person Thea had ever met. Her *what will be, will be* attitude was peaceful without being passive. Thea admired and deeply envied her.

'Well, I won't be long.'

'Take as long as you like.'

Encouraged on her way by Lilian's benign indifference, Thea retrieved her trainers from beside the door, put them on and stepped out into the small back garden. The air was fresh and the breeze off the sea was gentle. She walked down the path and through the salt-rusted gate. As she re-latched it behind her she looked back at the house, half hoping to see Lilian framed in the kitchen window, but of course Lilian was nowhere to be seen.

To begin with, Thea had the beach virtually to herself. The few people who were out kept their distance – which wasn't much of a challenge, given the huge empty sweep of the bay. Her only close encounter was with a scruffy terrier that cantered over to her with a chewed-up ball in its mouth, wanting to play. She declined, not wanting to touch the slobbered-on ball or to encourage the dog. But it persisted, dropping down on its belly and wagging its stump of a tail in anticipation.

A woman, presumably its owner, shouted, 'Pippin! Pippin, come here. Right this minute. Leave that poor lady alone.' The dog cocked its head, deciding whether to obey, then concluding that Thea was obviously no fun, upped and scooted, at speed, back across the beach to its owner.

Pippin. Not a bad name.

Ella had compiled a list of names for her possible dog, many of them deliberately preposterous. Her favourite changed often during the long months they did battle over the issue. At twelve, Ella had naïvely believed that the

303

perfect name would act as some sort of magic key, capable of turning her mother into a person who would countenance buying a dog to live in an apartment with no outdoor space, in a household comprising an easily bored pre-teen and a woman who worked full time. Despite the overwhelming evidence that pet ownership was a non-starter, Ella had not been easily deterred. Her campaign had been impressive and relentless, which sadly meant that the disagreement had gone on far longer than it needed to.

Perhaps Marc would buy Ella a pet, now she was living with him full time.

Of course he would, but he wouldn't merely go for a dog, he would go the whole hog and get her a puppy. The final garnish on his perfect family.

Thea turned and started to retrace her route back across the bay towards the town. The beach was a little busier now, but it was still only locals. It was too early for the day-trippers. Thea was aware it was a little rich to class herself amongst the residents, but so complete had been her adoption of Lilian's habits that she felt she could justify her claim. An honorary temporary resident perhaps? As she was reflecting on her submersion in small-town life, she noticed the figure of a lone man among the couples, joggers and dog walkers. Two things made him stand out. First, his smart trousers, which were obviously not designed for beachcombing and, second, his gait. Whereas everyone else was either strolling or running, he was walking with a strange, intense purpose that seemed odd on a beach. Her attention snagged, her eyes tracked him, her brain creaked and finally caught up. It was Simon.

No, of course it wasn't. What the hell would Simon be doing up in Bamburgh at this time on a Friday morning? He was at home, sulking.

Then he shouted her name.

Or he shouted something because, as the realisation of who it might be dawned, Thea turned away. She didn't want to risk an encounter with Denise's abandoned husband. She picked up her own pace, which was tricky on the powdery sand. She didn't look round, conscious that do so would indicate some form of recognition. There were no footsteps, but then again there wouldn't be – sand was good for stealth, but not for speed. After a few of minutes of ungainly progress she became aware of someone closing in behind her.

'Thea?'

There was no faking ignorance now. She turned toward him. 'Oh. Hello.' The surprise in her voice was nearly convincing.

'Didn't you hear me shouting?'

'No. Sorry.'

They were both slightly out of breath.

Simon looked different from the last time she'd seen him. Although his clothes were inappropriate and he was clutching his shoes like a total townie, the stubbly, dishevelled look suited him – it took his normally clean-cut appearance somewhere more interesting. Stuck for what to say next, Thea glanced down at his feet, which, like all feet, were thin-skinned and curiously vulnerable-looking.

'Have you spoken to my wife yet?' There it was. Virtually the first thing out of his mouth was clarification of ownership.

'Not this morning.'

'Ah.' He stroked his shadowed chin and flashed a knowing smile. It was almost laughable. He was acting like a TV detective. 'She's gone back to the house.'

That threw Thea slightly, but she matched his smile. 'I'll see her there then.' So that's where Denise had been: an early-morning tryst with her husband. Denise hadn't said he was coming up to Bamburgh. Was that because she didn't want Thea to know or because she hadn't known herself?

'To pack.' His smile was beginning to get on Thea's nerves. 'She's coming home with me.'

So that was why he looked so pleased with himself. Thea removed an imaginary strand of hair from her composed, untroubled face. 'Is she?'

'Yes.' He was obviously expecting more from her. And although she was feeling a little shaken by his news, she was damned if she was going to show it.

His smile dropped away and his expression became serious. 'I'd appreciate it if you'd back off a little when you get home yourself.'

Thea didn't deign to give his statement a response. She felt angry – with him, yes, but she also felt let down by Denise. So much for all her talk about taking control of her life and making changes. Half an hour with her husband and she was running home. He was still waiting for Thea to agree to forgo 'his' Denise. 'Back off?' she asked, faking confusion.

'I mean, give her a bit of space.'

'From?'

He obviously didn't want to say 'you!', although he plainly meant it. He repositioned his sinking feet – sand was such a bugger to maintain good posture on. 'You've been spending a considerable amount of time together, which I'm not averse to, but Denise has a lot on her plate and she has a habit of making time for other people, then having none left for herself.'

That was rich, coming from him. 'I wasn't aware that I was one of Denise's responsibilities.'

'That's not what I meant.' He looked agitated. 'I simply meant she has a full diary.'

'And it's surely up to Denise how she chooses to fill it.'

'Indeed it is.'

They stared at each other, the politeness that masked their dislike thinning by the second.

On reflection, he seemed to decide to dispose of his pretence at civility. 'This trip...' he gestured at the offending beach with his shoes, 'was your idea, wasn't it?'

'It was.' She smiled. 'I had planned to travel on my own, but I mentioned it to Denise and she was keen to come with me. And she seems to have enjoyed being away.' He appeared to be trying not to blink, literally and metaphorically. 'We're here, in Bamburgh, because *your* wife wanted to spend some time with *her* mother.' She pushed harder. 'Something she never seems to get time to do normally, given how busy she is with work, and the boys, and her many responsibilities,' she left a pause, 'including chasing around after *your* father.'

Simon's face stiffened, the inconvenient truths making his lips thin and his jaw jut. By the second, he was becoming less and less attractive. He pulled at his collar, loosening up for his next salvo. He pushed back. 'But the rest of it – the track day, the checking into random pubs, this midlife crisis masquerading as a road trip – is, I presume, all you!'

His rudeness fired her up. 'Oh that. Yes, all that "madness" is me.' She put on her best smile. 'But you're missing out some of the best bits. Hasn't Denise told you about the tattoo parlour?' Did Simon blanch beneath his tan? She liked to imagine so. 'And The Rage Rooms? They were a revelation. All that smashing and destruction. Very cathartic. It's something you should maybe consider. I'm sure carrying all that tension in your shoulders can't be good for your golf swing.' She was having fun now.

He plainly wasn't. 'Look, Thea. All I'm asking is that you give Denise and me some space. There's no need to get arsey about it.'

'Me. Arsey? I don't think I'm the one behaving like an arsehole.'

He looked at her and his eyes hardened. 'Look, just leave us alone.'

It was so childish that she laughed. 'Or else?' It was the laugh that seemed to tip him over the edge.

He flushed an unsightly pink and stepped towards her. 'You might think this is funny, but it isn't. My marriage is no laughing matter.'

Thea gave him her best indifferent shrug. 'Perhaps that's the problem, Simon. Not enough laughing all round.' Fury flashed across his face. She stood her ground. He stood his. Both of them poised, ready for another round.

After a second or two Thea became aware of a figure standing a few feet away. They appeared to have an audience for their puerile spat.

Denise.

'What's going on?' She looked confused, as well she might.

Simon was quick to reassure her. 'Nothing. I came for a stroll on the beach and I happened to bump into Thea.'

Thea looked from Denise to her husband, curious as to how this was going to play out. 'Simon and I were just discussing the highlights of our trip.'

Denise's response was surprisingly direct. 'You were arguing.'

'No.' Simon was swift in his denial.

Thea stirred the pot. 'Oh, I think we were, Simon.'

His colour deepened, revealing his struggling emotions. 'It doesn't matter.'

He took a step back, clearly wanting to break up their little conflab, but Denise didn't move. 'It does matter.'

Denise and Simon were staring at each with an intensity that Thea found unsettling, there was so much emotion compressed into it. She was suddenly assailed by an awareness that she was meddling in something she shouldn't be: namely, a marriage that was at a turning point. They needed to sort out whatever was going wrong in their relationship, and Denise could hardly do that while she was gadding around the country with her. Thea had no wish to contribute to another marriage imploding.

The only decent option open to her was to retire as swiftly and as gracefully as she could.

'Anyway. Nice as it's been chatting to you, Simon' – she still didn't like the guy – 'I have to be getting along.' There was an awkward pause. Neither of them looked at her. 'Bye.'

The bigger person walked away.

She started walking.

Chapter 50

DENISE WATCHED Thea stride away up the beach. She stumbled slightly in her haste to get away from them – from Simon. Who could blame her? Denise kept watching until her friend was a long way away and only then did she turn and face her husband. He was an odd colour, his skin mottled: a consequence of repressed emotion, or more accurately repressed anger. In that moment she was so disappointed in him that she had to look away. She turned instead to stare at the sea.

She'd heard his aggressive tone, his default to rudeness in the face of something he didn't like, and didn't understand. Upset or not, there was no excuse for him speaking to Thea like that. Or for blaming her for their current difficulties. The assumption that Thea was the root cause of the problem irritated her, deeply. It proved that Simon hadn't really listened to what she'd just told him about her feelings and her needs.

The longer she stared at the waves and ignored his pleas for her to 'say something', the angrier she became.

When she'd left him outside the pub her mind had been made up – it was time to go back, for the sake of her family and her marriage. It was not what she wanted to do, but it was what she believed was necessary, and right. The trip had restored her. It was time to put that new-found sense of herself to use, and she could only do that at home.

But the thought of returning to Lilian's small cottage and popping the lustrous bubble that she, Thea and her mother had created made Denise sad. And so she delayed, wanting to avoid breaking the news of her departure a little while longer. Instead she headed down to the bay and sat on a wall. The sun was coming up, the beach was dotted with early walkers and runners, the air was fresh. It looked idyllic. It *was* idyllic. She breathed deep, trying to take some small portion of the calmness and beauty into her soul to carry home with her. As she sat basking in the sun, she slipped her hand into the pocket of her cardigan and took out her phone. She brought up the photo Thea had taken of the two of them at Silverstone – their heads close together, their laughter captured in their wide smiles and their glittering eyes. It was an image of pure, unadulterated happiness.

It was a joy that she'd been looking for, for a long time, without even realising it. A joy she was reluctant to let go.

One last glance and she slipped her phone back in her pocket, something to treasure and aspire to. She looked out across the bay. It was a little busier now, people drawn out for an early-morning stroll by the sunshine – and amongst them were Thea and Simon. They were standing together halfway up the beach. Denise's surprise was tinged with a faint edge of hope. They were having a conversation. Their first without her presence. She watched, intrigued, trying to guess from the body language what was being said. Maybe meeting in person, in such a beautiful setting, would give them a chance to...

But no. They were arguing. Even from this distance, the negative energy between them was obvious. It was there in the stiffness of Simon's pose and in the whip of Thea's arms.

Her heart squeezed.

She stood up and set off towards them, hurrying to get there before something was said that could not be unsaid.

'Denise?' Simon was still waiting.

She turned back to face him. 'What?'

'Why are we still here? Why haven't you gone back to your mum's and packed up your stuff, like we agreed? I want us to go home, together.'

They both heard it in his voice: the uncertainty.

It mirrored her own. She knew she had to say something right here, right now, about her relationship with Thea – if she didn't, it would be tantamount to giving up on it.

'There was no need to speak to Thea like that.'

'I'm sorry, Denise, but I can't lie. I don't like her.'

'But I do.'

They looked at each other, silently testing limits that in the past they'd known so well, but which were now unclear.

Simon paused, then chose to assert his view. 'But you have to concede that she's come between us.'

'I do not concede that.' He opened and closed his mouth, but no words came out. 'Thea's friendship is important to me. I need you to recognise that.' She was not going to back down, not any more, and certainly not about this.

'But surely it's not more important than us.'

Why did it have to be either/or?

Why could she not have Thea *and* her marriage?

There, on the beach, with the sun on her face and Simon looking at her expectantly, Denise decided that she could, and would, have both.

Chapter 51

SHE WAS sad to see them go, but pleased they were leaving together.

Their adventure wasn't over yet.

A few years younger, and Lilian might well have gone with them.

Simon showing up had put the cat among the pigeons, but from what she could make out, it was the cat who'd fared worse, for a change. He'd left just as suddenly as he'd arrived, and the girls had lived on to fight another day.

They hadn't wanted her to get up with them, given how early they were leaving, but she'd insisted. She was used to rising with the sun, it was often the best part of the day. And today's dawn had been spectacular. A good omen.

They moved around the kitchen quietly, mindful of the neighbours, not speaking much. There was no need, they were comfortable with each other now. Their eyes met occasionally as they drank their tea and ate their toast. After they'd finished breakfast, Lilian presented them with their gifts. A cardigan each from her wardrobe, freshly laundered and finished with ribbon. The red one for Thea. The sky-blue one for Denise. A small part of her, to go on their journey with them. There was the threat of tears, but she averted them by saying she would accompany them to the car to say goodbye. Besides, the walk would be good for her, it would loosen her up for her swim.

Thea's Mini looked like it had been abandoned for weeks rather than a few days. The roof was covered in sap and the windscreen looked equally sticky. They stowed their bags and Thea slammed the boot.

'Have a good time.' Lilian hugged them both in turn. Thea was the one to hold on for a fraction longer than necessary. 'It's been lovely having you to stay. Come back soon.' Denise promised they would, and Lilian believed her.

Then there was a slightly strange moment when Thea offered the car keys to Denise. Denise shook her head and said, 'No. It's okay. You drive today.' In that moment something passed between the two of them – an understanding that was known only to themselves. Whatever they were to each other, it mattered.

Thea climbed into the driver's seat and pulled the door shut.

Lilian took Denise's hands in her own and gave her one last look. She was happy with what she saw. Whatever her daughter decided about her future, Lilian was sure, for the first time in a very long time, that it would be for the best – Denise's best, not everyone else's. 'I'm so glad you happened to be "in the area".'

Denise smiled. 'You never know, Mam, I might stray up north again next month. It's been lovely. It really has.'

'That would be good.' They kissed.

Denise climbed in beside Thea. Lilian stepped back, just in time to avoid the spray of water from the wipers. They squeaked as they laboured away, clearing the gunk off the windscreen. When Thea could see, she edged the car carefully out of its tight spot and drove away.

After they'd gone, the street fell silent.

Lilian turned and walked home, determined to do an extra two lengths of the bay in honour of their visit.

Chapter 52

THE SKY was filled with purple-tinted clouds.

The sun was coming up.

The roof was down.

The roads were clear.

Thea drove fast, following the smooth contours of the coast road with ease. Denise tilted her head back and felt the warmth of the new day hit her face.

They were mistresses of their universe.

As the sun rose higher, the road started to narrow and climb. After a few miles, Thea turned off. A plume of dust rose in their wake as they rolled and bumped along the unmarked track. Denise had no idea where they were. They drove on, away from or towards something – she no longer cared.

After another ten minutes or so Thea swung the car around a bend and brought it to a stop.

They'd reached the end of the road.

In front of them was a stretch of scrubby grass, the sky and the cliff edge. Away to the left, on the headland, sat a lighthouse, a curiously squat affair topped with a black-capped dome. Beyond it the coast unfurled in a seemingly never-ending series of rocky inlets. Denise heard the sea heaving and crashing somewhere far below. Above them the gulls wheeled and screamed.

'Where the hell are we?'

'St Abb's Head.' The wind whipped Thea's hair across her face. 'Isn't it beautiful?'

'It is.'

They sat, side-by-side, taking in the view. The grandeur of it silenced them both. They'd been travelling together for barely a week, but in that moment Denise felt closer to Thea than she had to anyone else in her entire life. She wanted Thea to know that. 'You're a good friend.'

Thea smiled. 'You, too.'

Denise breathed in the fresh, sharp air. She caught sight of her reflection in Thea's sunglasses: her hair a mess, not a scrap of make-up on her face, her nose and cheeks tinged red with sunburn. She looked good. Even more importantly, she felt good – the best she'd felt in a very long time. So much had changed since they'd left home, not least Denise herself. She was a different person, happier, freer, braver, and that was due, in large part, to the woman sitting next to her. Simon might be unsure about this new, assertive incarnation, but Denise liked her. She liked her a lot.

They fell silent again, reflecting on what they'd learnt about themselves, and each other, over the past few hectic, revelatory days.

Indifferent to the presence of such wise women in their midst, the gulls rose and fell at the cliff edge. Their screaming and flapping reminded Denise of the problems mounting and massing at their backs. Real life was going to catch up with them eventually. They couldn't keep running for ever.

Although up on that wild, isolated promontory, with the sun shining down on them, and the wind blowing in off the sea, it felt like perhaps they could.

'So,' Denise finally asked, 'what do you want to do?'

Thea looked at the limitless sky stretching out beyond the cliff edge and said, 'Keep going.'

Denise laughed. She got the reference: Thelma and Louise, holding hands as they chose oblivion over capture, the perfect ending – for a film. 'But that would be a waste of a perfectly nice car, and the rest of our lives.'

Thea opened her door. 'I'm going to take a closer look.'

Denise lingered; heights were not her thing. Thank heavens Thea had forgone the bungee jump in Middlesbrough. She watched Thea walk towards the cliff edge. When she ran out of ground she stopped and looked out at the view, her back to the car. Denise watched her raise her hands to her head and untie her ponytail. The wind grabbed her hair and whipped it around her head. In that moment she looked like the Greek goddess of her name. That whimsical thought was immediately followed by another, far less fanciful one – Thea was standing very close to the edge. Denise grabbed her jacket and went to join her.

The last few steps were a true test of friendship.

The drop was stomach-turning. Denise barely glanced at it. Sharp rocks, floating birds, churning waves. She quickly raised her eyes to the horizon and tried to regain her equilibrium. The urge to reach out and grab hold of

Thea was strong, but she didn't. Making any sudden moves seemed ill advised, this close to the brink. 'Wow, again.'

'Yes. It's something, isn't it?' Thea scanned the view, seemingly unperturbed by the promise of certain death only a few centimetres from her toes.

'Have you been here before?' St Abb's must mean something to Thea – why else was it on the itinerary?

'No.' A strand of hair blew across Thea's mouth. She left it there. 'Just another Google find.'

The combination of their precarious position and the racket from the gulls was getting too much for Denise. 'Can we walk on a bit?' Anything to get Thea away from the edge.

She finally stopped staring out at the horizon. 'Yeah. Sure.'

They backtracked, found the footpath and started walking along the clifftop. Denise felt her vertigo begin to settle. Thea was quiet. The views, from a safe distance, were spectacular. They'd been walking for a good ten minutes before Denise spoke again. 'It's sad that this is our last day together.' She had insisted on one last hurrah before returning home. Simon, though plainly disappointed and deeply irritated, had not been in a position to argue. She'd been very clear with him: Thea was part of her life now and he was going to have to get used to that – along with a few other changes.

Thea nodded, but said nothing.

'How long will you stay with your brother?'

'A couple of days, tops.'

'And then you'll head back?'

Thea shrugged and kept walking.

Denise had assumed that Edinburgh would be the last stop on Thea's trip, but she'd been sketchy about her plans all along. The vagueness and the shrug nibbled at Denise's subconscious. 'Are you planning on staying away for longer then?'

'I might.'

Denise picked up the warning tone, and she now knew that warnings shouldn't be ignored. 'But if you're tired, why not head home?'

'Who said I was tired?'

No one had, at least not out loud, but Thea still didn't look right to Denise. She was as beautiful as ever, but there was definitely something amiss. Why else did the shadows under her eyes seem to be getting darker each day? Why had Thea's energy evaporated?

But of course Thea was having none of it. 'I'm not sure I'm ready to go back yet. I quite fancy going seal-spotting off Orkney and drinking a skinful of malt whisky on the Isle of Mull.' Not for the first time, Denise thought she detected a note of forced jollity within Thea's ebullience. Simon's bitter description of their time away returned to her – a 'midlife crisis masquerading as a road trip'. Denise watched the high clouds scudding across the sky. As infuriating as his comment had been, it wasn't wrong. They had been running away, but whereas Denise now knew what she was fleeing in her old life – namely, her own uncertainty – and, perhaps, how to change it, Thea's motivations for the trip were still opaque. Denise simply didn't believe that turning fifty was what was driving her. It was obviously far more complicated than that.

Denise stopped walking. Thea continued, until she realised that Denise was no longer following behind her. She turned round. 'Have you seen enough majestic splendour for one morning?'

'No. Or, rather, yes. It's stunning, but the view's not what I'm interested in.'

'Denise, please don't go all cryptic on me.'

'I'm not the one who's being cryptic.' Thea made a despairing gesture with her hands and started to turn away. Denise felt a flutter of desperation. 'Thea, please talk to me.'

'I am talking to you.'

'Not about the view or your next adventure. I know there's something going on that you're not telling me.'

'What is this? On the couch with Denise?'

Denise literally stood her ground. 'If you want it to be, yes.'

Thea shook her head. 'There's no need, thank you. Please don't spoil our last few hours together by going all weird.'

'I'm sorry if you think I'm being "weird", but I'm worried about you.'

Thea smiled, a smile that was plainly calculated to throw Denise off the scent. 'There's no need.'

Denise was very aware that time was running out. If not now, then when? 'This has never been "just a little holiday", has it, Thea? Not for me, or for you. The list. All the "things to do before you're fifty" stuff. It's some sort of pilgrimage, isn't it? My concern is that there seems to be no end in sight.'

'You've got it all wrong.'

The awful realisation that she hadn't was growing inside Denise. Memories, images, fragments of conversation came back to her. Thea behaving so recklessly, and yet at the same time being so vulnerable, with the man at the hotel. The

322

symbolism of the little tree frog – a homage to a daughter with whom she seemed to have such difficult relationship. Thea's repressed anger as she smashed up her life with such clinical efficiency in The Rage Rooms. The look on Thea's face when she nearly crashed the car. Thea's bereft crying as they sat by that depressing lake at the motorway services afterwards. Thea's docile, dreamy passivity at her mother's home. And, most worrying of all, Thea standing dangerously close to the cliff edge, with her hair blowing wildly around her head.

'Then tell me what you're planning.'

'That's none of your business.'

'It is.'

'No, it isn't. We've had a blast, but you're going home and I'm not. If you're jealous of me being free to do what I want, when I want, with whoever I want... then I'm afraid that's your problem.'

Denise didn't flinch from Thea's sudden cruelty. She'd learnt some bravery over the course of the past seven days. She might not have conquered her fear of heights and needles, but she was no longer afraid of speaking her mind. 'I smell bullshit, Thea. This trailing around the country, having one mad experience after another, doing things for the sake of it. I don't think this is what you really want – not any more.'

They faced off on the path. Both, when all was said and done, were as stubborn as each other.

Below them the sea crashed. Above them the gulls screamed.

'How could you possibly understand what I what I do, or don't, want?' Thea shouted.

Denise knew the answer to that. 'Because I'm your friend.' She reached out her hand. 'And if you don't tell me what you're really running away from, then I swear to God, I'll never go home and you'll be stuck with me for ever.'

Chapter 53

Denise was a terrier, once she'd sunk her teeth into you there was no letting go – which was simultaneously intensely irritating and strangely touching. It was a long time since anyone had been so tenacious in their pursuit of Thea's innermost thoughts. Which was why, after a few long seconds of them glaring at each other, she allowed Denise to guide her away from the drama of the clifftop towards the placid shelter of some nearby rocks.

She sat down on the ground.

Denise plonked herself next to her. 'So?'

'God, you're persistent.' Thea pulled at the grass. It was so tough and well rooted that none came away in her hand.

Denise nodded. 'A few of your traits have rubbed off on me. That's a compliment, by the way.'

Hunkered down, in their semicircle of stones, they were out of the wind. It felt safe, but still not safe enough for Thea to fully offload the toxins she was carrying around inside her.

In the absence of the requested emotional outpouring,

Denise did what she did best – which was talk. 'This trip has been the best thing to happen to me in a very long time. You know that, because you've seen the impact it's had on me – on the way I think about myself, who I am. But we can't keep running for ever. It's not the way the world works. We have to go back and face our real lives. If we don't, nothing will change. Not really.'

Thea noticed and appreciated Denise's use of the plural. Female solidarity had its advantages and its comforts, but she needed to make it clear that Denise's chosen path was not her own. Denise had a chance of fixing the problems in her life. Thea did not. 'I know that you need to go back to sort things out with Simon, but I can't get out of the mess I'm in.'

'Of course you can!'

Denise sounded and looked so convinced that Thea had a sudden urge to lean over and kiss her. But one woman's restored faith in herself and her own superpowers did not guarantee a happy ending for everyone.

'Is this about Ella?' she asked.

Thea said nothing. Terrier Denise sat it out. Thea gave up on trying to uproot the turf. She found a small rock and threw it. It travelled a satisfyingly long way before disappearing into the rippling grass. She searched for another. Denise leant back and rested her hands in her lap, clearly indicating that she was in no rush, which was a sign of how much she'd changed – the 11 a.m. Edinburgh Waverley to London King's Cross wasn't going to wait for her.

After six more throws Thea started talking. Because? Because she trusted Denise. And that's what friends did, they shared. 'I told Ella about Marc being unfaithful. We've never said anything about it before. Infidelity wasn't cited as the reason for divorce, we went for irretrievable breakdown, to ensure everything stayed "amicable". We – I – have spent years lying, to protect her.'

'Why did you tell her now?'

'Because I panicked when she said she wanted to move in with Marc. I was frightened she was going to leave and never come back.'

'And you thought telling her might make her stay?'

'Yes. Or maybe I just hoped it would put a dent in her adoration of him.'

'But it didn't.'

'No.'

'Oh, Thea.'

'She was shocked, of course, but she was also furious – not with him; with me. I tried to damage her relationship with her dad because of jealousy and she was smart enough to see straight through that. The paperwork for him having full custody is going through now. So I achieved the exact opposite of what I wanted... at the time.' Thea closed her eyes for a few seconds.

'Why on earth didn't you tell me any of this before? I knew there was something going on,' Denise said.

'There was nothing you could do. And besides, it was my fault. I brought it on myself.'

'But she's living just across the street from me.'

'And that gives me some comfort. I like the thought of you being close to her.'

'Will you contest the custody arrangements?'

'No.' Thea picked up another rock. Hurled it. This time it dropped short of the grass.

'But she's your daughter. Given time, she'll come round.'

Thea held up her hand before Denise could reach for a reassuring platitude. 'I've come to the conclusion that she's better off with Marc.'

'You mustn't say that.'

'Why not? It's true.'

'But she will need you. You don't ever stop needing your mum. You must persevere. Let her know how much you regret the way you handled it. That you'll always be there for her.'

At that, Thea winced and moved away. 'That would be your way of dealing with it. It's not mine.' Denise was obviously about to come up with another of her other well-intentioned insights, so Thea cut in. 'I'm not the type of mother you are, Denise. Marc has always been the better parent.'

'That doesn't mean—'

'Denise! Please listen.' Her abruptness had the desired effect. Denise clamped her lips shut. 'It's always assumed that women are the nurturers, the carers, the home-makers; that we are maternal naturally, because of our biology. But I'm not. I never have been. I've always had to work at it. Getting pregnant was a struggle for me. Carrying Ella wasn't easy. Raising her has been hard. I'm just not suited to it. And please trust me on this, because the one thing getting older brings is some degree of self-awareness. I know that I need more than I give. I have in the past, and I will in the future. That's not good for any child, especially a teenager. It's not good for any marriage. For any friendship.' The hint was there. It was the end of the road for them as well.

But Denise being Denise, she chose to ignore the message. 'So your plan is to do what? Abandon your daughter and run away because you've had a bust-up? That makes no sense.' She sounded angry, which was perhaps unsurprising, because selflessness could look very like selfishness, if you didn't have the context. And poor Denise had only a fraction of the full story.

'I'm going to do whatever I want, at least for a little while.'

Denise slumped back against the rock, her exasperation getting away from her. Thea sympathised, but offered nothing to reduce it. Break-ups always hurt, but a swift and brutal end was better than a slow, lingering decline.

Suddenly, inexplicably, the sky above their heads cleared of the birds and the clifftop fell quiet. There was nothing but the wind and the sound of distant waves. Thea watched Denise. She imagined she could actually see the respect and affection they'd built up this week draining away. Denise refused to meet her eye. She was looking skywards, clearly trying to swallow down her disappointment. But when she did finally speak, it was calmly.

'I've known you for two months. It's nothing, in the grand scale of things. I appreciate that. I can't and don't presume to understand the complexities of your life and your relationships. And the pressures you're so obviously under. But after this past week, I believe that I've got to know the real you. And I know you're not a quitter.' She dropped her gaze so that it met Thea's. 'You said, when you were talking about Ella, *I achieved the exact opposite of what I wanted...*

at the time.' What I don't understand is why you're giving up *now*? What's changed?'

'It meant nothing.'

'I love you and respect you, Thea, but you're lying. There's something else going on. Something worse than what's happening with your daughter. However bad it is, I want you to tell me.'

Thea looked out at the view, thought about the cliff edge and the drop. What was bravery? What cowardice? She didn't know any more. And she was sick – so sick of holding it all in.

'My cancer has come back.'

Denise took hold of her hand, lightly, and pulled it into her lap. Thea did not resist. 'Sorry.' That was it – one word. Suddenly, finally, Denise appeared to have discovered brevity.

'You don't seem surprised.'

The frown that had been creasing Denise's forehead disappeared. She looked and sounded calm, pleased almost, like she'd finally worked out a particularly tricky clue on a crossword. 'Beneath all the bravado, I could sense you were frightened.'

'I was.' Simplicity had its virtues. 'But I decided, this time around, I had a choice. Go back to the oncology department and start treatment all over again, or head off on my road trip. I think I chose well.'

They looked around them. St Abb's was a truly spectacular setting for the confession of secrets.

Denise smiled and squeezed her hand. 'You did.'

They sat with their backs against the warm rock and the

hard ground beneath their backsides, content to share the moment for a while.

Thea was impressed. Denise managed to hold off the hope-counselling for a good few minutes, before, as expected, she cracked. 'You beat it before. And...' she added hastily, 'they haven't even established what the problem is yet, have they?' She had the sensitivity to sound hesitant.

Thea smiled, because what else could she do? 'I didn't "beat" it last time, Denise. I had it cut, and blasted, out of me.'

'But it worked. You recovered. You will again.'

Thea felt more tired than she'd ever done before. It was a fatigue that went way beyond the beginnings of her physical frailty. Hope was hard. Second time around, without Marc at her side, it felt impossible. 'No. I can't do it again. And I don't want to. I'm done fighting.'

'But you're the fiercest, feistiest person I know.' Denise was obviously, despite her composed exterior, shocked and upset – as Thea had known she would be.

This was another thing Thea couldn't face: other people's distress. Not Denise's. Not her mother's. And certainly not Ella's. She refused to put Ella through it all again. 'Thank you for the vote of confidence, Denise, but I really can't stomach the thought of the treatment, and all the endless waiting, and hoping, and the long slog of praying and obsessing about being ill. And I'm afraid your chances don't improve the second time round. It's one of those areas of life where experience, sadly, doesn't count in your favour.' She could see that Denise was struggling with her tone, but it was really the only way Thea knew how to cope with the situation she found herself in. She had to mock it and defy it – anything else would allow the panic to set in. And Thea was determined not to panic. She was going to maintain control, because it was all she had left.

It was time to convince Denise of that.

'Ella is settled with Marc and his new family. My mum is being well cared for. She'll be fine as long as someone keeps her supplied with gin. Maybe that's something you can do for me every now and again, when you're in seeing the old bastard? Work will be fine without me.'

'So are you saying you're never coming back?'

'That's the plan.' Thea watched as Denise's suspicions solidified. The darkness pooled between them, despite the clear blue sky. Denise actually shivered. Thea felt for her. What could she say? This was precisely why she hadn't told her. Why she hadn't told anyone. Not that she thought Denise would be able to talk her out of it, but because it was too heavy a burden to lay on a friend. It was time for the kind lie. 'I'm going to keep travelling as long as I can. When I run out of places to visit and things to do, I'll come back to Edinburgh. My brother will be around to help. I'll be fine until I'm not, then I'll be looked after. It's better this way. Ella will be used to not having me around by the time I can't be. I won't be missed. Well, not too badly or for too long.'

'I will miss you.'

Thea smiled. 'Yeah, I'm sorry about that, but you snuck under my defences when I was in a weakened state.'

'Please, Thea! Please think about the implications of what you're saying.'

'I have. I've thought of nothing else since I got the call from the hospital... well, apart from a few glorious times with you this past week. I know, in my bones, that I can't do it again. Not on my own.'

As Thea watched Denise struggle with her emotions she felt real sorrow, not for herself, but for her friend. It was cruel that they'd met too late for their relationship to properly take root and grow.

They would never get beyond this day.

This was it.

The end of their road.

And the end of their friendship.

The birds were back, adding their loud cries to Denise's silent ones.

Denise let go of Thea's hands. She scrubbed at her cheeks with her fists, lifted her chin and said, 'You're not on your own. You've got me.'

PART THREE

Chapter 54

FOR OCTOBER the weather was benign, dry and overcast, not cold. There was no need for scarves and gloves, which was a good job because Denise never could locate her nice black leather pair. The left-hand glove had hung around in the dresser in the kitchen for years, but its mate had never shown up. Every time she'd opened the drawer and seen it she'd been determined to throw it away, but somehow she'd never got round to it. It was probably still there, waiting for her to make up her mind.

Denise stood apart, watching the guests arrive in their smart coats and freshly shone shoes. They all had the same hesitancy that came with attendance at a funeral: the obvious keenness to get it over with, but also an acute wariness of getting the etiquette wrong. No one was ever certain whether it was good or bad form to wait until the arrival of the hearse before taking one's seat and staring at the empty space at the front of the chapel. Hence the appearance of the crematorium staff, who began encouraging the little knots of people inside to take their places. There would be another service within the hour – grief ran on a tight schedule. Denise watched until every one of the mourners had been gathered up and herded into the chapel, then she turned her attention to the sky. It was a canvas of oatmeal nothingness. How apt.

There was no putting it off.

She re-joined her family under the awning, slotting herself in between Simon and the boys. They said nothing, which was understandable. They were nervous. Denise was glad that pall-bearing was still a largely male preserve. She simply couldn't have done it.

The quiet was disturbed by the sound of a vehicle coming up the drive. She felt Simon stiffen in anticipation, but it wasn't the hearse. It was a car, travelling too fast for the occasion or the gravel. As it shot past the entrance to the chapel, Denise saw the driver mime an exaggerated apology. There were no nearby parking spots available. Undeterred, the driver bumped the Mini up onto a raised kerb alongside one of the formal flower beds, flattening a rose bush in the process. The engine died. Simon made a noise that conveyed disgust and expectation.

'I'm so sorry.' Thea clattered towards them, all jangling car keys, flapping coat sleeves and glossy handbag. 'I got lost.' She kissed Denise on both cheeks. She knew better than to do likewise with Simon or the boys. 'I'll just grab a seat at the back. See you on the other side.' The steward held open the door for her and she disappeared inside, trailing perfume in her wake. The phrase *she'd be late for her own funeral* popped into Denise's head. It took a huge amount of restraint to stop the smile in her heart from reaching her face.

On cue, the hearse appeared at the bottom of the driveway.

Showtime.

'You are coming back to the golf club, aren't you?' Simon asked afterwards.

It was the expected thing to do – drink weak tea or warm white, and make small talk with Simon's many elderly relatives – but she really didn't want to. If Simon and the boys had been distraught, she would have stayed close by them, of course she would; but it would be stretching the truth to the point of no return to claim that Eric's death had occasioned much sorrow. Life would be simpler and far less onerous for everyone without the old man in it. And whilst his passing – which, ironically, had been peacefully in his sleep, in the middle of the night – was sad, it was not enough to persuade Denise that her place was at Simon's side for the full duration of the wake.

'I'll be along in a little while.' She looked over at Thea. She was standing with her back to the crowd, looking out at the rows of headstones. 'I want to grab a word with Thea first.'

Simon said nothing. There was no reproach, no barbed comment, although Denise imagined that a few choice words must be forming in his brain. No matter how often they discussed her reasons for leaving – reasons that were deeply embedded in their marriage – Simon still preferred to blame their ongoing difficulties on Thea. This deep-seated enmity didn't trouble Thea in the slightest – the lack of respect and liking was mutual – but it did bother Denise.

Until Simon recognised her decisions and actions as hers, and hers alone, what hope was there?

'I'll see you in a little while.' She leant in and kissed his cheek. Old habits died hard: affection, familiarity, loyalty, even the lingering addiction to the smell of him. Time would tell whether such ties were strong enough to keep them together. His hand lingered in the small of her back for a second or two, then he released her, reluctantly.

She made her way over to Thea. They stood in silence, not out of respect for the dead, but out of a desire not to be overheard by Eric's departing mourners. Thea slipped her arm through Denise's. 'I spotted a bench at the top corner, if you have time.'

They set off. As they walked, Denise snuck glances at her friend. It was wise to try and assess covertly how well Thea was coping. She detested being monitored, said she got a bellyful of it at the hospital. Today her colour was okay and her pace brisk, but then again Thea was the arch proponent of faking it. The appointment on Thursday, with its dreaded update on her latest counts, would tell them more.

The bench had a covering of leaves. Thea swept them off and they deposited themselves on the creaky old slats.

'Sorry I was late.'

'Do you do it deliberately?'

'No!'

'You sure? The thought of winding Simon up didn't cross your mind?'

'No. Even I know there's no such thing as being fashionably late for a funeral. I've brought you a small gift, by the way. I thought you might be in need of some Dutch courage.' From the depths of yet another new handbag Thea extracted two Porn Star Martinis. They had such little habits, nods and catchphrases now, reminders of their trip together.

'My, you are spoiling me.'

They peeled back the ring pulls and clinked cans.

'Ding-ding!'

'Round...' Denise paused, 'what number are we on now?'

Thea smiled, tiredness suddenly writ large on her face. 'Oh, it's got to be at least a hundred.'

They took synchronised sips. Either Thea had bothered to chill the cans or they had been sitting in the boot of her car for days, because they tasted surprisingly good – sweet, cold, strong enough to hit the spot.

'Thanks for coming.'

'My pleasure.'

'Hardly,' Denise smiled.

Thea laughed. 'I wanted to double-check that the old bastard was absolutely, definitely dead.' Denise feigned shock and took another sip. 'Any change between you and Simon? Grief can, reputedly, make some people horny.'

Denise shook her head. 'We're doing okay. Taking it a day at a time.'

'That's hardly a ringing endorsement.'

'"Okay" is better than where we were. It's not his fault – it's me. I can't make up my mind what I want.'

'Has he stopped nagging you about the flat?'

'He wasn't "nagging". He just wants me to come home, for us to be a family again. He's actually being remarkably patient, although I think the effort is knocking years off his life.'

'Are you going to move back in?'

Denise took another swig of her drink. 'I have to decide whether to extend my lease or not before Christmas. She has another tenant interested.'

There must have been something in the way she said it, because Thea raised a querying eyebrow. 'You love that little flat, with its depressing view and totally inadequate wardrobe space, don't you?'

'I don't love it, but it's a been a good, practical stopgap while we sort things out.' Denise felt disloyal, preferring her spartan one-bedroomed box to the space and comfort of Prospect Crescent, but the truth was that she did. She liked the smallness of the fridge, and the okayness of said fridge sometimes containing nothing more than a bottle of wine and some cheese. She loved that one bath towel was enough, and that there was always hot water and Pears soap, and no one else's washing in the basket. She liked watching and eating and doing what she liked, when she liked.

She really was turning into her mother.

Thea's 'Yeah, right' put an end to the topic. They finished their drinks and Thea tossed the cans, one after the other, into the bin, getting them both in. With her back to Denise she said, 'I wanted to ask you something.'

'Shoot.'

She still didn't meet Denise's eye. 'I know you've got Thursday in your calendar.'

'I have.' Denise felt a draught of unease. Surely Thea couldn't be intending to skip the appointment. She thought they'd got through all that madness.

'It's just…' Denise started dusting off the old arguments. 'What I mean is… I appreciate each and every time you've come with me and held my hand through all this.'

'But…' Denise prompted impatiently.

'But Ella has asked if she can come with me.'

Relief flooded through Denise. 'That's great.'

'You think?'

'Yes. Don't you?' Yes, of course Denise did. As milestones went, this was an important one for Thea and Ella. One that it had looked extremely doubtful they would reach, a few months back.

Thea shoved her hands into her coat pockets. 'I'm touched she wants to come with me, but I'm worried that it'll all be too much for her. You know what Mr Tennant is like. Honest to the point of brutality. What if it's bad news? How will she cope? I don't want her worrying.'

'You mean more than she is now?'

'But it's different, isn't it? Being there. In the hospital. Seeing everyone with their jaunty headscarves and their polite desperation. I want to protect her from that.'

'You know her better than me, she's your girl, but I think if she wants to come with you, you should let her. It's going to be difficult, for both of you, but it might be important for your relationship. Perhaps you need to start being more honest with her. That's what she's been asking for, isn't it?'

Thea visibly flinched. Her history with Ella and the truth was obviously not good.

Denise tried to soften her last comment. 'What I mean is, protecting her from the reality of what you're going through could be seen as another way of shutting her out.'

'She's only sixteen.'

'Yes. I know.' Denise took Thea's hand. 'I do understand what you're saying. Being a mum is all about standing in front of your kids, absorbing as many blows as you can. But I've met Ella. She's strong, and sensible. Maybe even as strong as her mother.'

Thea looked off into the distance. Swallowed. Then screamed, 'Fuck!' – loud and furious.

Denise waited, expecting more. There was none. Just the rustle of the wind in the trees, and the faint strains of music coming from the next funeral service. 'Feel better for that?'

'Nope.'

'Would you like me to come with you and Ella to the hospital on Thursday?'

'Fuck, yes.'

'Feel like coming to Eric's funeral tea at a golf club in return?'

'Fuck, no!'

'Are you done with the gratuitous swearing?'

'Fuck, yes.'

'Want a hug?'

'Yes, please.'

Denise pulled Thea into her embrace.

And so they sat, on the rickety old bench at the top of the cemetery, as the leaves twirled down and 'One Step Beyond' rang out from the chapel below.

THE ENDING?

Chapter 55

'WHAT DID Lewis say when you asked him for the car keys?'

Denise's lips twitched, a sure sign that she was suppressing a lie.

'You didn't ask him, did you? You just took them.' Thea prompted.

Denise said nothing. The car swung round a blind bend. 'I *borrowed* them. I've left a note at the reception desk. They promised to give it to him when he comes down for breakfast.' She fumbled with the control panel for a few seconds, before finding the symbol for the windscreen wipers. They squeaked into action, increasing the visibility by a negligible degree.

Thea held on to the door handle. Loath as she was to admit it, her own love of speed had diminished with each passing birthday. It was one of the many consequences of ageing: a constant fear that Death was around the corner, sharpening his blade, getting ready to whip off your head when you were least expecting it. Denise seemed to have no such anxiety – despite the drizzle, the twisty country lanes and her seeming inability to find the de-mister. The word *dreich* drifted across Thea's brain. It was hardly blazing June. She contemplated asking Denise to let autodrive take over, but didn't, because she knew Denise was enjoying being back behind the wheel of a car, even if it was a Prius 2046.

At least there was no way they could get lost, despite the shroud-like weather. With the efficient precision that Denise's middle son seemed to do everything, Lewis had pre-loaded all their old haunts into the car's navigation system before they'd left St Albans, just as he'd helpfully made all their hotel reservations and pulled together their minute-by-minute schedule. It was a timetable that ensured he could fulfil his duties as chauffeur and still be done and dusted in time for him to fly out to his upcoming golf tournament in Dubai. This visit, unlike their last, all those years ago, was very much *not* a spontaneous event. It had been months in the preparation and the planning. People were so anxious, these days, about everything.

Hence Thea and Denise's decision to get up early, ditch polite, considerate but overly attentive Lewis and strike out on their own into the early-morning Scottish mist. This was, when all was said and done, their pilgrimage, not his.

Thankfully, as they drew closer to the coast, the sea fret started to lift and evaporate, revealing a glorious, closing-credits-worthy sunrise. The sky above them was filled with high purple clouds edged in red, through which the sun was beginning to emerge. Thea wondered briefly whether Lewis had somehow managed to order the perfect weather for them, along with everything else.

Denise took the climb up to the clifftop slowly – not out of caution, Thea suspected, but because it was too good a view to be rushed. She eventually rolled the car to a stop and killed the engine. Destination reached. They sat, side-by-side, in silence, looking at a view that had not changed in twenty-five years. It was as stunning as ever. St Abb's simply did not have it within its power to disappoint. Into their quiet contemplation the ghosts of the past came unbidden. They swirled and twisted together like ink in water. As before, sprays of black-headed gulls appeared and disappeared beyond the cliff edge like flung gravel. Sealed inside the car, Thea and Denise couldn't hear their cries.

Thea broke the spell. 'Well, we made it to old age.'

'Yeah, who'd have thought it?'

'Do you mind being old?'

Thea gave Denise's question some thought. She had no simple answer. After every bout of treatment she'd sworn to make the most of whatever lifespan she was lucky enough to cling on to, but with time and recovery, that promise had faded to a faint echo. Life had, as perhaps it should, been taken for granted, the more of it she'd been gifted. Squandered or just lived, it was not for Thea to say. The result – three grandchildren, a strong if still combative relationship with her daughter, a twenty-five years (and counting) partnership with a good man – who proved that nice was the best quality a lover could possess – and, perhaps most important of all, a quarter of a century of friendship with Denise. As a result of so much love and support, the years had flown by and had inexorably deposited Thea into old age, a hinterland she'd never imagined she would reach.

She'd been drifting. She refocused. 'It's not so bad. I like playing the mad old bird.'

'Playing?' Denise mocked.

'Fuck off!'

They both laughed, heard the cackle in their voices and laughed louder. Denise answered her own question, taking the pressure off Thea, as she increasingly did. 'Things are easier and simpler. A lot of the stuff I used to stress about doesn't seem to matter any more. Like my body. God, I used to be so unhappy about the way I looked. But I appreciate my body now. As it is – failings and all. I'm grateful to it, for keeping me going, for working, most of the time, after all that wear and tear.' Since her knee operation Denise had had a new lease of energy. She was doing Pilates and had joined a gym, much to her sons' and her grandchildren's amusement. At times her energy levels left Thea feeling exhausted.

The streaks of red in the sky lightened to a pearly pink. Thea drifted again. She was brought back by the sound of Denise's voice. 'Speaking of moving, are we actually going to get out? It's only the ill and infirm who drive to beauty spots and sit in their cars.'

And so they climbed out and wrapped their coats around them. There was still a chill in the air, despite the rising sun. They walked, arms linked, for affection and support. The closer they got to the cliff's edge, the more connected they felt, the pulse of their long friendship freshened by the sea air, the scream of the gulls and their memories.

The question, as ever, was where to stop?

Should they hang back where the grass was flat and the land solid under their feet?

Or should they edge forward to where the ground sloped away and frayed to a jagged lip?

Thea decided onwards, her steps steady if slow, and Denise kept pace with her. Thus they progressed until they ran out of earth.

At the cliff edge they looked down at the waves churning below them. As before, and as for ever, the red pillars of rock poked out of the white-capped, surging surf. The rocks looked like fingers reaching out to them. Thea held on to Denise. Her anchor. The wind was gentle, whispering through their grey hair, searching perhaps for longer, thicker locks. With the sun on her face, the sigh of the sea far below and the soft lace at the end of the earth in front of her, Thea felt the same yearning as she had all those years ago. The desire to lean further and further forward, until the decision was taken out of her hands. But Denise, now as then, had a firm hold on her.

'It's breathtaking, isn't it?'

'It is.'

'Why did you choose it?' Denise asked.

For a moment Thea was confused. Denise's son had brought them to Scotland, hadn't he? But then her friend added a vital clue. 'You claimed you simply stumbled across it, but that's not true, is it? You planned to come here all along, didn't you?'

Thea's lapse in understanding was replaced by a crystal-clear image of herself, sitting on the floor of her old, high-ceilinged apartment in Harpenden – God, how she'd loved that place – her legs crossed, her hair falling forward, a frown of concentration reflected in a computer screen, searching for the most dramatic places to kill yourself, and finding St Abb's. High cliffs. Long drops. Piercing volcanic rocks. A legend about a shipwrecked princess. All the ingredients for a spectacular exit.

'No, I was telling the truth. I read about it on a website. It sounded perfect.' She didn't need to add: *for what I intended to do*. Neither of them would ever forget that part of their story, it was the lock that bound them together. 'I'm glad I didn't go through with it.'

'So am I.'

'I'd have regretted it.'

Thea stood on the edge, watching the gulls and listening to the waves, seduced, once again, by the sights and the sounds of St Abb's until Denise summoned her, by tugging at her arm.

'Shall we go for a stroll?' She meant away from the edge.

Thea took one last look at what could have been her final destination and, with a touch of reluctance, let Denise steer her back to the path.

Now, as then, Denise felt more comfortable on the path than at the cliff edge. Heights and dramatic gestures were never her thing. It was, perhaps, strange that she and Thea could joke about something so serious, but time had that effect. It rubbed the sharp edges off the worst of times, as well as the best – and, between them, they'd had a lot of years to buff out most of the dings and scratches they'd picked up along the way.

'What about you?' Thea asked as they walked.

'What about me?' It was warming up nicely. Denise could feel the sun on her face.

'What do you regret doing, or not doing?'

Denise knew what Thea was getting at. It was the broken bone of contention between them that had never fully healed. 'Will you give it a rest? I went back to him because I wanted to. How many times do we have to go over this?'

'Oooh. Prickly! I wasn't necessarily referring to Simon.'

'Really?' She jostled Thea's shoulder to remind her that her support wasn't unconditional. 'Here's one regret. I regret that you two never got along. My life would've been so much easier if you had.'

'Wasn't ever going to happen.' Thea grinned. She could still look impish when she chose to.

'We had a happier marriage towards the end.' Denise would always defend her marriage. It was, after all, one of her proudest achievements, precisely because she'd put so much into it.

But Thea was unrelenting on the subject of Simon. 'You've been far happier as his widow than as his wife.'

Denise bristled. 'God, you are brutal.'

Thea merely shrugged.

Brutal she might be, but Thea was right. Denise's decision to recommit to her marriage had not delivered some grand, romantic Hollywood ending, but she and Simon had made their remaining years together count. That first trip away with Thea had shaken Denise's and Simon's foundations quite profoundly, but it was the shock they'd needed. Simon had woken up to the necessity to dedicate more time and care to their relationship, and Denise had learnt to live more in reality than in her head. Once she'd moved back home, they'd both made sure that their version of reality was more interesting and fulfilling. They didn't wait until the boys left home, they made changes immediately: they downsized the business, travelled, did more stuff together, listened to each other more – generally tried harder. And the mutual effort they put in had greatly improved their relationship, but did not revolutionise it. The problem was that the change Denise had started experiencing in her fifties kept on going, altering her opinion of herself and her expectations of her life. Whereas Simon, deep down, only ever wanted things to revert to 'before'. In essence he stayed the same man he'd always been, while she'd become a very different woman – and not only by virtue of the six additional years that she finally owned up to.

What sort of old man Simon would have become, Denise never got to find out, because in at least one crucial aspect he turned out to be more like his mother than his father.

His heart.

He dropped down dead on a golf course at the age of sixty-one, from a huge coronary.

Denise had been profoundly shocked. She'd mourned his untimely death and worried deeply about the impact on the boys. But after the dust and the grief had settled, Thea was right: she had gone on to live the life of the 'merry widow'. Was that brutal or brave? Shameful or admirable? She didn't worry too much either way any more.

They'd reached the point on the path where she and Thea had had their showdown. Off to the left was the semicircle of stones where Thea had finally set free her secrets and her pain.

Twenty-five years. Could it really be that long ago?

Denise suddenly felt tired. Or perhaps she just felt her

age. She stepped off the path onto the springy grass and made her way over to the rocky outcrop. There she leant back against the sun-warmed stone, tilting her face to the sky. She took a few slow breaths. Thea sat on one of the rocks and was sensitive enough to say nothing.

Neither of their lives had been without struggle, and their relationship had certainly never been straightforward. They had argued – often. They disagreed, fundamentally, about many things. Their choices and actions rarely mirrored each other. But not once, in all their time together, had Denise ever wished it to be different.

So there it was – the thing she would never regret: being Thea's friend.

'Hello!' Thea was waggling her fingers in front of Denise's face.

'Sorry.'

'You know senior moments are supposed to be my forte, not yours.'

Denise smiled. 'I was just thinking about how bloody ancient we are.'

'Speak for yourself.' Thea still liked to bring up the four-year age gap between them. 'Do you remember Cherry Trees?' she asked. Another blast from the past.

'I do.' Denise could readily conjure up the sense of claustrophobia, the feeling of time slowed to a crawl and – for some reason that eluded her – the smell of Blu Tack. She also had a very clear image of Thea and her long-dead mother swaying to Nat King Cole in a warm, sunlit room on a carpet dance floor.

'Do you think that's where we'll end up?' Thea asked.

'God, it can't still be a going concern.' Denise seriously hoped it wasn't.

'I don't mean there, as in the actual place. I mean somewhere like it. A facility with wipe-clean chairs and dinner at five-thirty. A place that's full of mad old men railing at the moon.'

The thought so horrified Denise that she made light of it. 'I've heard the one over at Broxbourne is really very nice. We should get our names down for adjoining rooms. You could cause trouble and blame it on me.'

The sun was fully up now, shining hot on their faces.

'Fuck that!' Thea reached into her handbag and swapped her glasses for her sunglasses. They were, of course, designer ones. Denise saw herself reflected in their lenses – an old lady. Perhaps in her future there was a home somewhere like Cherry Trees.

But for now...

The gulls were still wheeling and screaming.

The waves still restless and surging.

And the high blue sky still stretched to the distant horizon.

'Want shall we do now?' Denise asked.

And without hesitation Thea replied, 'Keep going.'

Acknowledgements

This book was inspired by my favourite film, *Thelma & Louise*, so my first thanks must go to Callie Khouri, who wrote the witty, powerful, moving screenplay, and to Susan Sarandon and Geena Davis, the stars of the show. All three are role models of the best possible kind. (My eldest daughter is called Geena, which is no coincidence.) The film stands the test of time – a sure sign of the quality of the writing, performance and production. If you haven't watched it recently (or ever!), please do.

Thea and Denise is my very English take on the central themes of the original film, namely female resilience, spirit and friendship. It's a story about keeping going – no matter what life throws at you – as much as it is about running away.

Which allows me to segue, neatly, into my thanks to the many interesting, resilient women in my life. À la an Oscar acceptance speech, there are quite a few....

First up there are the women in my family.

There's my sisters in-blood and law, Sue and Liz. They've both known adversity and battled it bravely and impressively.

357

Next there's my daughters, Rachel and Geena, my nieces, Hannah and Marissa, and my honorary daughters-in-law, Lauren, Lorna and Mary. I hope you all get to shape your worlds to fit your ambitions. Then there's the next generation, Issy and Daisy... who knows what the future holds for you? Apart from dancing and boxing!

I also want to mention two much-loved and much-missed women: my mum, Anne, and my mother-in-law, Norma. Sadly, neither made it to a healthy old age, but they lived their lives well, fully and with great kindness. Lilian is for them.

My friends are essential to my sanity and enjoyment of life. So thanks go to Linda S, Kath S, Sam and Jocelyn, my running buddies. I would be less fit, in mind and body, without you. Kath B gets a separate mention, as she, more than anyone else, has been with me from the beginning.

I also work with some impressive, thoughtful, talented women. Thank you Sarah, Judith, Kirsty and Hanna for your faith in my ideas and my stories, and for your professionalism.

From my days in research, I also know some deeply sound, life-juggling women; Jo P, Linda H, Naomi, Dawn, Roseann and Shazia. Respect ladies... and it's time someone sorted out a lunch date that we can all make.

And lastly, as with the film, the men in my life matter hugely. So, to Chris, Alex, Joe and Joseph, you are my Ridley Scott, Brad Pitt, Harvey Keitel and Noel L. Walcott III. Not forgetting Will, Head Honcho at Corvus, who, like Michael Madsen, is the unsung hero of the piece – without you I'd not have a career, or money for groceries!

Can't get enough of Caroline Bond?

Available in paperback and eBook